MASQUERADE

"All I seek is my fortune, Gypsy, and I'm told you can tell me that." She made no move to stop him as he reached out and gently removed her mask. "Is there no beautiful, dark-haired gypsy in my future?" he asked, his voice husky.

"No!" she replied.

"Ah. That's too bad, but then I've always been partial to a tawny-haired tigress."

"How many have you known?" she asked pertly.

"None, but I'm open to new experiences," he answered with a heart-stopping smile.

Claire breathed deeply and slowly, hoping to slow down her galloping heart. "That is fortunate, my lord, for I see events in your future that may have you questioning what you have always held true."

"Intriguing," he murmured, her movement drawing his attention to her bare shoulders. *I would like to kiss you all over,* he thought as he touched her soft skin.

"That would not do, my lord," said Claire, unaware she answered his thoughts.

"But it would be so pleasant." Lightly gripping her upper arms, he bent toward her . . .

ZEBRA'S REGENCY ROMANCES
DAZZLE AND DELIGHT

A BEGUILING INTRIGUE   (4441, $3.99)
by Olivia Sumner

Pretty as a picture Justine Riggs cared nothing for propriety. She dressed as a boy, sat on her horse like a jockey, and pondered the stars like a scientist. But when she tried to best the handsome Quenton Fletcher, Marquess of Devon, by proving that she was the better equestrian, he would try to prove Justine's antics were pure folly. The game he had in mind was seduction — never imagining that he might lose his heart in the process!

AN INCONVENIENT ENGAGEMENT   (4442, $3.99)
by Joy Reed

Rebecca Wentworth was furious when she saw her betrothed waltzing with another. So she decides to make him jealous by flirting with the handsomest man at the ball, John Collinwood, Earl of Stanford. The "wicked" nobleman knew exactly what the enticing miss was up to — and he was only too happy to play along. But as Rebecca gazed into his magnificent eyes, her errant fiancé was soon utterly forgotten!

SCANDAL'S LADY   (4472, $3.99)
by Mary Kingsley

Cassandra was shocked to learn that the new Earl of Lynton was her childhood friend, Nicholas St. John. After years at sea and mixed feelings Nicholas had come home to take the family title. And although Cassandra knew her place as a governess, she could not help the thrill that went through her each time he was near. Nicholas was pleased to find that his old friend Cassandra was his new next door neighbor, but after being near her, he wondered if mere friendship would be enough . . .

HIS LORDSHIP'S REWARD   (4473, $3.99)
by Carola Dunn

As the daughter of a seasoned soldier, Fanny Ingram was accustomed to the vagaries of military life and cared not a whit about matters of rank and social standing. So she certainly never foresaw her *tendre* for handsome Viscount Roworth of Kent with whom she was forced to share lodgings, while he carried out his clandestine activities on behalf of the British Army. And though good sense told Roworth to keep his distance, he couldn't stop from taking Fanny in his arms for a kiss that made all hearts equal!

Available wherever paperbacks are sold, or order direct from the Publisher. Send cover price plus 50¢ per copy for mailing and handling to Penguin USA, P.O. Box 999, c/o Dept. 17109, Bergenfield, NJ 07621. Residents of New York and Tennessee must include sales tax. DO NOT SEND CASH.

Alana Clayton

A Gifted Lady

ZEBRA BOOKS
KENSINGTON PUBLISHING CORP.

ZEBRA BOOKS are published by

Kensington Publishing Corp.
850 Third Avenue
New York, NY 10022

First Printing: July, 1995

Printed in the United States of America

For my sister, my one-woman band,
Carolyn Breaden,
with love and appreciation
for her enthusiastic support,
and because she liked the fog.

The mind is a dangerous weapon, even to the possessor,
if [s]he knows not discreetly how to use it.

— Montaigne

One

The fog that had descended on London on December 27, 1813, was settled onto the city as if it were an impoverished relative clinging to a warm hearth. It wrapped around the buildings and filled the streets, zealously guarding the shops and clubs and parks until it was the sole patron.

The smothering blanket of dense, white mist clung tenaciously to the city for eight interminable days, merging day and night into one continuous entity. It compelled the old year to end and the new to begin in darkness, a foreboding sign some would say.

And indeed the heavy vapor was a harbinger of the coldest stretch of weather experienced in recent memory. On February first of the new year, the Thames River would freeze solid and the last great Frost Fair would take place on its surface. Within a week, a plumber wheeling a barrow-load of lead would crack the ice and disappear forever into the frigid water, taking hundreds of sightseers with him.

But on New Year's Eve, the icy Thames still sluggishly flowed between its mist shrouded banks. Though the city was thin of company, several lavish entertainments were set to celebrate a year that would surely see the end of Napoleon's endless warfare. But the fog would have none of it.

Servants dined especially well that evening on suppers intended to feed their betters, while grim-faced hostesses stared at extravagantly decorated ballrooms empty of revelers. Their husbands, counting the vast sums uselessly spent, directed vehement complaints toward the inconvenience nature had inflicted upon their lives.

Quinton Courtney, marquess of Ransley, made his way carefully along what he hoped was Mount Street. Only a fool would be abroad in weather such as this, and Lord Ransley was no fool. What he was was a man whose pregnant wife insisted she must have sweets from Gunter's in Berkeley Square.

Thrusting aside his annoyance, Lord Ransley admitted he had no one to blame but himself for his unhappy domestic state. Against all advice he had wed a young, beautiful girl who, after five years of marriage, remained as self-absorbed as she had been at seventeen.

Lydia had borne their first child with great difficulty, and had been warned that another pregnancy could be life-threatening. Now, after one indiscretion, she was in a delicate condition again.

Since he had learned of the child she was carrying, Lord Ransley had acceded to every request his wife made. So it was not surprising that when she tearfully rejected the offerings from their own excellent kitchen and turned her beautiful blue eyes on him, he had instantly agreed to defy the vile weather and make the cold, damp trip to Berkeley Square. He was responsible for her condition; the least he could do was satisfy her cravings.

After reassuring her that he would return as quickly as possible, Lord Ransley shrugged into his caped greatcoat, settled his dark, curly-brimmed beaver atop his equally dark hair, and stepped through the door into the thick white fog that obscured the familiar landmarks of Grosvenor Square.

At last count, he had bumped into six disgruntled individuals, bounced off several substantial buildings, and apologized to innumerable lightposts during his tedious excursion along Charles Street and then Mount Street. So he was not surprised to hear a soft sound of protest as yet another person collided with his solid bulk as he approached Berkeley Square. The mist swirled around them, allowing Lord Ransley a glimpse of a woman, the hood of a fur-edged cloak obscuring most of her face.

He reached out to steady her, surprised to find a lady braving the murky afternoon unaccompanied. "My apologies, ma'am. Are you injured?"

"I'm fine, thank you, sir." A breathless catch caused her soft voice to falter momentarily. "I expected the streets to be empty this afternoon."

"It seems inclement weather isn't reason enough to bring London to a complete halt. Regardless, it isn't at all wise to be out alone. Perhaps I could accompany you home."

"Really, sir. It is I who should be offering my escort. I've been down this street so many times, I could tread it blindfolded." Lady Claire Kingsley resisted the urge to giggle in appreciation of her own wit. This gentleman would think her truly addlepated if she burst out laughing. He could not know that a thick fog or a sunny day made no difference, for her blindness made them equally as dark.

Intrigued by the lilt in her voice, Lord Ransley was curious to see the woman who found humor in such an unusual situation. However, the fog revealed no more than the glimpse of a small chin, and a delicate pair of lips with an old-fashioned beauty patch placed enchantingly at one corner. It was a shame the practice had gone out of fashion, he mused, for he found it extremely intriguing.

"Then perhaps you should offer your services to the prince regent. I heard just this morning he was forced to turn back on his way to Hatfield House, losing an outrider in a ditch on the return trip."

"I doubt even I could help the prince, he's much too substantial to be led around," she replied, laughing aloud at the thought of assisting the overweight regent in pulling his servant upright. "But I mustn't delay you any longer," she protested.

"Are you certain no damage was done?" Quinton asked. It had been some time since he had enjoyed bantering with a lady, and he was unaccountably reluctant to conclude their encounter.

"I assure you . . ." Her voice trailed off as the warmth of his touch penetrated her cloak. "Sir, you must return home," she suddenly insisted, her voice filled with trepidation.

He remained silent, puzzled at her abrupt change of mood.

"It's difficult, I know, but trust me," she pleaded. "If you continue, you face serious injury."

"I've done so this past hour and have survived," he joked grimly.

"Please, go home," she implored, "your life is worth far more than a box of chocolates." Her words hung ephemerally on the white mist between them, then without another word she pulled from his grip and was gone.

Unable to call out with no name to put to her, Lord Ransley proceeded cautiously into the square, incapable of dislodging her from his mind.

Tomorrow would be the first day of a new year, traditionally a time of hope for new beginnings, but he felt no stir of anticipation. He was a man who had put his wife's life in danger by forcing himself on her. If that was not enough, his daughter, Juliana, the joy of his life, had been silent these past three months, refusing to speak a word. Guilt washed over him; he should be concentrating on his family, not some mysterious woman in the fog.

A short time later, Lord Ransley brushed against an ornate bench that he recognized as being situated under a plane tree only two doors from the confectioner's. Drawing in a deep breath of relief, he congratulated himself on reaching his destination with no more than a few bruises to show for his effort. Once again he was jolted from behind and swore silently. It seemed all of London was on the streets, determined to bowl him over.

Before he could utter an apology, he felt the sharp sting of a blade as it entered his back. He had experienced the feeling once before on the peninsula while under Wellington's command. Then it had been expected, a distinct possibility he lived with daily until it held no surprise when it actually occurred. But he never expected to be stabbed on a foggy street in London while fetching sweets for his wife.

He pitched forward into the mist, and as the last vestiges of consciousness flickered from his mind, he wondered how his nameless lady knew about the chocolates.

Two

"My dear, you must resist this tendency of yours to snoop around in other people's minds without good cause."

Claire Kingsley turned from the fireplace and smiled at the woman ensconced in a rose covered chair in the small sitting room. It had been nearly a year since Claire's sight had returned, but she still remembered those dark days when she thought she would never see her grandmother again. She offered thanks every day for the miracle that had restored her vision. Putting aside her thoughts, she gave her full attention to the older woman.

There was an air of youthfulness about Hanora Maitland, duchess of Kenton, that served to keep her younger than her sixty-five years. Her dark hair was barely touched with silver threads. She had remained slim and active over the years, and though it wasn't a daily ritual, she still sat a good seat on her favorite mount.

"I do not snoop, Grandmama! Well, not exactly," she amended, observing the older woman's dubious expression. "And I did think I had the best of reasons. I cannot bear to see unhappiness if I can alleviate it."

"People can seldom assuage unhappiness unless it is their own, or a purely physical need such as hunger," contended the duchess, searching through a basket of brightly colored silk thread for the shade she needed in her needlework. "Just look at what you've caused by thinking Margaret Lacefield was languishing to be alone with Mr. Gentry."

"But her expression was filled with such yearning," protested Claire, "and when I heard her longing to have him to herself for just a few minutes . . ."

"You couldn't resist giving her the opportunity to meet with the man you thought she admired," finished the duchess. "And now Mr. Gentry, who aspires to being the pink of the *ton,* has seen his purple waistcoat embroidered with red flowers, green vines, and rainbow-hued hummingbirds, and his yellow coat and unmentionables utterly ruined by iced cakes."

"Margaret was very apologetic about allowing her plate to slip," said Claire, intent on redeeming her friend's good name. "Indeed, she was in tears."

"I am sure," mocked the duchess drily.

"You're right, of course," admitted Claire. "I should have been certain I knew all the facts. If I had only looked long enough I would have known she thought him an insufferable prig."

"You should not have been intruding at all," her grandmother chided.

Claire made an agitated trip to the window to stare out at the barren picture winter had created in the small courtyard at the back of Kenton House. "How can you say that after all you've told me about your escapades?"

The duchess could see a little of herself in the slim figure framed by the deep rose window hangings, and hoped that her experiences could make Claire's life easier.

"What I did came from youthful ignorance. I was too

much a child to realize the gift I had inherited should not be misused. In fact, I didn't understand it at all, and with my mother dead I had no one to explain it to me as I did to you.''

The primrose skirt of Claire's morning gown swirled around her ankles as she returned and dropped into a chair near the fire to face the older woman. "It must have been frightening," said Claire, remembering her own initial reaction.

"It was," her grandmother agreed, allowing the thread to fall unnoticed in her lap. "When I first began hearing others' thoughts and seeing events that were yet to happen, I feared I was losing my mind. Then I tried to make a game of it, exposing people's private feelings when they were better off left unsaid. I was very nearly ruined."

"But the duke saved you," Claire added softly.

"Yes, he did," she admitted, a tender expression stealing over her face.

"I wish I had known him," Claire said, remembering the tall, fair-haired man she had seen only once in her life.

"As do I, my dear," said Hanora, picking up her threads again and sorting through them. "The two of you would have gotten along very well. He was an extremely intelligent man, and when he realized I had an unusual talent, he did not desert me. Instead, we married and went on a grand tour where I learned people were often admired for the very thing that practically ostracized me from society here in England."

"He must have loved you very much, Grandmama. I can't imagine any of the men I have met marrying a woman who could see into his mind."

The duchess held up two shades of green to examine in better light. Selecting the darker of the two, she replaced the other in the basket and took up her needle.

"Claire, I will not try to deceive you. Life can be very lonely for people with our gift. That's why you must strive to be discreet until you find someone confident enough to accept who you are."

Claire watched her grandmother thread her needle and commence stitching again before speaking. "I doubt that will ever happen," she said, her usually bright voice devoid of hope.

"Don't despair, you're young yet. Somewhere there's a strong man who will cherish you," the duchess replied, setting perfect satin stitches to form a rose leaf in her design.

"I'm thankful my ability didn't surface while John was alive. I cannot believe he would have tolerated it." Claire's fingers touched the corner of her mouth where a small black mark lay cleverly concealed beneath cosmetics. Some labeled it a beauty mark, but John had called it a witch's brand and insisted she hide it from view. In light of this reaction, he would have surely condemned her for being able to read thoughts.

"John was a good man from all that I know, but you probably have the right of it," agreed the duchess. "Most Englishmen are fed beef and potatoes— both physically and spiritually— all their lives, so it should come as no surprise that they're unwilling to accede to insubstantial theories."

Claire was quietly bemused for a moment. "Do you think he would approve of what I'm doing?"

"With the children?" inquired her grandmother momentarily looking up from her embroidery. "Of course, my dear, your work is admirable."

"And with Matthew Templeton?" she asked with studied indifference.

"No, Claire, I do not think he would condone it," she answered truthfully. "And I can't say that I do, either. But I understand your motivation. You've lost your husband and experienced injury yourself at the hands of someone who was also betraying our country. You have every right to feel as you do. Revenge is a powerful force, and when the means are so readily at hand, it's difficult to refrain from using it.''

"I wonder if I will be successful?" Claire murmured, staring into the red-gold flames of the fire.

"Even I cannot see that," responded the duchess. "But it would appear your chance has diminished with peace declared."

"The war is not over for me," Claire asserted fiercely, pushing herself erect, "and it never will be until John's murderer pays for what he's done. The Congress is meeting, and an opportunist could do well supplying information between the allies, if one can call them that at this point."

"Like dogs over a bone," muttered the duchess, referring to the brangling going on over the realignment of the continent.

"Exactly," agreed Claire, rising and wandering restlessly around the room. "Then there's Bonaparte himself. Some want to move him further away; others seek to free him. It's possible the person I'm looking for will be greedy enough to take a last chance at lining his pockets— and I intend to know about it."

"You must be extremely careful," warned the duchess. "If anyone discovers your purpose you could be in grave danger, and revenge is not all that sweet if you die in the trying. I would hate to lose you when we have just found one another again."

Claire gave the older woman a hug. "Don't worry, Grandmama. I intend to be inordinately circumspect until I find the man responsible for John's death."

Hanora Maitland loved her granddaughter and did not want to see her exposed to danger. But Claire's solitary upbringing had molded her into an independent spirit, loyal and devoted to a fault to those she loved. The most Hanora could hope for was to wring a promise of discretion from Claire.

"Then will you agree that meddling in your friends' affairs is not an inconspicuous occupation?"

"Indeed, Your Grace. And I promise to respect their privacy, and to be modest and unassuming in the future," she recited solemnly, but with a twinkle in her eye.

"I only asked for some restraint, Claire, not a miracle."

"Will you attend the Montfords' rout this evening?" Claire asked quickly, more than ready to end their discussion of her unfortunate miscalculation.

"I think not," she replied, knotting, then snipping off the green thread. "Tony's agreed to keep me company. We'll have dinner and a game of cards in front of the fire while you're shivering in the Montfords' underheated rooms."

It didn't surprise Claire that Anthony, Lord Moreland, would be her grandmother's companion that evening. The two had spent many evenings together during the winter, and she envied them their accord. "If it turns into a crush, there should be enough bodies to heat the rooms," she said, wondering whether she should choose a gown more for warmth than fashion for the evening.

"With the Montfords' pinch-penny ways, I doubt whether there are that many people in town yet. However, those who are here are surely dying of boredom and will most probably attend. Will Ashford escort you?"

"Yes, he insisted," replied Claire, not bothering to conceal her annoyance.

"What's wrong, my dear?" she asked, encouraging

Claire's confidence. "I thought you quite liked Hamilton."

"I do. He was John's best friend, and has stood by me during my illness. I appreciate his support, but now I'm fully recovered and do not need to be indulged any longer. I would be satisfied to be his friend, not a helpless female," she said with rising impatience.

The irritation in Claire's voice caused Hanora to smile. What would have broken the spirit of most women had strengthened her granddaughter. She had seen her husband die at the hands of a hired killer, and had been seriously injured in the carriage crash that followed. The accident had left her blind and she had suffered months of darkness and uncertainty before finally regaining her vision.

After recovering, Claire had not indulged herself with the pity that, in light of the tragic events, would have been her due. Instead she had directed her anger and sorrow into a campaign to find the man behind her husband's murder— an endeavor that many men might evade. The duchess was proud of her granddaughter, but she also feared Claire would end up in a coil before the matter was over.

"I wouldn't attach too much significance to it," she replied, concealing her concern. "Ashford will soon recognize you no longer need a nurse."

"I hope so. Sometimes I feel stifled he hangs over me so. I fear others will get the wrong idea," she confessed, pink suffusing her face.

"And would that be so bad?" asked her grandmother, having often speculated about her granddaughter's feelings toward her attentive gallant.

"Of course," replied Claire sharply, lifting her head to meet her grandmother's penetrating gaze. "I consider Hamilton a good friend, but he's too closely entwined with John for me to think of him elsewise."

"Then perhaps you should discourage his constant attendance," suggested the duchess.

"Yes, I can see that I should," agreed Claire, her fine features looking rather drawn as she considered the problem, "but it will be difficult to do without hurting his feelings."

"I'm confident you can manage it if anyone can, my dear," responded the duchess in a supportive manner. "Now, I think I'll rest awhile before dinner. Come and see me before you leave."

Claire watched her grandmother leave the room, a fond smile curving her lips. Although the duchess would scoff at the thought, she owed the older woman more than she could ever repay.

Claire's childhood had been a solemn one. Her mother, Naomi, had married the Earl of Grantham when she was but eighteen and he near forty. The duke and duchess were both against the match but Naomi was adamant and, rather than see their stubborn daughter marry over the anvil at Gretna Green, they finally relented.

The young countess gave birth to Claire within the year, but she was the only child of the mismatched pair. After it was apparent that Naomi was unable to produce a male heir, she and her daughter were sent to one of the earl's minor estates in the wilds of Yorkshire. Claire seldom saw the dark, brooding man she called father, since he preferred to conveniently disregard his wife— whom he blamed for lack of an heir—and return to the vices of town life.

Naomi became increasingly bitter as the years passed—faulting everyone but herself for her unhappy marriage; relegating her daughter's care to a string of governesses. Claire had seen her grandparents only once when the duke and duchess had travelled from London to Yorkshire on the occasion of her sixth birthday. She had escaped from the nursery and had spent an enjoyable time with the visitors before her mother arrived and ordered them from the house.

The countess told her they were evil and she would never see them again, but Claire remembered them as a bright spot in her otherwise bleak childhood.

It was surprising, therefore, when Naomi stirred herself to demand the earl give Claire a Season. By then the countess had become a virtual recluse and left it up to a cousin of the earl's to take charge of Claire's come-out.

At the time, Claire had wondered at her mother's decision, but later learned that the Duke of Kenton had died and the duchess was in mourning at their country estate. Her mother had been confident she would not meet her grandmother, and had taken the opportunity to rid herself of the visual evidence of her failure.

Having little experience with affection of any kind, Claire fell victim to the ardor of her first suitor and accepted his offer of marriage. John Kingsley was the second son of a viscount, but his prospects were good and he was a lighthearted young man who sincerely loved Claire. They were married almost immediately and left London for his new government post.

The Earl of Grantham paid little heed when his wife died shortly thereafter from what the doctor attributed to a disinterest in living. It was not long before Grantham followed her to the grave after a night of heavy drinking and gambling. Having no direct heir, he had been determined to leave as little as possible for his distant kin who would inherit, and had succeeded admirably at the time of his demise.

Claire received the news of her parents' deaths calmly. While she had never gone in want of creature comforts, neither of her parents had furnished the love a child needs. She had become self-sufficient during her childhood, only beginning to learn what it was to give and receive affection when she married John Kingsley.

After the accident that took John's life, the duchess brought Claire to Kenton House to recover. Claire remembered the paralyzing fear that gripped her when she had awakened unable to see. The sound of her grandmother's soothing voice and her comforting touch had been invaluable at that time in her life.

Hanora Maitland had given Claire the strength to survive John's death and to endure the months of darkness that followed. Finally, she had explained the strangeness when unwanted thoughts began tumbling through Claire's mind.

Blinking the tears from her eyes, Claire rose and smoothed her skirts. It proved no good purpose to relive the memories. She must concentrate on circulating throughout the *ton* to discover the traitor who was responsible for her husband's death. It was a vow made in anger, but one she meant to keep. Mounting the stairs, she set her mind to what she would wear that evening to appear a fluttery female with nothing more pressing on her mind than the latest fashion.

Some hours later, Claire entered the Montfords' Palladian style home on the Honorable Hamilton Ashford's arm. They made a handsome couple, Claire wearing a gown of golden gossamer satin with a parure of topaz and diamonds, and Hamilton in black evening clothes with a diamond flashing fire in his exquisitely tied cravat.

The youngest son of Viscount Rawleigh, Hamilton was blessed with blond hair lighter than her own, and eyes that were as blue as a summer's sky. He had been born especially to please women, John often teased, and Hamilton had taken great care to prove him right.

Claire had seen scores of ladies fall captive to his spell since she had first come to know him.

Hamilton had spent a great deal of time with John and Claire after their marriage, and the three had been the best of friends. After the accident, Claire thought nothing of Hamilton running tame in Kenton House, but his manner had become increasingly proprietorial since she had regained her vision. It was more annoying than ever this evening, and she was determined to begin breaking the bond she had not sought.

"Town is dreadfully flat this time of year," drawled Hamilton as he surveyed the press of people in the room through his quizzing glass.

Contrary to his reflections, Claire was pleased to see that Lady Montford had invited the fringes of society to insure her rooms were filled. It was more likely she would find her man here than in the cream of the *haut ton*.

"I'm certain we can rub along tolerably well for a few hours even though the company is not all to your liking," replied Claire, still out of sorts with his possessive attitude.

Hamilton accorded her a probing glance at her acerbic reply. "To be sure, my dear," he agreed amicably, choosing to accept her words at face value.

Glimpsing Margaret Lacefield across the room, Claire quickly took leave of Hamilton and made her way through the press until she reached her side.

Claire had initially met Margaret during her first Season, and they had promptly become friends. Margaret had called after the carriage accident, and their relationship resumed as if years had not passed since their last meeting.

"I'm surprised to see you alone," commented Margaret. "Is Ashford engaged elsewhere this evening?"

Claire made a face. "No, he's here, but I slipped free

as soon as I could. I'm determined to establish my independence from him. He's been a very good friend, but that is all I mean it to be. Grandmama reminded me today that the longer I allow the situation to continue the worse it will be to break."

"I see that having a handsome man's devotion may not be all it's rumored to be, but I'll admit it's a problem I wouldn't mind experiencing," teased Margaret.

Claire studied her friend. Margaret was not a diamond of the first water, but she was no antidote, either. She stood several inches taller than most women, but carried her slim body with a willowy grace that Claire envied.

Her brown hair was short and curled naturally around her face. Dark brown eyes below finely arched brows were her most striking feature, and Claire knew that more than one gentleman had composed a poem to them in hopes of gaining her favor.

Tonight she was complete to a shade in a deep blue velvet gown with a low-cut square neckline. A single sapphire on a finely wrought gold chain and matching earrings were her only adornments. Her simple elegance of dress made her stand out from the crowd of beruffled, jewel-laden ladies.

"Do not try to gammon me, Margaret. I know several gentlemen who would be more than happy to toss their hats over the windmill for you."

"But would they be willing if I were poor?" Margaret queried bitterly. "I will not turn over control of my life and income just to avoid being a spinster." Her smile was forced, and Claire detected a trace of sadness beneath her words.

"You are not yet breathing your last, Margaret."

"I have twenty-four years to my account which puts me firmly on the shelf."

"And I have twenty-five, yet you do not see me donning a cap, do you?" protested Claire.

"Your situation is altogether different. You've been married." Margaret placed a hand over her mouth in dismay. "Oh, botheration! Forgive my runaway tongue, Claire. I didn't mean to bring up unpleasant memories."

"Don't fret, Margaret. I'm well over public displays. But you're right, being married does make my situation different, and not all to the good. Many men harbor the thought that widows are as readily available as any lightskirt."

"That cannot be pleasant, I will admit. But at your come-out you attracted the admiration of gentlemen without effort, while it was only my money that drew their interest."

"I cannot credit that," scoffed Claire. "You are merely more particular in selecting a husband than most women. Keep in mind that you have much more to offer than any green girl, and I don't mean your money," she insisted loyally. "You'll find a man worthy of you yet."

Margaret considered Claire's words before answering. "Perhaps you're right, but I hope it's soon, while I'm still able to totter down the aisle on my own."

"I'm convinced that this season will see you happy," replied Claire optimistically.

At that moment Hamilton approached with two strangers in tow. "Lady Kingsley. Miss Lacefield. Allow me to introduce Forrest Harcourt and Tyler Carrington."

Harcourt, still on the sunny side of forty, was the older of the two. His dark complexion in England's cold January brought to mind warm foreign places. Bright blue eyes glittered in a handsomely chiseled face, framed by dark hair winged with silver. His exotic ap-

pearance attracted his share of attention, and Claire noticed covert glances being cast in their direction from
several bored London ladies.

Tyler Carrington was an altogether different creature.
From his perfectly arranged dark blond hair to his expertly tailored clothes, he was a flawless example of a
young man of wealth. His face was perfection itself,
with impeccably proportioned features. While women
might flock to Forrest Harcourt with lust in their
hearts, they would worship at Carrington's elegantly
shod feet.

"Are you newly arrived in town?" asked Claire, directing her question to Harcourt.

"We reached London only a few days ago," he confirmed. "Carrington and I met in France, then decided
to travel on to England together."

"And do you find it changed much?" she inquired,
taking the opportunity to focus on his thoughts.

"Not until now," he said, a curious expression of surprise and amusement flickering across his face as he
observed her intent concentration to his reply. "But after meeting two such lovely ladies, my stay has brightened considerably."

Claire's fleeting probe had not uncovered a scrap of
his thoughts. Feeling uncomfortable under his close
scrutiny, she quickly turned her attention to Mr. Carrington who was discussing poetry with Margaret while
Hamilton looked on in a mild state of ennui.

"I met up with Byron not long ago and we agreed
that much of what is written today cannot be considered
seriously," said Carrington, taking a pinch of snuff after
offering it around the circle.

"And do you also write, Mr. Carrington?" asked
Claire, unable to picture the moody and somewhat scandalous Lord Byron in a *tête-à-tête* with this exquisite
flower of manhood.

"Oh, I dabble a bit," replied Carrington modestly. "Nothing I boast about, you understand, but Byron seemed well taken with my scribblings."

"I should be interested in reading your verse if you would consider sharing it," said Claire, concentrating on his answer.

Devil take it! I should have left well enough alone. I could not rhyme two words if my life depended on it. "Ah, well, some of my trunks were misplaced and I'm afraid all my writing was in one of them."

Claire repressed the giggle that threatened to bubble past her lips. She would not let him get away with puffing up his consequence that easily. "I'm sorry to hear that, Mr. Carrington. Perhaps when your trunks catch up with you, we can persuade you to share your talent with us. I could hold an afternoon reading and invite all the ladies. They would be all agog to hear one of Bryon's proteges."

Blast it! How am I to get myself out of this mess? "Ah, I would not exactly say that we are that close," replied Carrington, dabbing a bead of perspiration from his brow with a monogrammed handkerchief.

Claire had thoroughly intended to keep her vow and not use her talent in such a frivolous manner, but Mr. Carrington could not truly be considered a friend and, therefore, surely was not protected by her promise to the duchess. So it was with a clear conscious she replied. "Oh, I'm certain you're too modest, sir. It would be my pleasure."

Carrington remained silent and Claire brought her concentration to bear on his thoughts again as his face took on a pleased look.

Perhaps it would be useful after all. A man says all manner of things to his wife, and a bit of flattery might reveal some useful information. I could hire someone to write a bit of drivel to read. Yes, it just might work. "Perhaps we could come to an agreement after all, Lady Kingsley," he said, granting her a smile designed to weaken her knees.

"Wonderful," she replied, fluttering her eyelashes just enough to make it appear she had fallen for his charm. "I shall count on you to let me know what is convenient," she replied, her mind racing with what she had heard.

Carrington was more than he appeared, but just how much more she wasn't sure. He didn't seem strong enough to be the man she sought, but he might lead her to him. It was also more than possible that he was working for Harcourt— a man who clearly fit the picture she held of a successful spy.

After a few additional minutes of conventional conversation, the men took themselves off to the card room.

"I have never met a more fascinating man," remarked Margaret, staring after the departing trio.

"I will admit nature has been generous with Mr. Carrington," agreed Claire, accepting a cup from a passing footman, "but I can't believe you would fall victim to looks alone."

"Carrington," Margaret uttered scornfully, "is nothing more than a preening popinjay. It is Harcourt of whom I speak."

Claire choked on the punch she had just sipped. "Harcourt? Margaret, it's dangerous just to be in the same room with such a man. You cannot truly admire him?"

"Indeed I do. Harcourt is the embodiment of my fantasies," she replied sheepishly, industriously waving her fan before heated cheeks. "It's reassuring to know such a man exists."

Claire gulped the rest of her punch, sure Margaret had lost her senses. "I suppose I must agree that he could inspire a certain amount of admiration. He is appealing in a dangerous, dark sort of way."

"Oh, don't think I'm all about in the attic, my friend. I'm fully aware that a man like Harcourt isn't interested in boring English spinsters, but there is nothing that says I cannot admire what has passed me by." Margaret's laugh was unnaturally gay, and Claire found she lacked a witty reply.

Leaving Margaret with the promise to see her later, Claire moved around the room, chatting aimlessly with men whose patriotism endured in direct proportion to their declining fortunes. Their desire to impress a well-heeled widow could lead to a loose tongue, and Claire meant to use every means at her disposal to see they had an attentive, admiring audience. It was not long until her dance card was filled and she was being whirled around the floor with varying degrees of expertise.

"I have heard an amusing tale, my dear Lady Kingsley," said Lord Davenport, peering at her over the high points of his collar as he led her onto the dance floor.

Davenport was a small man with an inflated opinion of himself. He teetered through the complex steps of the Quadrille on silver buckled, high-heeled shoes that barely brought him level with Claire's moderate height. His stout body was encased in a puce velvet coat and a gold embroidered waist-coat whose seams were nearly tested beyond endurance. Cloying perfume hung in a cloud around him and Claire was thankful the figures of the dance did not allow for a lingering closeness. How the man had the breath to dance with stays squeezing him like a sausage was a miracle in itself.

"And will you be generous enough to share this tale with me, my lord?" Claire simpered coyly. It was times such as this that she questioned her ability to continue. Only by the strictest measure of self-control could she meet Lord Davenport's confident smirk with an encouraging smile.

"Of course, my lady. I have been saving it just for you." Looking quickly to either side, he leaned closer. "It is said that Napoleon is planning to escape from Elba. How do you like that?" His cackling bray of laughter rose above the music.

"And where did you hear such news, my lord," asked Claire casually, again smiling into his overheated face.

"Oh, dunno, my lady. Might have been Easterly, or Fordyce. Dashed if I remember for sure," he responded lightly, shrugging off her question as unimportant.

"But if I recall, your lordship— and I readily admit a mere woman's mind is far inferior to yours— " she rattled on, attempting to look as hen-witted as possible, "that rumor has been around before."

"Just so," agreed his lordship condescendingly, "but this time it's said there's power behind it, and money and men enough to follow through. No need to worry though," he assured her, taking the opportunity to squeeze her hand, "that Corsican devil won't escape us."

Claire searched his mind to see if he was holding anything back, but only encountered his lascivious thoughts of what he would like to do with her. Subduing a shudder of revulsion she rejoiced when the dance forced them apart.

"How could I be afraid with men such as you to protect me," Claire replied, when they came together once again, confident Lord Davenport would never associate her comment with levity.

Quinton Courtney, marquess of Ransley, observed the activity in the Montfords' ballroom. It had been several years since he had been socially active in the *ton*, but the scene hadn't changed at all. The women's gowns were a swirl of color amidst the men's evening wear as they moved through dance steps or congregated on the sidelines to exchange the latest *ondits*.

Tonight was no different than countless others he had suffered through. Scheming mothers pushed their marriageable daughters to attach an eligible man, fortune hunters looked for a desperate heiress, married men and women planned secret assignations that would be common knowledge before the next day was out.

He had ventured out this evening in sheer boredom. With the rest of his family still in the country, his town house was much too silent after his daughter had been put to bed. Now he wondered if his impulsive act was wise. It brought back unhappy memories of endless evenings spent watching his lovely wife flirt outrageously with every man present.

He knew, as well as any other, that the *ton* allowed a married woman freedom in such things. And while outwardly he had acquiesced to Lydia's comportment, his private feelings were something else entirely.

It was also the way of society that he was pursued for his title and fortune; however, he had desired to wed for more than social advantage. He wanted to experience the same kind of love his parents had shared, and thought he had found it with Lydia. But not far into his own marriage he realized what he had taken for love had been an expert act on Lydia's part.

Unwilling to continue reliving the past, he searched the room again. Yes, there she was on the far side of the dance floor. A striking beauty dressed in a shimmering golden gown, surrounded by admirers. She was as lovely as he had first concluded, and probably readily available to the man who could best flatter her self-esteem.

He watched as she tapped one man playfully on the arm with her fan, tipped her head and smiled enchantingly to another, before being led onto the dance floor by that overstuffed fop Davenport.

Golden highlights in her tawny hair shone as she passed beneath the glittering chandelier lighting the room. The mass of curls were gathered up and allowed to fall artfully to her nape in careless abandonment, revealing the sweet curve of her chin and throat.

She was monopolizing his attention and he shook his head in disgust. She was everything he detested, everything he wished to avoid, and her flirtations reminded him too much of Lydia for comfort.

It was not late, but he decided to return home. There were more unpleasant memories here than in the quiet town house. Tomorrow his daughter would see Dr. James, and perhaps she would soon be able to speak again. His spirits lifted at the thought, and he left the room determined to have as little as possible to do with the ladies of the *ton*.

The morning after the Montfords' rout Claire swiftly penned a message detailing Davenport's news, stuck it in her reticule, and took herself off to Hatchard's Book Store on Picadilly. There she took great delight in selecting a book on manners, slipped her message between the pages, and gave directions for its delivery. Leaving the shop, she smiled for the first time that morning, wondering in what spirit Matthew Templeton would receive her latest offering.

Claire had first met Templeton when he called to offer his condolences on the death of her husband. It was during that visit, when she was still unable to control the unsettling experience of hearing another's thoughts, that Claire discovered the "highwayman" had actually been after important documents John was bringing to London.

Shocked at her discovery, Claire had blurted out that she knew her husband's death was intentional, and she meant to expose his murderer. Seeking to calm her, Templeton had pledged that the War Office was doing everything possible to ascertain John's killer.

In his effort to soothe her, Templeton inadvertently admitted that they knew the man was a member of the *ton,* and assured Claire it would be only a short time until he was brought to justice. But Claire was adamant in her determination to complete her husband's final assignment by revealing the spy and, in doing so, avenge his death.

Claire smiled, thinking of Templeton's frustration when he could not persuade her to forego her crusade, and his surprise when not long thereafter she brought him information of some significance concerning the battle of Vittoria. Since then he had come to respect her ability to uncover reliable information.

Her smile faded as she climbed back into the carriage. If Davenport's rumor was true and Napoleon successfully escaped, it could mean more years of war for England, a critical drain on the country's dwindling resources, and continuing loss of lives. Claire prayed her information would serve to prevent the escape if, indeed, it was a reality.

Three

Nothing more I can do. . . . Nothing more I can do. . . . Nothing more I can do . . .

Simple words, but powerful enough to reduce the blocks of hope he had unwisely built to a rubble of dull despair. His gaze drifted around the well-appointed room as he absorbed the doctor's pronouncement, adding yet another tragedy to those crowding his life this past year.

Oak paneling gleamed faintly in dim light that eluded the dreary January day and crept through the tall windows facing Brook Street. Mahogany and burgundy leather furniture enhanced the professional aspect of the room, while a floor to ceiling expanse of weighty medical tomes filled the wall behind the doctor's substantial form. And in none of these, thought Quinton Courtney, lies the answer to one child's problem.

"Your daughter is physically healthy," the doctor stated emphatically. Although he sympathized with the man sitting across the desk from him, no pity showed in his voice. Ransley was well known for neither asking nor giving quarter. But for all his strength, for all his wealth and power, what he wanted most was out of reach.

Lord Ransley met the slightly magnified gray eyes behind wire rimmed spectacles. "Then why isn't she able to speak?" asked the marquess, his blunt question shattering the gathering tension.

"There is so much we do not know about the workings of the mind," lamented the doctor, removing his eyeglasses and rubbing the faint mark visible on the bridge of his nose. His movements were deliberate as he settled the earpieces into place before continuing. "It's my opinion your daughter has suffered a shock so threatening that she's taken refuge in silence. I've seen similar situations in our men coming back from the war."

"So have I," acknowledged the marquess, "but it usually wears off. Juliana's been this way for over a year, with no indication that she's getting better."

"If we knew the cause, then perhaps . . ." The doctor spread his hands and shrugged black-clad shoulders.

The marquess reviewed the shambles of his life, wondering how the anticipation of a future with his beautiful bride six years ago had come to this. "There was my stabbing and my wife's death, but Juliana's silence commenced months before either of those occurred. I wasn't even in the country when it began," he confessed, remorse altering his expression.

"Have you spoken with the servants?" Dr. James inquired. "Possibly they know of something."

"I interviewed them extensively when I returned. They all denied knowledge of anything unusual transpiring, as did my wife. I have no idea what could have caused Juliana to stop talking. She was only four at the time, and her chattering was non-stop." Thinking of his vibrant daughter endlessly repeating each new word she learned, his sadness deepened. "The only thing I discovered was that she awoke one morning and would not speak. She's been silent since then."

"We may never understand the cause of your daughter's problem, my lord, but I do know there is no medicine that will cure her. We can only hope that time will heal." His inadequate words would not bring solace to the marquess, nor speech to the young girl waiting silently in the next room; but they were all he had to offer.

"At this point my hope is nonexistent," Lord Ransley admitted in a defeated voice.

Dr. James, uncommonly affected by this unusual display of vulnerability, considered a suggestion he would not otherwise propose to a gentleman of rank. "There might be a chance," he began reluctantly.

"What is it?" the marquess demanded, a dim spark of hope temporarily alleviating the weariness in his dark eyes.

"I hesitate to suggest it— many people would scoff— but since there is nothing more . . ." The doctor paused, then dauntlessly continued. "And it certainly couldn't harm the child."

"Out with it, man!" commanded Lord Ransley, impatient with the doctor's quibbling. "I'm desperate enough to try the devil himself!"

"You may consider this just as bad," Dr. James jested weakly. "There's a woman who's had some success working with children."

"A woman doctor?" the marquess asked incredulously.

"No." James pulled out a handkerchief, blotting the cold perspiration from his forehead. He had gone too far to cry off from an explanation, but he wondered how to rationalize such an insubstantial theory, and cursed himself for being fool enough to mention it in the first place. He had previously only offered this treatment to women whose children would not respond to medical care. Women, he had learned in his years of practice, were more receptive to unconventional ideas, particularly when it came to their children's welfare.

The marquess shifted, impatient with the lengthening silence. "This woman has an extraordinary gift for communicating with children," began the doctor. "It's no use to ask me how she does it for I don't know, but she reaches them on some level and gains their confidence."

Lord Ransley sank back into his chair. "Juliana cannot share her fears," he conceded, disappointment robbing him of all animation. "You forget, she's unable to talk."

"Being unable to speak isn't the problem, my lord, only the result. We need to reach the cause, and that's what this woman may be able to do. With the other children, she's been able to discover their secret fear and convince them nothing dreadful is going to happen if they return to normal. I've seen her work wonders with children I had given up on.

"She met my first patient by accident in the waiting room. The child would not eat and had wasted away until she had only a short time to live. When the lady I am recommending saw the child, she asked if she could visit the little girl at home. After several visits she had coaxed the child to begin taking thin gruel, then increasingly solid foods.

"She later confided that a nursemaid had told the child a terrifying story about a little girl who had been poisoned. The child had taken the story to heart and would not eat for fear of dying the same torturous death that the maid had described. The lady convinced the child there was no danger of poisoning and persuaded her to eat.

"That's only one story of her remarkable ability. There are others that have ended with the same success."

Ransley forced himself to seriously consider the doctor's words. Luther James was a highly esteemed doctor, the best London had to offer, so it was said. If there were a solution for Juliana's condition, he would know it, Ransley had been told.

"Who is she?" the marquess asked, still unable to summon any enthusiasm.

"I'm afraid I'm not free to reveal her name until I speak with her," Dr. James replied, casting him an apologetic look. "With your permission, I'll explain the particulars of Juliana's case. All in strict confidence, of course. That way, if either of you decides not to proceed, your privacy and the child's will be safeguarded. If she feels she can help Juliana then I will set up a meeting between the two of you."

"This all sounds rather like a childish game," complained the marquess, unwilling to expose his daughter to a quack, no matter how highly regarded she might be. "If the woman is such an expert, surely she would benefit by becoming known."

"She is a lady of quality, my lord, and has no need of money or fame. I assure you, her concern is strictly for the child."

The marquess was surprised by the admission. "I need to think about it," he remarked slowly, his fingers drumming against the mahogany chair arm.

"Do so," advised the doctor. "If you decide to meet her, let me know, and I'll make the arrangements."

With an effort, Lord Ransley pulled himself from the deep leather chair. He had pinned his hopes on this visit, only to find it was another dead end: another possibility that had begun with optimism and ended in vain expectation. He must face reality; he had no other option.

Lord Ransley had reached the door, his fingers gripping the handle before he turned. "I have no choice, doctor. If you think enough of the woman to recom-

mend her, I'll take your word for it. Will you arrange
a meeting between us?''

"Gladly, my lord. And you may set your mind at rest
as to her character. When you meet her you will find
she is not an eccentric, merely an exceptional lady who
has a remarkable way with children.''

"Claire," hissed the Duchess of Kenton, "do not even
consider pouring sherry down Mr. Amberson's neck.
Lady Carlson would never forgive such a disruption during her musical, especially when her daughter is singing," she concluded, lips parted in a pleasant smile.

Claire glanced down at the glass she held, then toward Freddy Amberson's starched neckcloth. "Grandmama, you have broken your promise," she accused
under her breath.

The two women were seated on the last row of gilt-
edged chairs in Lady Carlson's drawing room, speaking
softly to avoid disturbing the audience.

"I certainly have not," she answered firmly. "We
agreed it would be impossible to live in the same house
if we intruded on one another's thoughts, and I always
keep to my bargains."

"Then how did you know?" Claire asked, glancing
again at the man seated in front of her.

"Because I can see him pressing his knee against that
silly chit sitting next to him— Fitzgerald's youngest, I
believe— and I know exactly what you're planning. If
I'm not mistaken, a similar situation occurred last
month during the Harrisons' ball between Viscount
Shiffield and Emily Harrison where you accidentally
spilled champagne in his lap."

"Shiffield is a depraved man old enough to be her
father," Claire replied as heatedly as the situation would
allow.

"And rich enough to save Lord Harrison from debtor's prison," interrupted the duchess.

"Nevertheless, if you had heard the designs he had on Emily, you would have done far worse," murmured Claire fiercely, nearly spilling the hotly contested sherry on her gown while venting her indignation.

"Perhaps," agreed the older woman, "but you have only delayed his plans. Before the Season's over Shiffield will have the girl and Harrison's pockets will be plump again."

"I know," sighed Claire "but . . ."

"You could not help yourself," finished the duchess, patting her hand. "Come along, my dear," she commanded, as Arabella Carlson finished her song to a smattering of polite applause. "I feel a headache coming on."

Claire's hand trembled with longing as she stood for a moment behind Mr. Amberson. Overcoming the inclination that would surely put her in her grandmother's black books forever, she set her glass down on a nearby table and followed her from the room.

Three days after agreeing to Dr. James's suggestion, Lord Ransley was again ushered into his office. Having had time to reconsider his rash decision, he had prepared a speech to thank the lady for coming while courteously refusing her help if she looked too much the charlatan.

"My lord," said Dr. James, rising from behind the mahogany desk, a smile spreading across his angular face. "I'm pleased you could make it at such short notice. Lady Kingsley should be here any moment."

"Lady Kingsley being the woman who may be able to help Juliana, I presume?"

"Yes. Claire Kingsley, daughter of the late Earl of

Grantham, and granddaughter of the Duchess of Kenton."

Lord Ransley's dark brows raised a fraction, his doubts increasing at the news. "Dr. James, are you certain about this? I've never known a lady so highly connected to concern herself about anything more weighty than the cut of her gown."

"I assure you, Lord Ransley, Lady Kingsley is not amusing herself at your child's expense. As I told you, she has restored several of my patients to a normal life when medical procedures were ineffective."

"Doesn't her husband object to her activity?" inquired the marquess, unable to disregard his curiosity toward a lady of the *ton* who performed good deeds without demanding public adulation for her works.

"He was killed in an accident several years ago," replied Dr. James. "Since then Lady Kingsley has resided with her grandmother. Both ladies are generous to a fault."

Lord Ransley rubbed his hand across his face. It seemed there were no barriers but his own doubts to keep Juliana and Lady Kingsley apart. "And she is my only hope," he stated, watching closely as the doctor nodded in assent.

"Very well, I suppose I should at least meet her after bringing her out in this weather. I suppose we can expect her to arrive fashionably late?" he asked impatiently, settling himself more comfortably into the chair as a knock sounded at the door.

Dr. James pulled out his pocket watch and flipped it open. "As usual, right on time," he proclaimed proudly.

"Lady Kingsley," announced the nurse, pulling the door wider and stepping aside.

Claire Kingsley was not at all what Lord Ransley expected. She was no thin, pinched spinster, nor did she look as if she wore blue stockings.

The light coming through the arched windows today was laced with weak rays of winter sun. It struck her fur-trimmed cape, accentuating the golden brown color. She pushed back the hood and the marquess's gaze was drawn to the tawny shades of hair pulled into a loose chignon at the back of her well-shaped head.

She was beautiful, composed, and every inch the lady . . . something she was not the last time he had seen her cavorting at the Montfords' rout. Suddenly he was unreasonably angry. Infuriated that she was both his only hope and all that he detested. Furious at James for getting him involved, and at himself for responding to her beauty despite his knowledge of her true character.

Before being wed, Quinton Courtney had been as susceptible as any man to a pretty face, but his marriage had been a rude awakening. He had learned without a doubt that beauty could hide more faults than the most homely countenance.

And while this purported miracle woman did not have the porcelain doll beauty Lydia boasted, she exhibited an outward appearance even more threatening in Lord Ransley's estimation. There was a warmth about her that invited a man to approach and bask in her presence, encouraging him to lose all reason and submerge himself in the captivating sensation of her femininity. That, coupled with her behavior at the Montfords', warned him that Claire Kingsley was a woman to avoid at all costs for a man who wanted no entanglements.

Dr. James stepped forward in greeting, helping Lady Kingsley with her wrap before escorting her across the room toward the tall, dark-haired man who had risen from his chair.

It was not auspicious, Claire thought, that he had not

spoken, but stood staring as if she were some strange specimen to study.

He was an imposing figure, tall and broad in the shoulders beneath the blue superfine of his coat, showing a superior length of leg encased in buff inexpressibles above glossy black boots. If he had known his face reflected suffering he would surely have managed to conceal it, she mused, for he was a man who would display no weakness. He had accepted what life had dealt him and gathered it tightly inside, determined to control it.

The doctor's jovial voice cut short her thoughts. "Lady Kingsley, may I present Quinton Courtney, Marquess of Ransley."

"Lord Ransley," acknowledged Claire, extending her hand and praying it would not tremble, for suddenly it was important that they deal well together.

The marquess touched her fingers still chilled from the wintry day and met her gaze. Her eyes were of a green difficult to describe. It was not the bright green of spring leaves, nor was the hue faded with shades of gray or blue, but more like the sea he had observed in his travels. The color was rare, occurring only in the most exotic spots, but it had always mesmerized him.

"My lady," he replied stiffly, with a slight bow. "Dr. James has been singing your praises."

"Not too loudly, I hope. I would be extremely uncomfortable attempting to live up to such high expectations." Claire smiled at him, thinking perhaps he was not as dour as he looked.

If he had been less experienced and if he had not seen her at the Montfords' she would have fooled him, would have made him believe she was asking for his good will instead of flattery. However, Lydia had cured him of such illusions. He would never again be drawn to a woman for beauty alone.

"I gave up expecting miracles long ago, my lady," he responded abruptly, allowing her to infer the unspoken words.

Rude and cynical, judged Claire, as the essence of his message reached her, dashing her hopes for an amiable relationship.

"Perhaps we can restore your belief, my lord," she replied, craving to prove him wrong.

"I trust that you may," he answered bluntly. "It is the only reason I'm here."

The marquess was dismayed by his conduct. No matter how provoked, he had never offered insult to a lady of quality, and this woman had done nothing to warrant it. She was well respected by Dr. James and was here as a favor to him and his daughter. She did not deserve to suffer his churlish behavior because of her comeliness or personal pursuits. Now that he was back in town, he would meet many lovely, flirtatious women, and could not insult them all.

"Please excuse my abruptness, madam. I can only blame my impertinence on the anxiety over my daughter's condition."

Claire was certain that while he was sincere in his apology for his brusqueness, Lord Ransley's belief in her ability was still nonexistent. "Think nothing of it, my lord. It is not the first, nor, I doubt, will it be the last time I have met with skepticism."

"Then I hope you will not take it amiss . . ." he began, and she knew he was going to refuse her help. At that moment his eyes caught the doctor's glance and held.

The temptation was too great for Claire to resist. Silently asking her grandmother's forgiveness for breaking her promise she succumbed. With only the slightest encouragement their thoughts were hers. *Nothing more I can do. . . . Nothing more I can do. . . . Nothing more I can do.*

So they both knew Dr. James could not help the child. Then why not give her a chance? Claire stormed inwardly.

The marquess caught himself just as he was ready to refuse her assistance, remembering that there was no choice. It was a situation he seldom encountered and did not relish, but accepted in this instance for his daughter's sake. Clearing his throat, he continued in a much different vein than he had begun. "I hope you will agree to see my daughter, Lady Kingsley. Dr. James is convinced you are Juliana's only hope."

Claire released a sigh of relief. "You must understand, my lord, I cannot make any promises. Perhaps you should reconsider before committing your daughter to me."

"I have already done so," he admitted frankly. "And I ask that you work with Juliana."

"Then I will do my best, Lord Ransley. Rest assured I will continue until I am convinced there is . . . nothing more I can do."

The marquess felt as if he had taken a blow to the chest. Searching her sea-green gaze he observed sympathy and caring, and just a bit of satisfaction at the shock her words had caused.

Claire stepped into the carriage and settled herself comfortably on the plush squabs. Lord Ransley disapproved of her, of that she was sure. But why? It did not make sense that he had taken an instant dislike to her for no reason at all. Giving him the benefit of the doubt, she attributed his attitude to the stress he had suffered over his daughter's illness. Things would be right between them the next time they met, she determined, as the coach came to a halt in Berkeley Square.

Meanwhile she was not so poor-spirited as to allow him to cast her into a fit of the dismals.

"Where is my Grandmama, Biggersleigh?" asked Claire, as she entered Kenton House and removed her outer garments.

"Her Grace is in the small sitting room, my lady. She has been waiting tea until you returned."

"Capital! Precisely what I need after being out in the weather this afternoon," she exclaimed, continuing down the hallway to the small room toward the rear of the house. Furnished with an eye toward comfort rather than style, it was made cozy by a well-laid fire.

Claire bent to kiss her grandmother's cheek, then moved to warm her hands in front of the flames.

"Was your meeting satisfactory, my dear?" inquired the duchess, setting aside her embroidery in order to give Claire her full attention.

"As well as can be expected. There was the initial resistance, but we finally agreed I'm to begin seeing the child Tuesday next. I met her before leaving Dr. James's office today, but we spent only a few brief moments together. Juliana is lovely, but so small and silent. I yearn to hear her laugh, yet fear it will never happen."

The duchess waited until tea had been arranged on the table in front of her before responding. "That's just your usual insecurity cropping up, my dear," she responded after the footman and Biggersleigh had departed. "Once you begin, you will overcome it."

"I pray you are right," said Claire, taking a seat across from her grandmother and accepting a cup of tea. "I feel an urgency that I have not felt with any of the others. Perhaps it's her father; Lord Ransley has more belief that his horse will fly than I will help Juliana speak."

"Lord Ransley?" asked the duchess, the teapot suspended in midair. "Juliana is Quinton Courtney's child?"

"Yes. You sound surprised."

"I am," she admitted, then continued pouring tea. "Ransley's been buried on his country estate this past year. I wonder what brought him to town so precipitously."

"Evidently Dr. James was his last hope for Juliana." A blush rose to Claire's cheeks and she avoided the older woman's eyes. "I'm afraid I broke my vow," she confessed. "It was impossible not to. "Nothing more I can do," was practically written in the air between them. Even with that conclusion from Dr. James, his lordship was ready to refuse me."

Her grandmother looked at Claire inquiringly.

"No, I did not invade his thoughts again, his decision was apparent by his countenance. But at the last moment he changed his mind and, after meeting Juliana, I can only be glad he did. She's such a sad, quiet little girl. I can't bear to think of her living in silence the rest of her life."

The duchess passed a plate of cakes to Claire. "Is Ransley as handsome as he once was?" she inquired.

Claire accepted a slice of saffron cake before answering. "I'm unable to judge since I didn't know him before, but he's a nice enough looking man."

"Ransley cut quite a swath in his salad days. He was wealthy, and heir to a respected title. His smile has been known to make women swoon," the older woman reminisced.

"That was certainly not the case today," replied Claire, remembering his tight-lipped expression. "He was as stiff and somber as if he was being led to the gallows. His countenance can certainly not encourage Juliana's well-being."

"Why, that doesn't sound like the Quinton Courtney I knew," exclaimed the duchess. "He was always able to coax a smile from the most nervous girl. It had to be his marriage and all that followed that changed him. He made the mistake of marrying a pretty face and thinking of little else," she lamented, staring into the flames.

Claire was unexplainably downcast at being reminded the marquess was a married man. "His wife did not accompany him," she offered unenthusiastically.

"She died a year ago," the duchess explained. Observing Claire's inquisitive expression, she continued. "Lydia Grey was her name. She was of the gentry, but not his equal. At the time of their marriage she was only seventeen and he probably ten years her senior. He was old enough to know better, but not strong enough to resist her obvious charms. I understand his family and friends attempted to convince him to wait, but Lydia was determined to marry into titled wealth. With the help of her scheming mother, she rushed him into marriage, and to be fair, he did not fight it."

"It sounds as if their love overcame many obstacles. I'm sure they were very happy."

Her grandmother uttered a very unduchess-like snort. "*He* may have been blinded by love, but *she* certainly had her eye on the main chance. She used her beauty to snare him, but I doubt whether any emotion other than greed entered her thoughts. Shortly after their marriage Quinton's father died, and Lydia had everything she had dreamed of for so long. However it was soon apparent she was unequal to the station she had married into.

"Rumor had it that the new Lord Ransley was discontent before the honeymoon was over," continued the duchess, warming to her subject. "His bride was oblivious to anything and everyone but her own beauty and desires. The very thing that had captured Quinton Courtney drove him away. Soon after their child was born, he began making trips to the continent. It was said he travelled a great deal in order to avoid the emptiness of his marriage. He returned suddenly and word circulated that his daughter was unwell, and his wife was increasing. He had been back just a month or so and tragedy struck again."

"What could be worse than Juliana's problem?" asked Claire, setting down her cup and putting aside all pretense of interest in tea.

"You wouldn't remember. It was at the time you were regaining your sight and I'm sure much of what was happening passed you by."

"Yes. Each day a little more of the world was revealed. I was so engrossed in seeing again that everything else was of little import."

"I understand, child." The duchess reached over and patted Claire's hand. "I'm certain I would have felt the same." She gave her granddaughter a reassuring smile before continuing. "It was after Ransley returned from the continent, about a year ago if I recall correctly. He was attacked by footpads and left in the street for dead. Fortunately, he was found quickly, but his life hung in the balance for weeks before he came about.

"Then before he was fully recovered his wife suffered a fall down a flight of stairs, killing both herself and her unborn child. Since then Ransley and his family have lived quietly at his country estate. I had heard he had changed, but not that he had lost the smile that at one time turned every woman's heart."

Claire felt guilty for having judged the marquess too harshly without knowing the circumstances. "I think he feels responsible for Juliana's silence," she said, more to herself than to the duchess.

"That wouldn't be unusual for any parent, particularly for a man alone in his grief. Perhaps you'll be able to heal them both."

"At all events, I would not attempt to approach the

marquess, Grandmother. He holds himself too far apart to even attempt it."

"He's been hurt, Claire. Perhaps more so in heart and mind than body," replied the duchess. "If you're successful with his daughter, I own you'll see a totally different person. I cannot help but remember that engaging young man, and I'm convinced that side of him is still there."

"Perhaps, but I'll leave it for someone else to discover, and concentrate on Juliana," decided Claire.

The next evening Quinton Courtney stood in the shadow of a sickly looking palm at the edge of the Forsyths' drawing room, scanning the crowd until he spotted Claire Kingsley's graceful form.

Tonight she wore a green gown, with ribbons of the same color threaded through her hair. Emeralds sparkled at her neck and ears as she made her way through the various groups of guests.

The marquess had not been free from thoughts of the tawny tigress since their meeting at Dr. James's office, and a sliver of anger bubbled beneath his calm demeanor. He had sworn desire would never enslave him again, but here he was casting sheep's eyes at a woman he knew to be all that he abhorred.

It was essential he determine the true character of the woman who would be in close contact with his daughter, he told himself as he followed her progress around the room. He could not argue with her loveliness, but she was entirely too frivolous for her own good. It was also not to her credit that the men upon whom she chose to expend much of her charm were of questionable character.

While not widely known, Lord Ransley's travels had been in the service of England and, thus, he was well aware of the spying going on at all levels of society. Entree to the upper ten thousand did not guarantee loyalty to the crown.

In fact, many Englishmen admired Bonaparte's ability as much as his French followers did, and women were no less susceptible to his appeal. It was common knowledge that ladies sent gifts to the disposed emperor on Elba, hoping to make his exile less tedious. Lady Kingsley would not be the first person caught up in what began as an innocent desire to right what appeared to be a wrong.

Good God! What was happening to him? If every woman who flirted was a spy, England would have been overrun by the French long ago.

Once again, he wondered whether he had made a mistake in asking for Claire Kingsley's help with Juliana. She had seemed respectable in the doctor's office, and James heartily approved of her. Yet there had been more than a touch of insolence in her eye, as if she knew he questioned her competence and meant to prove him wrong.

Lord Ransley sighed in resignation. He was bent on giving Juliana every possible advantage for recovery. If it meant accepting the flighty Lady Kingsley, then so be it. He would keep a vigilant eye on her when she was with Juliana. He smiled, his gaze travelling the length of her gown as she stood conversing with the duchess and Lady Barringer— at least it would not be an unpleasant duty.

"Oh, come, Hanora," demanded Lady Barringer, "I remember how you pretended to tell fortunes when we were both girls. You did remarkably well, and we must add something of interest to the occasion if it is to be a success."

The duchess was sorry she had not seen Lady Barringer in enough time to avoid meeting her. They had never been bosom bows when they were young, as the overbearing woman continually implied. Now she was insisting that Hanora "lend her considerable talents to a good cause."

Lady Barringer considered herself a charitable minded woman who helped the downtrodden of society. Therefore, each season she held a benefit to assist the foundling home in London. The event had much in common with Almack's in that the refreshments were weak and bland; however, the surroundings were much more lavish than the exclusive rooms in the building on King Street.

"Yes, do agree," begged Claire, an impish light in her eye.

Her granddaughter was having too good a time at her expense, thought Hanora as she smiled sweetly. "I'll be happy to, Augusta, if Claire will agree to join me. She has been fortunate enough to inherit my talent for guessing futures."

"Oh, I am most happy to accommodate the both of you, to be sure," gushed Lady Barringer. She glowed at the opportunity of having two well-placed fortune-tellers at her entertainment. It was certain to be her most successful venture once it became known.

"What an unscrupulous trick," accused Claire, as their hostess bustled away no doubt to begin spreading the word.

"Why, my dear," replied the duchess innocently, "you seemed to think I would enjoy it so much I could not leave you out."

Claire burst out laughing. "You are a complete hand,

madam," she said, bringing her mirth under control. "I suppose I deserve as much."

"Of course you do, and before this affair is over you will wish you had told her I was breathing my last and unable to do nought but pray."

"You look far too healthy for her to believe such a Banbury tale. I'm sure it will not be nearly as bad as you make it out."

"I will be interested in your opinion when it's over," commented the duchess, leveling her a look that implied she was a bird-witted hoyden.

"If you will excuse me," said Claire making a quick getaway.

Lady Kingsley left the duchess and strolled in Lord Ransley's direction. The marquess was not eager to converse with the woman who had taken up so much of his thoughts, and he prepared to withdraw before her attention diverted to him. As he made ready to slip away, he was surprised to see Matthew Templeton approach her. The marquess had worked with Templeton occasionally during his service to the crown, and he allowed curiosity to overcome good manners by remaining well within listening distance of the two.

"Mr. Templeton, how lovely to see you."

"Lady Kingsley," responded Templeton with a slight bow. "I trust you are well this evening."

"I would hardly be out in such weather if I were not," Claire simpered.

The admiration in Templeton's eyes expressed his appreciation of her acting ability. "Let us hope tomorrow will be better. Staying indoors can dampen one's spirit."

"Indeed, sir. In fact, I am determined to visit Hatchard's no matter what the weather. I understand

they have a novel by Sir Walter Scott that will soon be
all the thing, and I simply must be the first to read it."

"Then I would suggest you wait until afternoon to
brave the elements, my lady. It will surely be warmer
then and you will have less chance of contracting a chill."

"You are so solicitous, Mr. Templeton," gushed
Claire, personally convinced he would urge her to swim
the icy Thames if it meant procuring information for
his office. "I'll take your advice and delay my excursion
until after luncheon. Now, I must take leave of you. I
see Miss Lacefield has arrived and I need to speak with
her." Fluttering her lashes one last time, Claire withdrew with a provocative swish of her skirts, passing Ransley without a glance.

The marquess was vastly irritated with the smile of
appreciation that spread across Templeton's face as he
watched Claire walk away. Ransley had often observed
a woman in the same way, and it was not the weather
he had been thinking about at the time. The relationship between Templeton and the woman who would
soon befriend his daughter deserved to be scrutinized,
he decided, and what better place to expand his knowledge than at a bookstore.

A few minutes later, Claire absently nodded in agreement with Margaret's assessment of Lady Rushmore's
scandalous dress, all the while watching Lord Ransley
speak politely to his hostess before departing. Too late,
she had observed him leaning against the wall near
where she and Templeton had paused. Had he overheard anything damaging? Reviewing the conversation,
she thought not, but she knew better than to underestimate the marquess.

She tapped her foot impatiently against the polished
floor. Now it was not only Hamilton, but also Lord Ransley,
who jeopardized her chances of success. She must tread
carefully around the two men; neither were fools.

Four

A short time later the marquess stepped out of his carriage on St. James Street and entered Brook's for the first time in more than a year. Time had stood still in the elegant club. He was greeted and served his favorite port with the same smooth service that had made Brook's the most prestigious club in London.

"Quinton! By God, it's good to see you again!" came a gruff voice from over his shoulder.

The comforting ritual of habit enfolded him. It never failed, he thought, accepting the hand extended to him, that sooner or later Andrew Stanford would toddle into Brook's before finding his way home each evening.

Andrew had been a friend since Quinton had rescued him at Eton from a gang of bullies who were looking for easy prey. Besides growing taller and broader, he had changed little since then. His unruly sandy hair still verged on red, and light freckles scattered across a slightly crooked nose that had been broken more than once. His face nearly always wore a good-natured smile, which had caused many men to underestimate the intelligence it hid. He and Quinton had enjoyed a friendship that had gotten them both out of more than a few sticky situations over the years.

After leaving school, they had remained close until the marquess's marriage, when Lydia had taken an unaccountable dislike to her husband's comrade. Quinton had urged Andrew to ignore her obvious snubs, but their friendship had suffered nonetheless.

"Sit down and have a drink if you can spare the time," he invited, indicating the wingback chair near his.

"Always have time, Quin," Andrew replied agreeably, accepting a glass from his friend and taking an appreciative swallow of the rich port. "Heard you were back in town."

"I owe you an apology for not answering your letter," said Quinton.

Andrew waved aside his words. "No need. Didn't expect any unless I could help. Dashed difficult time you went through. Wanted you to know I was there if you needed anything." He cleared his throat and stared at the toe of his boot.

Quinton smiled in amusement. Andrew had never found it easy to voice his feelings, and he doubted the man would ever marry for that reason alone. He could not imagine Drew finding the courage to declare his undying love to a woman. But that did not mean Andrew Stanford was not awake on every suit. Despite his retiring nature, Drew invariably knew the latest *ondits* of everyone worth knowing.

"I could always count on you," remarked Quinton, thankful their friendship had endured such a lengthy separation.

The two sat in companionable silence for a moment, savoring the renewal of a relationship they had both missed.

"Meant to call round after you got settled in," said Drew, raising his glass to Quinton in a salute.

"There wasn't much to settle," replied the marquess, lifting his glass in return. "I only brought Juliana with me. My mother and sister are still in the country and Jason's gone off to check on his estate.

"I've just left the Forsyths' soiree," continued Lor
Ransley leaning back in his chair. "I had forgotten ho
wearing the *ton* can be."

"Believe in jumping right in, don't you?" chuckle
Drew. "Forsyths' have a reputation for holding the mos
boring routs in town."

"Well, they certainly didn't jeopardize their positio
tonight."

Viscount Stanford laughed and helped himself to an
other glass of port.

"I saw Matthew Templeton this evening," Quinto
remarked casually.

"Good man. Worked with him, didn't you?"

"He was my contact on several occasions, but we ha
no opportunity to know one another well. He sper
some time with an extremely attractive lady tonight b
the name of Lady Kingsley."

"Ah, Claire Kingsley," said Stanford, encouraged tha
his old friend was showing some interest in the petticoa
line. "A widow, and very well off, so I've heard. No
that a beauty of her stature needs a fortune to attrac
a man."

"Which entices Templeton most?" asked Ransle
swirling the port in his glass.

"Neither. Templeton and her late husband wer
friends, worked together."

"They looked quite cozy this evening," commente
Quinton.

"Nothing serious in it," concluded Drew. "Been i
one another's company quite often since Lady Kingsle
started going into society again. Don't seem to go be
yond friendship."

"You're probably right, since she arrived with Ham
ilton Ashford."

"Same there," stated Drew. "Boyhood friend of he
husband's. Same school, that sort of thing."

"I heard Ashford was rolled up long ago," Quinton remarked casually.

"Not a feather to fly with," confirmed Drew, nodding emphatically, "make no mistake about that. Being the youngest son he'll probably never attain the title, and his father's profligate ways have all but depleted the family fortune."

"Sounds like an uncomfortable position," commented Quinton, frowning into his glass.

"Would think so," agreed Drew, stretching his legs out before the chair and crossing them at the ankle. Exhaling a sigh of contentment, he continued.

"Born to a lavish way of life, but no means to support it. Relied on his wits for years. Then had a run of luck at the tables. Made some excellent investments with the blunt, so he says. Lived fairly high since then. Can't seem to get gambling out of his blood though. Can usually find him here in the gaming room several times a week."

Ransley wondered if Lady Kingsley could be seriously involved with a man who made his living from gambling. She would probably enjoy the fast-paced life, but a run of bad luck and Ashford could go through her fortune and his in an instant, leaving them penniless.

"If your interest lies with the lady, Quin, don't worry about either of them. Lady Kingsley's shown no partiality toward anyone. Probably waiting for some fellow like you to come along and sweep her off her feet," joked Drew, smiling loosely at the marquess.

"You've had far too much port if you think I'm ready to become a tenant for life. It will take more than a pretty face to bring me up to scratch again," he vowed.

Since birth, he had taken a wife and family, along with his title and fortune, for granted. Every marquess before him had followed the time honored path and kept the family line intact. He felt a certain sense of

failure that so far he had been unsuccessful in his per
sonal life.

Oh, he had accepted the responsibility of the hold
ings and increased the family fortune, there was no
doubt about that; but he had chosen a wife who, he
was now willing to admit, had been unsuited to her
position. That he might have been the cause of her
death was something he did not wish to consider at the
moment. He rubbed his hand wearily over his face, then
stared at it as if blood from long healed scratches might
have suddenly reappeared.

Lord Ransley shared another glass of port with Vis
count Stanford before finding his way home. He had
learned nothing unfavorable about Lady Kingsley, but
his suspicions would not be laid to rest so easily. He
added what he had learned to his meager store of
knowledge before succumbing to a restless night of
sleep.

Matthew Templeton was not far wrong on his forecast
for a pleasant day, thought Claire, as she stepped out
of the carriage in front of Hatchard's the following af
ternoon. Although the day was crisp, the bright sun
brought much needed warmth to the city.

This time last year, London had experienced tem
peratures colder than many people had ever seen, but
much more had changed since then. At that time, the
darkness had only begun lifting for Claire, revealing
tantalizing glimpses of gray shadows wisping about
much like the fog that had lain so long and heavily over
the city. Now she raised her face to warm rays, enjoying
the beauty of an unusually pleasant day, and the color
and sights of the city in the brilliance of the sun.

Lord Ransley regarded Claire as she lingered outside
the store. In her green velvet pelisse and matching

green bonnet with curls sparking gold around her face, she looked like a hesitant jonquil leaning into the sun.

He had arrived some twenty minutes earlier, taking up an inconspicuous spot that would allow him an unrestricted view of the entrance while remaining obscured by the shelves. His instincts had remained reliable, he reflected smugly, as Matthew Templeton entered Hatchard's a short time after Claire.

The two met with the pleasantly surprised faces of old friends coming upon one another unplanned. Picking a book at random, the marquess moved closer to the couple who were now earnestly engaged in serious conversation. The hum of a busy afternoon's trade did not allow him to overhear their low voices from a distance, and he risked discovery by edging even nearer while directing his attention to the book in his hand. But his luck ran out when a chit just out of the schoolroom bumped against him, no doubt at the insistence of her mother who hovered nearby. Murmuring his apologies, he turned to find Templeton's and Lady Kingsley's attention focused on him.

"Lord Ransley," Claire trilled in a falsely frivolous tone. "I did not expect to see you here."

Claire was inexplicably shaken by her unexpected meeting with the marquess. She had been engrossed in her conversation with Templeton concerning the increasing rumors of Napoleon's escape until they were distracted by the disturbance nearby.

"Why so, Lady Kingsley? Did you imagine I could not read?" he retorted.

Claire flushed under his quizzical regard. The man obviously thought to transform her into a quivering peagoose with one searching perusal from his dark eyes. Gathering her composure she met the challenge of his intent gaze. "No, my lord, but I *am* surprised at your selection of reading material," she replied, tilting her head slightly to read the title of the book he held in his hand. *"The Compleat Book of a Lady's Complaints,"* she intoned gravely, looking to him for confirmation.

Ransley held her gaze, ignoring the choked laughter from Templeton. "For my mother. I'm afraid she doesn't understand that a man might lose his dignity by executing such a simple errand."

Claire felt a measure of satisfaction at catching him unawares. "Then it shall be our secret, Lord Ransley, and will go no further. Will it, Mr. Templeton?"

"No, of course not," her companion agreed in a strained voice.

"My thanks to you both," said the marquess, holding her gaze a moment longer before turning to the other man. "As I remember, Templeton, you are unmarried and your parents reside in Suffolk."

"That's true, my lord," the other man confirmed in a puzzled tone.

"Then, may I assume your selection is for your own enlightenment?"

Templeton looked down at the volume in his hand, *Sermons for the Edification of a Sinner's Soul.* At each meeting, Claire took great delight in presenting her information to him in outlandish reading material. In the past, he had left the bookstore with gothic novels, feminist writings, and books on new farming methods. He had accepted them with a wry smile, knowing she was exacting retribution from him for ever doubting her ability. But suffering Ransley's ridicule was more than he was willing to endure.

"Ah, Lady Kingsley was good enough to recommend it," he replied, sparing a sharp glance for the woman by his side. Abruptly offering his goodbyes, he made his way to the front of the store, quickly paying for the book and disappearing onto the crowded street.

"He actually bought the thing," said the marquess in disbelief.

"Of course, my lord. Some men do not put themselves above taking suggestions from a woman," she quipped, still smarting from his earlier shot.

"No we do not, ma'am," he agreed pleasantly.

"You, my lord? That I cannot believe," she replied, feigning amazement.

"You are seeing my daughter because you suggested you could help her, did you not?" he answered smoothly.

Drat, the man! Why did she lose all sense around him? "Of course. And I appreciate your confidence," she admitted, unwilling to risk her chance at helping Juliana because of an excess of conceit.

"Then I will bid you good day, Lady Kingsley. Juliana and I will look forward to seeing you Tuesday next." He was gone as quickly as Templeton, his grimace as he paid for the book discouraging any comment from the clerk.

Too keyed up to go home, Claire directed the coachman to Margaret's house on Upper Grosvenor Street. She arrived just as Margaret and Forrest Harcourt descended the steps of the brick town house.

"Claire," Margaret called out in a welcoming voice. "Mr. Harcourt has just invited me to drive in Hyde Park. Please join us."

Margaret exhibited an inner glow that made her eyes sparkle and the very air around her crackle with excitement.

"I wouldn't want to impose," protested Claire.

"It would be no imposition, Lady Kingsley," assured Harcourt. "We would be happy to have your company."

"I'm sorry, but I really must decline," she repeated,

feeling decidedly *de trop*. "I have only a few minutes before I'm expected back at Kenton House. I thought merely to say hello and be on my way. I imagine I'll see you tonight at the Barnstables' rout, won't I?"

"Yes, I had planned on attending," said Margaret.

"And I would deem it an honor to escort both of you ladies if you would allow it," offered Harcourt, a devastating smile on his handsome face.

"Well . . ." faltered Margaret.

"We would be delighted to accept your offer," said Claire, not happy with the situation, but unwilling to leave Margaret alone with him in a dark carriage.

"Then we'll see you this evening, my lady," replied Harcourt, handing Margaret into his curricle.

Margaret gave a worried look over her shoulder as they drove off. She well knew Claire had more to say than hello.

Claire reentered her carriage and ordered the coachman to return to Berkeley Square. Her life had become increasingly difficult of late and her head was spinning with its complications.

When she had begun her search for John's murderer, she never thought she would be seriously considering a man her best friend admired to be the guilty party. Claire pressed a hand to her temple, admitting that even though Margaret seemed taken with Forrest Harcourt, she could not eliminate his as a suspect.

In addition, she was failing in her attempt to convince Matthew Templeton to take the latest rumor of Napoleon's escape seriously. Perhaps she was setting too much store in her ability. Grandmama had warned her it could not always be relied upon. But in this instance she knew with a certainty that Bonaparte would escape his small pile of rocks in an attempt to become emperor in more than name only.

Then there was Juliana, a child so frightened that

she could not share her fears with anyone. It was a grave responsibility to have Juliana's future resting in her hands. And the marquess might prove to be the largest obstacle in her path. Even though he had agreed to have her work with Juliana, his apprehension was evident. Claire was determined he would be begging her forgiveness for his skepticism before she was finished.

The well-sprung carriage came to a halt and Claire gathered her dark green skirts to step down to the cobblestones. There was nothing she could do about Lord Ransley or Juliana at present, but perhaps she could keep Margaret's heart intact if she acted quickly. Claire hurried into the house to change before joining her grandmother for tea.

A short time later, dressed in a gown of Bishop's blue, Claire handed the duchess a cup of Bohea tea. Pouring another cup, she settled back into the chair, stirring her tea and staring into the fire until the older woman looked up to discover the reason for her silence.

"For heaven's sake, Claire, you take nothing in your tea. So put down that spoon and tell me what's bothering you and be done with it."

Claire came alert with a start. "I'm sorry, Grandmama, but I'm worried about Margaret."

"Never say she's been decorating other gentlemen with iced cakes," responded the duchess, calmly sipping from the gold rimmed cup.

"Of course not. Just the opposite is true. I'm afraid she's taken a particular liking for a certain gentleman."

"Is there no in between for the girl?" chided the duchess mournfully.

"This is serious, Grandmama!"

"Then I see no problem. It's high time Margaret found a man she can admire. I should think you would be happy for her."

"I would be if the gentleman was worthy of her, but from what I can see he's a scoundrel who would bring her nothing but sorrow."

"Margaret is no green girl, Claire. She's a level-headed woman of an age to make decisions for herself."

"Normally I would agree, Grandmama, but she is so completely taken with Forrest Harcourt she has lost all common sense. I think if he asked her to leave with him tonight she would not even take time to pack her portmanteau."

"Harcourt?" pondered the duchess. "I don't recognize his name."

"No one knows anything about him," complained Claire, "except he's dark and exceedingly attractive to women."

"And are you taken by him also?"

"He holds no appeal for me."

Hanora Maitland studied the rosy blush stealing across her granddaughter's face. No doubt another dark, handsome man had been taking up her thoughts lately.

"I wondered, Grandmama. Would it be too presumptuous to see how he feels about her?"

"After your last disastrous venture into those waters you wish to set sail again?" the duchess asked skeptically.

"Only for Margaret's good. I can't sit by and watch her make a mistake that could ruin her life."

"Claire, I learned long ago that even my gift could not save the people I care for from going their own way and sometimes making a shambles of their lives. Much of the time people will resent your advice no matter how well intended or knowledgeable. The sooner you accept that you must be selective and discreet in offering help, the more content your own life will be."

All that broke the silence was the crackling of the fire, and the duchess knew her answer was not to her granddaughter's liking. It would take time for Claire to realize she could not solve all the sorrows of the world, no matter how great her gift.

As the silence lengthened, she sighed in resignation, knowing her advice had fallen on deaf ears. "Has the man approached her with an unworthy proposition?" she asked.

Claire looked up, a flare of hope springing to light in her face. "None of which I'm aware. They converse when they meet of an evening, and today they were going to drive in the park."

"Then I see nothing untoward in the situation," the duchess said gently. "You attach too much significance to Margaret's admiration for the man. I'm sure she will conduct herself in the proper manner."

"But, Grandmama—"

"Claire, you asked for my opinion and I have given it to you," she said resolutely. "I cannot force you to take my advice, but I ask you to remember my early days in London. I would hate to see you suffer the same fate, especially if someday you have children of your own."

Claire fell silent. "My mother hurt you terribly, didn't she?"

"Yes. She didn't mean to, and I can understand her feelings. Naomi only wanted a normal life— one without a parent whose unusual abilities made grist for the *ton's* gossip mill. Instead, she found herself getting glimmerings of our gift."

"But it can be a wonderful gift," replied Claire, thinking of the children she had helped.

"Not for Naomi. She was frightened she would be ostracized from society, and fought the curse that she deemed would ruin her life if she gave in to it. She ignored its existence, married against our wishes, and moved away from London."

The duchess was silent for a moment, taking a sip of tea while she regained her composure.

"It was worse when you arrived," confessed the older woman. "We were not allowed to see you at all. Only once were we able to slip by her guard. We tried, Claire, I hope you understand how much we wanted to see you."

"I do," said Claire, taking her grandmother's hand.

"Why did it take such a tragedy to bring us together?" the duchess asked, tears shining in her eyes.

"I don't know, Grandmama, but we cannot change the past. I regret the years we've been apart, but we must make the most of what we have now. And if it will make you happy, I'll forget all about Margaret and her regrettable *tendre.*"

"I'm happy just having you with me, my dear, but perhaps we can solve your quandary in a more accepted way. I will see what I can find out about Mr. Harcourt."

"Oh, thank you," said Claire, kissing the duchess's cheek enthusiastically.

Claire's spirit rose during the evening. After escorting the two women to the Barnstables' rout, Harcourt was distracted by Carrington, who asked him to make up a table in the card room. Even though the women did not see him again until shortly before they were to leave, Margaret did not seem dejected by his negligence. Perhaps her grandmother was right; perhaps Claire had made too much of Margaret's attraction to the man.

The marquess arrived late in the evening accompanied by a sandy-haired gentleman. Both were perfectly attired in black evening dress, but Lord Ransley had an air about him that commanded attention, or so Claire thought. He nodded across the room when their eyes met and she acknowledged him, but neither made a move to seek one another's company.

The exchange didn't go unnoticed by Viscount Stanford. "Met Lady Kingsley, I see."

"Yes, it was unavoidable," said Lord Ransley, amused at his friend's obvious interest in his personal life. "We had some business to transact."

Drew quirked an eyebrow, took out his quizzing glass, and peered through it. "Business ain't what it used to be. Usually wrinkled old men smelling of cigar smoke. Not lovely ladies in blue silk."

"Don't try to gammon me after all these years," said Quinton with a smile for his friend. "It's private and thoroughly above board I assure you."

Drew gave him another quizzical look, but said no more on the subject. "Ashford's here this evening," he observed, looking toward the door. "Met him yet?"

"I know him only by reputation, but I'm relying on you to remedy that oversight."

"More business?"

"In a manner of speaking."

"Private?"

"Andrew, your insight is exceptional." A roguish smile lit the marquess's features. "Now, let us accidentally bump into the Honorable Hamilton Ashford."

Claire watched apprehensively as Viscount Stanford introduced Lord Ransley to Hamilton. She did not need either man in her life; one smothered her with unwanted attention, while the other looked at her with cynical disbelief. Breathing a sigh of relief when they parted a few minutes later, she turned the full effect of her charm on her next dancing partner, making him wonder what he had done to deserve such a radiant smile, and how he could do it again.

* * *

Claire's apprehension increased during the week before her first meeting with Juliana. She had seen the marquess nearly every evening at one event or another, but they had exchanged no more than polite comments. She did not know what had caused him to take her in such dislike, but she was sure that if it weren't for Juliana, he would cut her without a second thought.

Claire had agreed that Juliana would feel more comfortable in her own home, and arrived in Grosvenor Square on Tuesday afternoon to be met by Lord Ransley in the marble floored entrance hall. The marquess's hair looked as if he had run agitated fingers through the dark strands, and Claire speculated he had been pacing while awaiting her arrival. She felt somewhat appeased that she was not the only one overly concerned with this first meeting.

Suspicion fairly radiated from Lord Ransley's large figure as he led her into the drawing room where his daughter awaited them. Juliana was wearing a white dress with a blue sash and shoes which set off to perfection the blue of her eyes and the dark curls bouncing around her shoulders.

A small tea table had been brought in, and Claire was reminded of her own childhood as Juliana precisely positioned a cup and saucer at each chair. Claire remembered the long, lonely years spent on the Yorkshire estate where her only companions had been her dolls. They had shared all her secrets and had become as real to her as any playmate could be. She recognized herself in Juliana and was saddened that another child had to endure the loneliness she had experienced.

She watched as Juliana set out matching dishes filled with cakes and thinly sliced bread and butter. At times such as this, Claire gave thanks for her gift, and the opportunity to bring a child happiness.

Although Claire would have preferred to be alone

with Juliana, she did not dare suggest it while the marquess was so obviously in high dudgeon. Fortunately the drawing room was large and his lordship withdrew to the far end where he sat like a threatening thundercloud.

Claire attempted to ignore his presence and concentrate on Juliana. The child was withdrawn at first, her mind hiding behind the wall that protected her, but as Claire took tea with the dolls gathered around the miniature table, she detected a slight thawing in Juliana's attitude. Questions crept through as Juliana's guard dropped.

Who are you? What are you doing here?

"I'm here to be your friend," Claire said, calmly lifting a lilliputian teacup to her lips. She smiled at Juliana's startled glance, seeing the same suspicion she had observed in the marquess's eyes a short time earlier.

"Do you believe in magic, Juliana?" She had the child's full attention. "Well, I have a magic gift, you see. I know that for some reason you're afraid to speak, and I know that you probably miss talking a great deal. Why, you cannot sing or talk to your dolls or even speak to your papa."

Juliana's eyes were glued to Claire's face in rapt attention. "But you may talk to me, Juliana."

No. No, I can't. Can't talk at all or bad things will happen.

"That's not true, Juliana, but I know you believe it to be. And until you feel safe again I have a grand surprise for you. You will be able to talk to me without saying a word out loud. So you'll still be safe, but you won't be alone anymore."

Juliana looked at her with disbelief for a long silent moment before turning her attention to the tea table again, her lower lip jutting out in stubbornness.

Not true, not true.

"Of course, it's true," repeated Claire gently, reach-

ing out to touch the small shoulder which held a weight
far too great for its size.

Juliana met her gaze again, alarm apparent in her
face. "Don't worry, darling. This will be our secret. No
one need know except the two of us." Out of the corner
of her eye Claire saw the marquess check his watch and
shift restlessly in his chair.

"It's time for me to go now, Juliana, but I'll be back
to see you soon. Remember, you're not alone anymore.
I want you to think of all those things you've wanted
to say and tell me the next time I'm here. Will you do
that for me?" she asked.

There was no response from Juliana, but Claire
thought she noticed a flare of interest in the dark eyes
as the maid led her away.

As soon as Juliana left the room, Lord Ransley made
his way to Claire's side, the expression on his face thunderous.

"Is that all you plan to do?" he demanded. Seated
in a remote corner of the room, he had been unable
to distinguish what was being said, but Lady Kingsley's
words had elicited no overt response from Juliana. "I
don't know what kind of rig you're running, but I won't
have my daughter become an *ondit* for your amusement," he stormed.

"I've done exactly what I had planned," Claire replied calmly, drawing on her gloves. "I became acquainted with Juliana. What did you expect?"

Her unruffled reply infuriated him. "I don't know,"
he admitted truthfully. "But more than just talking. *I*
can talk to her."

"But I *listened*, my lord," she responded reasonably.

"What do you mean?" he growled. "I saw everything.
She said nothing."

"Yes, she did. That's what I can do that no one else
can; I can listen to her. Most adults are too busy telling

children what is right or wrong to actually hear what they say. The difficulty is increased tremendously with a child who has a problem like Juliana's," continued Claire, meeting the marquess's gaze without flinching beneath his heated glare. "She cannot speak, but there are other ways to converse, and I can understand them. You must trust me when I say that I can listen, that I can learn her fears and help her overcome them."

Ransley ran an agitated hand through his black hair. "Dammit! I don't understand what you mean."

"I know, there are few who do," she said, filled with compassion at his confession. How she wished she had the confidence to disclose her ability to him, but it was much too early to consider such a move, if ever. And that thought, too, brought on sadness. "That's why I'm extremely careful about the children I help. If word got out about my unorthodox behavior then I would be the *ondit*, not Juliana. So if you feel threatened by me, then I am equally threatened by you."

The marquess paced to the window and back, pausing directly in front of her, his frustration turning to anger at the lack of any acceptable explanation. "I have had the unhappy task of watching you nearly every night this past week. You are a consummate flirt, madam," he stated harshly, "concerned only with a good time. You consort with men of such questionable allegiance that I would not invite them into my home, all for the sake of their flattering words. Yet you are my last chance." He grasped her shoulders in an iron grip, glaring into her eyes as if to sear her soul. "Listen, and listen well. I won't have Juliana's name bandied about. If I hear one breath of gossip about my daughter, I will make you sorry you ever heard my name."

"I already am, sir," she replied, striving to remain unruffled in the face of his anger. "And if it weren't for Juliana you would never see me again. But the child needs me. With your permission, I will be back in two days time, my lord. If you would absent yourself, you would do us both a favor."

Pulling from his grasp, she marched stiffly to the door. Turning, she subjected him to a head to toe scrutiny which stripped him bare and made him understand why women detested it so.

"I may be all that you despise, but at least I have not forgotten that life is for living. That's something you have misplaced somewhere along the way. You might think of your child and reconsider your attitude."

With that parting shot she stepped into the hall. He stood listening until the heavy outside door closed behind her, his hands clenched with the effort of exercising control over his emotions.

Was ever a man caught in such a quandary— where he must consort with a woman not only of questionable virtue, but also of suspect loyalty to her country? He paced the room again, unable to remain still while recounting the scene just past.

His decision was a foregone conclusion, wearing a hole in the carpet would not change it. There were times when pride must be set aside, and this was one of them. He had told Dr. James he would try the devil himself if there was a chance that Juliana would speak again. Now he must insure that the devil was still willing.

Five

Needing time to think before she returned to Kenton House, Claire ordered the coachman to drive through Hyde Park. If she returned home immediately, her grandmother would certainly see that she was upset and demand to know why. And Claire did not know herself.

Others had doubted her and she had not become angry. But to be honest, it was not the marquess's misgivings about her ability to help his daughter that had vexed her, but his criticism of her conduct. Until now she had felt no scruples about her deportment, content in the belief that finding John's murderer prevailed over all else. For the first time she saw herself from a stranger's point of view and she did not like what she saw.

By the time Claire returned to Berkeley Square she was outwardly composed. Changing quickly, she joined her grandmother in the small sitting room for tea.

"You look chilled, my dear. Here, this will warm you," she said, handing Claire a steaming cup of tea.

"Thank you, Grandmama. It was so sunny a few days ago, I thought surely that spring was arriving early this year. Now it is as cold as it was before."

"The vagaries of the English clime, my dear. But surely the weather isn't causing such deep thinking on your part."

"I saw Juliana today."

"Ahhh."

Claire clasped her hands in a white-knuckled grip. "I felt so helpless, Grandmama. I should have been able to reach her and I couldn't."

"You're too impatient, Claire, and much too hard on yourself. You cannot expect Juliana to immediately trust you with all her secrets."

"If only my skill was more developed. There are times that I cannot probe any further despite feeling that I could if I just knew how. I glimpse incomplete pictures and wonder why I can't see them fully," she replied peevishly.

"It will take time, Claire. You've come a long way in the short time you've been aware of your ability. Eventually you'll learn to open your mind and direct the force of your power, but it won't happen overnight. Remember, too, that even though you gain knowledge of what is going to happen, it doesn't necessarily mean you can control it," she cautioned. "So don't chastise yourself for what you perceive as shortcomings. Be proud of what you've attained thus far and the lives you've helped. You have nothing to be ashamed of, my dear. I'm very proud of you."

"Oh, Grandmama, I don't know what I would have done without you," replied Claire, tears glistening in her eyes.

"Hush, child, and have some more tea before we both become watering pots."

The duchess poured them another cup, and they made an effort to lighten the mood by exchanging gossip from the previous evening's entertainments.

"Tony has invited us to the theatre," imparted the duchess, and was rewarded with a radiant smile. "I told him you were already promised for tonight and tomorrow, so he's planning on the evening after if you're free. He included Margaret, too."

Claire took inordinate pleasure in the theatre, and it would be a welcome diversion from the problem Lord Ransley posed to her. "A night at the theatre sounds wonderful. I'll ask Margaret tonight when I see her. Lord Moreland is an extremely thoughtful man, Grandmama," said Claire, the last hint of tears disappearing. "If you don't watch closely, someone will steal him away from you."

"Don't be impertinent. We are just very good friends," she replied sharply, a light blush rising on her cheeks.

"Well, in case you change your mind, I would not at all take exception at a step grandfather of his calibre," teased Claire.

"You may be too old to turn across my knee, young lady, but I can still send you to your room," said the duchess with mock severity.

Claire laughed and left the sitting room in a much lighter frame of mind. She would put Lord Ransley and his stiff-necked disapproval out of her mind and look forward to the evening's entertainment.

There was a sameness to the evenings that could not be avoided no matter how enthusiastically the hostess attempted to vary the motif and atmosphere.

The Bellinghams' soiree was much like the last one Lord Ransley had attended, except tonight he had come to apologize to Lady Kingsley, not stand on the sidelines and mentally criticize her every move.

London was filling up quickly, and every new arrival must be packed into the Bellinghams' ballroom this evening. Ransley had been working his way through the crush nearly a full half-hour before he spied Claire's tawny curls. His mouth tightened as he recognized the man with her.

Lord Burton, Earl of Westfield, was one of the most corrupt beings he knew. The man indulged in every debauchery known in the hell holes of London. He had run his estate into the ground and had come within an Ames-ace of fleeing from England because of his debts. An aging uncle had saved him and he lived on expectations that the elderly man would die before his pockets were to let again. It was rumored he would do anything for money, not excluding murder. Lord Ransley's lip curled into a sneer as he watched Burton whisper in Claire's ear.

"Lady Kingsley," he greeted, presenting himself in front of her. "Burton," he added almost as an afterthought.

Claire nodded stiffly, her eyes wary, until she realized she was permitting the marquess to intimidate her. Her indignation immediately flamed into life again. She would not allow one suspicious, disagreeable man to ruin her evening, no matter how handsome he was, nor how often he commanded her compassion as well as her anger. Breathing deeply she lifted her chin and met his gaze, the sparks from her eyes threatening to singe his perfectly tied cravat.

"My lord, I am surprised to see you. It was my understanding you had a distaste for the questionable conduct exhibited by some members of the *ton.*" She was gratified by the hint of color marking his cheekbones, but his gaze did not waver from hers.

"I believe you were ill advised, my lady," he replied calmly, curbing his urge to pull her away from the blackguard who was standing far too close to her. "With your permission I'll spend the next dance acquainting you with the truth of the matter."

Claire had been dreading their meeting. He was a proud man and she had greatly insulted him in his own home, but she had not changed her mind. She still thought him deserving of every word she had uttered, and had not been able to bring herself to pen an apology. She knew perfectly well there was more behind his request than a dance, and she prayed he was not going to deny her meetings with Juliana. She had been unable to detect the child's problem during their brief time together, but she had felt the sadness and despair that filled her small body, and the spark of happiness she could not completely conceal when Claire had conversed with her.

Murmuring a hasty farewell to Lord Burton, Claire accepted Lord Ransley's arm and walked quietly beside him. "The dance floor seems quite crowded, my lady. Shall we tour the gallery instead?"

Startled green eyes met his, and he realized with a small stab of shame that she was afraid of him. Had Lydia looked at him that way before she died? He could not think of it now.

"I promise you will be quite safe with me, my lady. I only mean to talk; you have my word."

She nodded and he led her through the room and into the hall. Silence enveloped them as they climbed the stairs to the long gallery filled with Bellingham ancestors. Several other couples seeking privacy were too preoccupied to pay them heed as they strolled slowly down the length of the room.

"Bellingham considers himself something of a collector. He has a Turner here that might interest you." They stopped in front of the landscape, studying it for a time before the marquess spoke again.

"I'm here to apologize, Lady Kingsley, in hopes that you will forget that regrettable scene yesterday."

His words were not at all what Claire expected. "There is no need, my lord," she objected, surprised to find she did not like his being humble after all.

"There is every need," he answered sincerely. "I had

no intention of engaging in a battle royal with you, nor
any right to cast aspersions on your character. It's true
I was disappointed," he acknowledged with a contrite
quirk of his lips, "not that I expected Juliana to suddenly start speaking," he said, waving his hand dismis-
sively. "But perhaps I was looking for a sign that would
assure me things would come right in time."

"You were so angry." she murmured, watching him
closely.

"Yes, and frightened, too," he admitted with an honesty most men would eschew. He looked unaccus-
tomedly vulnerable, his face free from the rigid mask
of self-control he usually kept in place. "I try not to
think about Juliana never speaking again," he confessed. Turning, he took both her hands in his, studying
them as if they contained a secret he could not unravel.
"It's disturbing for me to know I'm helpless and that
her future rests in these small hands."

A short time earlier Claire would never have thought
she could feel compassion for Lord Ransley again, but
she was helpless as it spread insidiously through her
body, supplanting the anger that lingered there.

"Physical stature is not always the best measure of
success, my lord. I cautioned you earlier that I won't
build your hopes and tell you for a certainty that Juliana
will be all right, but I have a great belief that I can
help her."

"Then I pray you have not taken such an aversion to
me that you will cry off."

"I had no such intention," she confessed, and saw
the tension begin to ease from his large frame. "I would
have called and allowed you to make the decision
whether to admit me."

"Shall we cry peace then, and accept one another as
we are for Juliana's sake?" His forthrightness was rewarded with a dazzling smile.

"Of course, my lord," Claire readily agreed, banishing the last of her anger. "After all, we need not be lifelong friends, but surely we can contrive to be amicable until Juliana is well again."

Intent on their conversation, she looked an entirely different person from the beautiful but flighty woman who had graced the ballroom only a short time before. For the moment, he forgot his objection to the men whose company she sought, and the manner in which she comported herself. He craved to hold her, to absorb her faith that Juliana would be whole again.

Releasing her hands, he grasped her shoulders, prepared to pull her into his arms. But she cringed beneath his touch. "My pardon, madam," he said stiffly, releasing her. "I didn't mean to frighten you."

"No, my lord, it isn't that. It's just that my arms . . . I mean they're . . ." Her protestations died on her lips and she looked at him as if to beg his understanding.

Suddenly he was afraid he understood only too well. Touching the rich material of her dress he inched the sleeve down until the beginning of a dark bruise showed against her fair skin, confirming the strength of his grip the day before. His lips thinned, opening only to utter an oath of disgust.

"I'm sorry, Claire," he said, oblivious to his familiar address in the emotion of the moment. "Damn, that's altogether inadequate. I never meant to hurt you. I've never hurt any woman before."

"It's of no consequence, my lord," Claire assured him, stepping back to escape his touch. She felt much safer dealing with the arrogant Lord Ransley than with this man who was so obviously distressed at the results of his action. He aroused feelings she had thought were long dead, feelings she was not yet ready to acknowledge. Claire was all at sixes and sevens and knew she must escape before making a complete fool of herself.

"Since we have made peace I prefer to forget everything that happened," she uttered briskly. "Now I must return, I've promised the next dance to Lord Burton." She turned away and hurried down the room hastily adjusting the sleeve of her dress so it covered the bruise again.

The marquess stood alone in the gallery, wondering. Had he never harmed a woman, or did this prove conclusively that he could, if strongly provoked? Were the rumors true? Had he killed Lydia?

The great horseshoe auditorium of the King's Theatre in Haymarket was filled to capacity. The boxes glittered with jewels and fine silks and satins of the ladies and the Fashionable Impures, while the pit was filled with dandies strutting about dressed in the extremes of fashion. The prince regent and the royal dukes often frequented the theatre, but were not in attendance tonight. Which was fortunate, thought Claire, because there was not an empty space for the corpulent regent to squeeze into.

Claire was pleased that Margaret had been able to join their party at the theatre, hoping they might find a private moment to discuss Harcourt. She agreed with her grandmother that she was being presumptuous, but she did not want to see her friend hurt. And what she had seen of Harcourt did nothing to reassure her of his suitability.

Catalani was singing and the first act ended in thunderous applause before the real business of coming to the theatre began. People visited from box to box and promenaded in the corridors to display escorts, clothes, and jewels, exchanging the latest *ondits* and watching others occur before their eyes.

The occupants of Lord Moreland's box elected to stay

where they were instead of entering the crush in the hallway. Claire had just summoned the courage to approach Margaret about Harcourt when Lord Ransley entered the box with the same sandy-haired gentleman who had accompanied him at the Barnstables' rout.

She did nothing to hide her surprise. "Lord Ransley."

"Lady Kingsley, I observed you from our box and thought to pay my respects." Taking her hand he bent over it, his lips leaving a trail of warmth where they touched.

"May I present Andrew, Viscount Stanford?" he said, indicating the sturdy figure standing next to him.

"Pleasure, ma'am."

"My lord," Claire acknowledged. "I'm sure you're acquainted with the Duchess of Kenton and Anthony, Lord Moreland. And this is Miss Lacefield," said Claire completing the introductions.

"It's been some time since I've seen you, Lord Ransley," said the duchess.

"My loss, Your Grace," he replied smoothly. "I shall try to rectify the situation in the future."

Hanora laughed at his blatant flattery. "Do that, you scoundrel. Now I have changed my mind, Tony, I think a stroll would be just the thing."

"Of course, my dear, allow me." The earl offered her his arm and they disappeared into the hall leaving the younger people alone.

Viscount Stanford and Margaret were soon engaged in a discussion on the merits of Catalani's performance, leaving Claire and Quinton to entertain one another.

"You look quite fetching this evening, Lady Kingsley." Her gown, which was white gauze over a slip of white, was sprinkled with diamantes that sparkled in the dim light of the box. More diamonds glittered around her neck, at her ears, and in her hair. Juliana would think her a fairy princess from her favorite bedtime story, he thought, and a smile hovered about his mouth threatening to break through.

"Thank you, my lord. How is Juliana?" she asked before the pause could lengthen into awkwardness.

"She seems to be happier, and I attribute that to you."

"Come, Lord Ransley, I know we have agreed to get along, but you need not flatter me so outrageously," she chided.

"I am not flattering you," he replied, his face serious. "I truly believe that Juliana seems more at ease since she saw you. She gazes out the window a lot; I think she's watching for you."

Claire experienced a small sense of satisfaction at his words. "Please reassure her that I will be back."

"I've already done so," he confessed. "Several times, in fact, and she smiles each time."

Quinton held her gaze for a moment, sharing the small success. Like proud parents, he thought, before they were interrupted by the return of the duchess and Lord Moreland.

It was with a much lighter heart that Claire changed for bed and drifted off to sleep that night, her dreams filled with the tall, dark-haired marquess, which she did nothing to vanquish.

"I promise never to tease you again," whispered Claire as she and the duchess stood inside Lady Barringer's ballroom.

"That is comforting, my dear, but unfortunately comes too late to change our current situation. You must admit, however, that Augusta does not stint on decoration."

Lady Barringer had decided on a country fair theme

for her rout, and had created a scene more opulent than any country lass could imagine. Rich, colorful fabrics were draped from ceiling to floor, creating private booths around the edge of the ballroom. Large plants and seats were arranged on the dance floor to produce the idea of a village square. In the center was a fountain where live ducks splashed in the pool surrounding it, filling the air with their raucous quacks.

"Silly looking birds," grumbled the duchess. "All noise and no brain. Well adapted for survival in the *ton*," she remarked with a mischievous glint in her eye. "I do believe that large one sounds suspiciously like Augusta's first husband. I would not blame him for returning as a duck; it would be a far better bargain than being wed to her."

"Grandmama, hush," warned Claire, turning her laughter into a small cough. Searching the ballroom for a diversion, her attention was caught by the tables of refreshments scattered around the room, each overseen by a footman dressed in Lady Barringer's idea of country clothes.

"I wonder how many farmers wear velvet?" remarked Hanora, barely disguising her laughter.

"Could we not just slip quietly away?" Claire asked, hoping she could contain her grandmother's high spirits until they were in private.

"My dears," trilled Lady Barringer, approaching them with outstretched hands.

"Too late," muttered the duchess, "we are truly caught. Smile, my dear, remember this was your idea."

Claire was to rue the thought a half-hour later standing in front of the chevel glass dressed in the costume Lady Barringer had provided her. She wore a long, red full skirt, pulled up on one side to show a white lacy petticoat trimmed with red bows. The blouse was no better. It was red, also, with black fringe around the

low-cut neckline which exposed far more of her flawless
skin than usual. Long, red paste earrings dangled pro-
vocatively from her ears, while several strands of beads
hung round her neck.

Augusta had insisted she color her cheeks and lips
and let her hair flow freely down her back. That was
the gypsy way, she had said just before darting out of
the room to check on the preparations.

Turning, Claire inspected her grandmother's dress.
"You are at least costumed with a little more dignity,"
she charged.

"If you call purple satin and a turban with an os-
trich feather dignified, then I suppose I am," the
duchess replied. "But look at this," she said, holding
out a myriad-colored shawl, trimmed with a deep
fringe that would blind anyone who stared at it more
than two minutes.

Claire could not help herself. She giggled at the sight
and could not stop. Soon the two women were doubled
over in laughter at the scrap they had gotten themselves
into.

"Well, madam, our audience awaits," gasped Claire,
finally getting herself under control.

"Lead on, my dear," replied the older woman. Link-
ing arms, they made their way to the ballroom.

Claire's tent was fashioned with draped red silk,
which blocked out most of the light from the ballroom,
leaving the interior dim and mysterious. A black fringed
cloth covered the small round table which held a large
crystal ball. Near the entrance, there was a cut-glass
bowl where anyone availing themselves of her talents
was expected to deposit a contribution. The duchess
was ensconced in a similar brilliant purple tent across
the floor.

Lord and Lady Mansfield were the first to enter. The
two were newlyweds just back from their honeymoon.

Lord Mansfield seated his giggling bride and stood behind her.

"Nothing would do for my wife but to see what our future holds," he said, placing his hand affectionately on her shoulder.

"If you will concentrate, my lady," Claire said in a dialect she felt confident belonged to no known country or race.

The young woman, attempting to look very solemn, closed her eyes in concentration. She could have saved herself the effort thought Claire, because the news of her pregnancy was uppermost in her mind.

"You will have a long, happy life filled with love," predicted Claire, following her grandmother's instructions of foretelling love for the ladies, and great fortune for the gentlemen.

Lady Mansfield reached up and placed her hand over her husband's.

"I see a happy event in your future," continued Claire. Not wanting to make her task look too effortless, she stared into the crystal ball frowning. "It is not exactly clear yet, but . . . wait! Yes, I see it now! In a short time you will be blessed with an addition to your family."

"How could you know?" gasped the young woman, her face pale with shock.

"Violet, you were aware of this?" demanded Lord Mansfield.

"Well, I . . . that is, I was not exactly certain," she stammered out.

"But you were not going to tell me until after the hunt next week, were you? You knew I would forbid you to endanger our child. I cannot believe you would be so devious," he said, stomping out of the tent.

"How could you do such a thing?" cried Lady Mansfield, tears streaming down her face. "You have ruined my marriage," she accused, hurrying after her husband.

Before Claire could order her thoughts, another figure entered.

"Ah, Lady Kingsley, what a lovely fortune teller you make."

"You should not recognize me this evening, Mr. Templeton. I am a mysterious gypsy here to tell your future."

"If your crystal ball could tell me whether Napoleon is planning escape, I would be satisfied."

"Have you heard it from other sources?" she asked eagerly.

"Yes, but I cannot give it credit unless I have at least a scrap of substantial evidence. All I have now are whispers of an escape, and that we've heard before," he fumed, unable to contain his frustration.

"Surely you cannot ignore even a possibility?" Claire asked anxiously.

"Of course not, but there's little I can do. I don't have enough evidence to ask for additional troops to guard that infernal pile of rocks." His fist clenched as if to strike the table in futility, but instead he took a deep breath and spread his fingers on the black cloth.

"A pile of rocks that houses the most dangerous man of our time," added Claire after ascertaining he was under control.

"There are few in government who would argue with you, my lady. But since he has been incarcerated on Elba, many think Napoleon's teeth have been drawn and do not consider him a worthy opponent without his army."

"But don't they know that his marshals would most likely pledge their loyalty again if he were free? They've been faithful to Napoleon for fifteen years; Louis means nothing to them in comparison. And what of his soldiers and the French people?" she entreated. "There are thousands who think that he offers them freedom from the corrupt institutions that governed them before. They would support him again if given the chance."

"You argue a good case, and no one agrees more than I. Our only hope is to pin down the force behind the plot— if there is one— and render it powerless. I count on you to help me do that." With a pensive look on his face he took his leave, far too preoccupied to drop a coin in the bowl.

"Not a single contribution," complained Claire, "and I have been here almost an hour."

"Talking to the spirits, madam?" came a familiar voice from the gloom.

"Just remarking on the vagaries of the human race," replied Claire.

"There are many, or so I've found, and impossible to comprehend." Moving closer to the table, Lord Ransley seated himself across from her. "I'm glad to see you've recovered," he said, his gaze travelling over the creamy skin exposed by her costume, searching for the marks left by his hands.

"Please don't trouble yourself over the incident any longer, my lord. I didn't suffer, it's just that I bruise very easily. I assure you it looked worse that it was."

"I will remember your delicacy in the future. I wouldn't like to harm anyone so lovely." He stared a moment longer, then cleared his throat. "Will you see what your crystal ball has to say for me?" he asked.

Claire's emotions were too jumbled to sort out as she stared at him, unable to believe her own eyes and ears. He had actually complimented her and she thought she had seen desire flame in his dark eyes, but surely she was mistaken. Despite his remorse at bruising her, he was still merely tolerating her for Juliana's sake.

"Surely my future is not that shocking," he said, breaking the silence that had surrounded them too long.

"I'm afraid my predictions would be no more to your liking than they were to my other customers," Claire replied, attempting to sound normal. She did not want to read his thoughts and uncover the true nature of his feelings for her. No matter what they were, she was not strong enough to face them at the moment.

"Ah, Lord Mansfield and his wife. I saw him tear out of the ballroom with her close behind. Never say you were indiscreet?" he queried, a slight smile curving his lips.

"How was I to know she was not being completely honest with him?" Claire replied, pleased his attention was diverted from her fortunetelling.

"Many wives aren't," he observed.

"Nor are husbands," she responded.

"Granted," he said, nodding slightly. "Did you and your husband enjoy honesty in your marriage?"

The question was far too personal for him to be asking, but she was not affronted by his forwardness. "Yes. We were always forthright with one another. Perhaps, with time, things would have changed, but I like to think we would have continued as we began."

"I'm certain you would have, and I envy you for that. I was not so fortunate in my marriage." But Claire would be loyal, he thought, with sudden insight. She would stand by her husband's side no matter what the situation. Reaching across the table he covered her hand with his. "Claire . . ."

"I know she's here somewhere, Mr. Harcourt. Lady Barringer said this side of the ballroom." Margaret appeared in the doorway, shattering the intimacy of the silken tent. "Claire, there you are. I've looked everywhere . . . Oh, I'm sorry," she apologized as

Lord Ransley rose to his feet. "I didn't see you, my lord. It's so dim in here."

"That's quite all right, Miss Lacefield. I was just leaving. It seems the crystal ball holds nothing for me this evening." Giving a slight bow he disappeared through the entrance.

"I'm dreadfully sorry," Margaret repeated.

"There's no need to be so apologetic, Margaret. Lord Ransley was just on his way out," Claire said absently, wondering what he would have said if they had remained private.

"We are here to have our fortunes told," Margaret said as Forrest Harcourt stepped into the small space.

This was no time for woolgathering decided Claire, and directed her attention to the matter at hand. "Well, I do hope you intend to contribute for there's not one farthing in my collection bowl yet."

"Of course," said Harcourt, dropping a generous number of coins in the bowl, and pulling out the chair for Margaret to be seated.

"Are you sure you want to risk this," Claire asked. "My fortunes have not been welcomed so far."

"Nothing you say could upset me this evening," said Margaret, fairly glowing with happiness at being in Harcourt's company.

"If you insist then," agreed Claire, staring into the crystal ball and concentrating on Margaret's thoughts. It was as bad as she guessed; her friend was madly in love with Harcourt and was ready to fly in the face of convention at his bidding.

Claire switched her attention to Harcourt who was standing behind Margaret's chair staring down at her. For once his thoughts were transparent. *You are very tempting, my sweet Margaret. More than you know. After we get Boney settled, perhaps there will be time for us if you are still willing.*

Claire's indrawn breath caused Harcourt to look across the table at her. His eyes narrowed and he held her gaze for an instant before a smile crossed his face. "Is your crystal ball still empty, madam?"

"It seems so. Would you please excuse me," she said hastily, rising and moving around the table. "There is something I must attend to immediately. If you'll return later, I'm sure your fortunes will satisfy you."

Claire left them in the tent staring after her. Moving quickly through the increasing crowd, she made her way to the chamber where she had dressed. She needed time alone to slow her thundering heart. She had searched so long, and now there was a good possibility she had found the man responsible for John's death and Napoleon's forthcoming escape.

Willing herself to be calm, she took deep, slow breaths, attempting to think logically. Templeton would be more likely to lock her up if she told him she had read Harcourt's thoughts and believed him the traitor. No, she needed solid proof before she made any accusations. She must also think of Margaret. How could she tell her best friend she was in love with a murderer?

Shadows fell across Lord Ransley's face as he sat in the wing back chair placed discreetly in the corner of the drawing room. The *Post* lay on a small table at his elbow, but advertisements for the latest prime bits of blood on the market did not appeal to him any more than the lists of guests attending the preceding evening's soirees.

His attention was held by the woman and child settled in front of the fire some distance away. A miniature tea set was arranged before them and they were taking tea with two of Juliana's favorite dolls: Maria, a bedraggled creature who showed years of use, and Lady Jane, of a rather more recent vintage, but still in need of new apparel.

At first he had watched this ritual performed over the past weeks with frustration. As far as he could see, the woman merely carried on a one-sided conversation with Juliana and the dolls, occasionally sipping tea from a thimble-sized cup, and pausing as if to listen to answers from her silent companions. He did not see how his daughter could be cured by playing, but his frustration had gradually given way to acceptance as he observed Juliana's solemn face curve into a smile that always charmed him.

It was obvious that his daughter bloomed in response to Claire's warmth, and he realized how much Juliana missed a woman's attention. No, not just a woman; she had a doting grandmother and aunt. She was surrounded by nursery maids, coddled by the housekeeper, spoiled by the cook and every other female member of the staff. No, she missed someone devoted particularly to her; she missed a mother.

He gazed longingly at Claire's tawny hair, sea-green eyes, and womanly figure, imagining her in the role. Then cursing himself roundly, he reminded himself that Juliana was just a temporary cause for Lady Kingsley. She evidently felt the need to perform a useful deed occasionally and had been fortunate enough to have the capability to indulge her whims.

But at heart he knew her to be a creature of society, devoted to attending every entertainment, large or small. It had been a fortnight since he had found himself falling under her spell in that red silken spider's web. If Miss Lacefield and Harcourt hadn't interrupted when they had, who knows where his loose tongue would have led him.

He had realized then that he harbored a weakness for her that must be governed. He must also protect

Juliana, for Lady Kingsley would be far too busy during the height of the Season to be concerned with a child who was no relation to her. His thoughts were interrupted by the end of the tea party, and he rose as his daughter and Lady Kingsley joined him.

"My lord, perhaps I've been precipitate," Claire admitted with a melting smile, "but I've invited Juliana and Maria to tea at Kenton House."

Lord Ransley looked down as Juliana gave a sharp tug on his coattails. She smiled up at him, nodding until her dark curls bounced around her face.

"I see my daughter is already in total agreement," he said, wondering what magic Claire had worked. While Juliana had joined him on outings, she had never shown such marked enthusiasm.

"She's accepted for herself and Maria, now we're only awaiting your endorsement. Of course, you'll join us, as will the duchess."

"Are you certain Her Grace will welcome a child to her tea table?"

"Certainly, my lord. In fact, she's been urging me to invite you for some time now, but I wanted Juliana to feel entirely comfortable with me."

"Then we shall be pleased to accept, my lady."

"Good! Do you hear, Juliana?" she asked stooping down to the child's size. "You and Maria and your father will take tea with us the day after tomorrow. We shall have your favorite cakes, and my grandmother has some dolls from her childhood you will enjoy seeing." Smoothing back the child's curls, she stood.

"Thank you, my lord."

An air of formality lingered between them, as if they both knew that danger lay in anything less. "It would take a harsh man to refuse two such convincing ladies," he replied, taking her hand and smiling.

Despite her silent admonishment that he would respond to any woman in like manner, Claire's heart felt like a butterfly batting its wings against a cage as she met his dark gaze. It was all she could do to remove her hand and murmur a hasty goodbye.

Six

The tea party had been a great success. Claire and the marquess stepped into the hall while the duchess bid goodbye to Juliana.

"Juliana has captivated my grandmother," said Claire. "I haven't seen her so lively since I've been with her."

"Observing the world through a child's eyes can make everything seem new again," he replied, smiling.

"And when Juliana speaks again it will be like seeing the light after a long darkness," Claire declared passionately, remembering her own period of blindness.

"Are you so confident she will speak?" he asked. "There's no doubt you've made her happier," he hastened to add, "but she hasn't uttered a sound yet."

"She will, my lord. Every case is different. Sometimes it takes longer with one child than another, but I'm certain Juliana will eventually speak again. You must give me time," she said, a worried expression on her face.

"You may have all the time you want," he assured her, wondering anew at his strong response to a woman he did not completely trust. "And if our ultimate goal is not reached, I still owe you thanks for making Juliana happier than she's been since my return. I seldom saw a smile until she met you." He fought the urge to reach out to her— an urge that was growing stronger each time they were together.

His dark eyes, intent on hers, were warm with gratitude and perhaps something more, she thought. Tempted, she focused on him just long enough to feel his agitation, and wrongfully attributed it to Juliana's situation.

"Do not be so faint-hearted, my lord. With patience we shall be successful yet."

"Patience has never been my strong suit, and I admit the little I possess is sorely strained." And for more reasons than Juliana's well-being, he added silently.

"Then I shall furnish enough for both of us." She smiled up into his eyes, forgetting for the moment to keep her distance, allowing their common purpose to bring them close in spirit.

Ransley surrendered to his craving and reached for her hand, but his words were cut short as Biggersleigh approached carrying a bouquet of deep red roses.

"What lovely flowers, Biggersleigh."

"They just arrived, my lady, for you."

"How sweet," she said, breathing in the fragrance of the blooms. "They are so welcome in weather such as this. It reminds me that summer will soon be here.

"Would you have them put in water?" she asked, removing the card from the bouquet.

Lord Ransley did not need to strain his eyes to see Hamilton Ashford's signature scrawled across the buff-colored paper, and a flash of unexpected anger surged through him. He had watched her dance with Ashford the night before, his blond head bent to her tawny curls. He did not know what Claire saw in Ashford, and the thought of her tying herself to such a man added fuel to his ire.

"It seems we're keeping you from your admirers,

Lady Kingsley," he remarked stiffly, "Perhaps we should cease our visits before your social life is ruined."

Claire was stunned by his sudden attack. They had been in such accord only moments before and now he was glaring at her in an accusing manner.

Juliana arrived at their side in time to hear her father's threat. Throwing herself against Claire, she burst into tears.

At that Claire lost her temper. "Now see what you've done! You've probably destroyed all the confidence I've been building up these past weeks," she railed before turning her attention to Juliana. Dropping to her knees she gathered the child in her arms, rocking and crooning to her, assuring her that her father was only teasing when he said they could not visit again.

By the time Juliana was quieted, Lord Ransley felt a veritable ogre, and wondered how he had allowed a few posies to crack his formidable control. He apologized to Claire and left her house with peace uneasily restored between them.

Afterward he could not escape the worry that his daughter was becoming too attached to Claire, a woman who kept close company with Hamilton Ashford.

For the most part, the *ton* was unaware that Ashford's reputation was not all it should be. They saw a handsome, agreeable man, most probably on the lookout for an heiress to support his expensive habits, not an unusual circumstance in their circle. But the marquess knew Ashford was not particular about the manner in which he earned his money.

Then there was Claire's connection with Matthew Templeton. Even though Drew had assured him that Templeton was an old friend of John Kingsley, Ransley sensed something more in their relationship, and the alternative to friendship was exceedingly distasteful to him. If they weren't yet lovers, Claire could be skillfully seducing the man in order to gain secrets vital to the Congress now going on. Or she and Templeton could be in league passing intelligence directly to the enemy.

No matter how lovely or agreeable on the surface, Claire Kingsley could be hiding all manner of secrets beneath her faultless complection. It was his duty to learn how deep her connection with Ashford and Templeton ran, and whether it put his daughter, and the country, at risk. He was too stubborn to add his heart to the list.

It was no great surprise for Lord Ransley to discover from Drew that Ashford preferred Brook's over the other clubs. There a gentleman would find the steepest games of chance, and despite his claim of investing on the exchange, it was clear that gambling was a significant source of income.

The marquess had been in and out of the club over the past several days without running into his prey. Tonight he had made it a point to arrive late, when desperate men made a final hopeless gambit to avoid ruin.

His patience was rewarded by detecting Ashford seated at a table with five other men, three of whom had already tossed their cards onto the green baize. An interested audience surrounded the table, their faces reflecting various degrees of disgust or pity for the individuals remaining in the game.

Drawing near, the marquess identified Ashford's opponent as a youth who had not been on the town more than a Season. His cravat was loosened, and his hair rumpled where agitated fingers had disturbed the once carefully arranged locks. Beads of perspiration dotted his forehead above bloodshot eyes, and the light showed his pale countenance to no great advantage.

It was no secret that the young man had been playing

deep in hopes of recouping his losses before his father found out. So far he had been lucky enough to keep ahead of the game, but from his expression he had met his match this evening.

The end came quickly as the young man threw down his cards and scribbled his vowels on a scrap of paper, which he thrust across the table at Ashford before weaving his way out of the room. The marquess spared a moment's pity for him. He was acquainted with his father and knew he would pay dearly for his indiscretions if forced to confess his folly.

The group broke up, many mumbling about Ashford's luck or lifting questioning eyebrows as the blond-haired man collected his winnings.

The marquess moved toward the table as the area cleared. "It seems luck favored you tonight, Ashford. Would you have a brandy with me in celebration?"

"Lord Ransley," acknowledged Ashford, his pale blue eyes flickering over the marquess in surprise. "I'd be delighted, but I insist you join me in my good fortune."

The marquess nodded and the two men made their way to a small table flanked by two comfortable chairs. Ashford ordered a bottle and soon they were sipping the club's best brandy.

"I don't think I've seen you here before, my lord," remarked Ashford, stretching his legs out toward the fireplace with its glowing embers.

"I've been in a few times since I've come to town, but usually earlier than this. I was on my way home from the Castletons' rout and needed something to regain my spirits."

Ashford scooted lower in the chair, resting his fair head against the back. "Deucedly dull, I'll wager. Couldn't bring myself to accept."

"When I saw Lady Kingsley there alone I thought you might be under the weather."

"Never felt better," Ashford replied, patting his bulging pockets. "Call it hen-hearted if you will, but there are some entertainments even Claire cannot entice me to attend."

Lord Ransley's hand clenched around the glass stem, resenting the other man's familiar address. "You must have great powers of resistance, for she's a lovely woman. Have you known her long?"

Ashford finished his brandy and poured another. "Six or seven years now, since she first became engaged to her late husband." He relaxed in the chair, the brandy loosening his tongue. "John and I were boyhood friends. We went to the same school and came to town the same Season. Swore we'd set London on its ear. And we did, until he met Claire."

The marquess kept silent, hoping that Ashford would forget he was there and continue his reminiscing.

"Nothing else would do but that they marry right away. No long engagement for the two lovebirds." Reaching for the bottle he filled his glass again. The long night and the liquor were exacting their toll.

"John took a position with the government office and off they went," he continued, his words slightly slurred but still intelligible. "London was flat without John, so I travelled, too. Met up with the happy couple and toured with them on and off until . . ."

The silence lasted so long Lord Ransley thought Ashford had dozed off. "Until?" he urged.

"What? Oh, until John was killed," he finished dully. "We had spent some time at Bath, all of us together. John and Claire left early one morning. I had quite a head and couldn't rouse myself until later in the day. Didn't even see them off," he mused.

"By the time I reached London, John was dead, shot by a highwayman, and Claire was lying unconscious. I swore then that if she survived I would watch over her for John. I owed him that much at least." Ashford closed his eyes.

Lord Ransley removed the brandy glass from Ashford's limp fingers. The man's grief seemed sincere. Perhaps there was nothing more between Claire Kingsley and Ashford than her husband's ghost and Ashford's guilt that he had not been there to save his friend. Lady Kingsley could be entirely innocent of Ashford's shady dealings, but then again that could be exactly what she would want others to think.

Out of countenance with his confused thoughts, he looked for a footman to help get Ashford to his feet. Before he could call for assistance, Viscount Stanford appeared in the doorway and made his way across the room.

"Conversation must have been sadly flat to put a man to sleep," he commented, a smile splitting his face.

"Sorry to disappoint you," replied Quinton with a wry grin, "but it's brandy, not my dull wit that floored him. Help me get him into a hackney or else he'll lose everything he gained this evening."

Drew positioned himself on the other side of the chair from Quinton and between the two of them they heaved Ashford to his feet. "Good to see the milk of human kindness hasn't dried up," gasped Drew, slinging Ashford's arm across his shoulder and securing a hold around his waist.

Quinton had taken the same stance on the opposite side. "I think I have enough left to get him outside," Quinton remarked as they struggled toward the door with their burden.

"The Season is not yet in full swing and I'm already fagged out." Claire leaned her head against the tall back of the Queen Ann chair and closed her eyes.

"You're doing too much," said Margaret, taking in the apathetic posture of her friend, and privately agreeing that she looked frazzled.

The two were alone in the small sitting room at Kenton House and Claire had relaxed the strict vigilance she kept on her true feelings when in public.

"Nonsense, I'm just getting old." A feeble smile flitted briefly across her face, barely disturbing the fatigued expression which had occupied her countenance for the past few days.

"Not long ago you were telling me neither of us was ready for caps," Margaret reminded her. "Now you sound as if we're past praying for. What changed your mind?"

"I suppose the sameness of it all, the endless energy expended with no visible results except bouquets arriving each morning and cards filled with insincere compliments stuck amongst the blooms."

"You certainly are blue-deviled to deal yourself such a slight," observed Margaret, surprised at the depth of her friend's cynicism. "I'm sure the gentlemen are sincere in their tributes."

Claire gave a short laugh. "I also told you there were men who were interested in more than money, but now I doubt my own words. I don't think there's a man of my acquaintance who does not calculate the advantage of an alliance when he looks at a woman."

"And are women any different?" challenged Margaret. "They come to London expressly to snare a husband."

"But women do not enjoy the same advantage," Claire argued. "How many poor women marry wealth? Not many," she said, answering her own question. "But men without a feather to fly with have their choice of heiresses if they possess a title."

"And so it has always been in our society. Why are you commenting on it now?" probed Margaret.

"Because I'm tired of this endless parading of oneself, because I'm bored with the stale compliments and politely false facades, because . . . because . . . because . . ." she chanted.

"It doesn't by chance have anything to do with a certain dark-haired marquess, does it?" inquired Margaret, cutting to the heart of the matter.

Now that the subject had been broached, Claire was reluctant to discuss the man who consumed her thoughts. "I don't know what you mean."

"I am speaking of Lord Ransley and you well know it," accused Margaret. "A man who looks as worn as you do, I might add. He hovers on the edge of every event you attend, watching you constantly, and you're as nervous as a green girl when he's around. It would be much easier on the two of you if you would admit to an attraction and see where it leads."

"There's nothing between us," protested Claire indignantly. "There isn't," she sputtered, seeing Margaret's look of disbelief. "I've been seeing his daughter several times a week, that's all."

Margaret knew Claire occasionally worked with children who suffered problems, but out of respect for the child's privacy, had never pressed for details. "Perhaps, but I'll be bound there's something more. John has been gone for some time now, Claire. It wouldn't be disloyal if you were attracted to another man."

"I don't know what I feel for Ransley," admitted Claire, abandoning her defensive air. "He confuses me, stirs up all manner of feelings, then turns away without a backward look."

"It sounds as if he's as confused as you are. I understand he hasn't had an easy time of it this past year or so. It's obvious you're taken with one another, but I don't think either of you is willing to risk your heart again."

"I believe in being careful, Margaret, and I think you should, too," Claire responded sharply.

"You mean Harcourt, I assume," she said, her serene composure at odds with Claire's high dudgeon.

"I've never known you to cherish a tendre for a man such as Forrest Harcourt," charged Claire.

"I've never cherished a tendre for any man," she retorted with a bubble of laughter, "and it's high time I did. Unlike you and your marquess, I'm more than willing to follow my inclinations. I don't care a fig about propriety when it comes to Harcourt," she admitted, a feverish look in her eyes. "I've been cautious far too long, Claire. Perhaps I've waited too late, but I have a chance at happiness and I intend to take it if it's offered."

"Margaret, don't do anything foolish," begged Claire, alarmed at her friend's passionate outburst.

"Is it foolish to want to experience love?" asked Margaret, rising to her feet and pacing before the fireplace. "I have never known a man, and I want that," she confessed, her face flushing. "My parents have been gone since I was a child, and except for a few far-flung relations I've been alone nearly all my life. I want the closeness that comes from marriage."

"But will he give you that?" Claire asked gently.

"I don't know." Margaret raised her head proudly. "But if he cannot, and offers me something less, I would accept. I will not spend the rest of my days mourning the chance of fulfillment, no matter how brief."

"There are things you don't know about Harcourt," cautioned Claire, remembering his thoughts about Napoleon.

"We all have secrets, and Forrest is no exception. Neither am I, nor you, for that matter. Sometimes it's better to leave that secret side alone and enjoy what we can."

Claire was surprised by her friend's attitude. Since the beginning of their acquaintance, Margaret had been a practical person, and now she was willing to risk everything, even scandal, for love's sake. "I wish I had your courage," said Claire. "And I wish you well, for you deserve to have all that you desire." She rose and gave Margaret a quick hug, wondering why she couldn't settle her own uncertainties as calmly.

"Ahem." Biggersleigh stood in the doorway. "Lord Ransley has called, Lady Kingsley. Should I tell him you are not at home?" he asked, observing the confidential air of their conversation.

Margaret laughed. "Send him in, Biggersleigh." As soon as he was out of sight, she returned Claire's hug. "Now is a good time to begin following your inclinations and find out what exactly it is you feel for the marquess. And I plan to make myself scarce so that you can do so without an audience."

"I can't entertain him alone," protested Claire weakly.

"Don't be foolish. You're no Bath miss fresh from the school room, Claire. Take advantage of the opportunity, it doesn't happen often. No doubt I'll see you tonight and you can tell me what progress you've made," she whispered, as the sound of booted footsteps approached the sitting room.

"Lord Ransley, I was just leaving," said Margaret, as she offered her hand to the marquess.

"My loss, Miss Lacefield," he replied bending over her hand. "Don't let me chase you away."

"I've stayed overlong as it is," she explained. "I'm already late for an appointment with my modiste."

"Not a person to offend, so I'm told," he responded, according her a smile that Claire envied.

"Exactly. I shall end up looking a perfect dowd if I don't hurry."

"That could never be," he declared gallantly.

"I would rather not test the veracity," Margaret rejoined gaily. Waving goodbye to Claire she disappeared into the hall.

"An admirable woman," Lord Ransley remarked, strolling farther into the room.

"Yes, I treasure our friendship," responded Claire, observing how much smaller the room appeared with his presence.

"You're looking well as always, my lady," he said, running a practiced eye over her deep rose gown.

"Oh, botheration!" Claire was still unsettled after her discussion with Margaret, and his patent flattery vexed her. "I am not in looks at all, my lord, and you well know it. I'm tired and there are circles under my eyes and I've just encouraged my best friend to follow a path that could well lead to her ruin. So don't stand there and offer me Spanish coin, I am not in the mood for it."

Lord Ransley stood quite still for a moment staring at Claire, then burst out laughing. She stamped her foot in a temper, fists on her hips, looking a veritable termagant.

"You're absolutely right," he said, quickly bringing his merriment under control and moving closer to her. His hand reached out to touch her hair. "Your curls are in disarray," he said, letting the tawny strands slide through his fingers. "There is a slight touch of lavender just here," he continued, the rough pad of his finger tracing above her cheekbone, and you look as if you would definitely benefit from some time in bed." His eyes darkened at the suggestion.

"I'm not here for your enjoyment, my lord," she said stiffly, endeavoring to overcome her anger at an *entendre* that, coming from anyone else, she would have shrugged off as being of no consequence.

"Then perhaps I am here for yours," he suggested, bending down until she felt his breath against her face.

His thoughts were scandalous, and she blushed beneath his scrutiny. She desperately wished for Margaret's resolve to take what was being offered without questioning, without wanting more, but she could not. There were too many doubts in her mind to allow herself that liberty.

"I apologize for my outburst," she said, pointedly ignoring his remark. "Please take a seat, my lord. Would you care for some refreshment?"

A man might think this intriguing baggage was truly a gypsy who could read his mind, thought Ransley, observing her rising color. "No, thank you," he said, in a subdued tone, accepting her rebuff gracefully. "I promised Juliana I would seek you out," he said, settling into a chair opposite her."

She looked at him inquiringly.

"I'm afraid I bribed my daughter with a trip to Astley's in order to get her to London," he confessed self-consciously. "Now she insists that I beg you to accompany us. I attempted to explain that ladies do not look upon a visit to Astley's with anticipation, but nothing would do but that I put the idea to you."

"My lord, you may tell Juliana that I am not one of those ladies who are so high in the instep, and that I would be delighted to accompany her. I did not grow up in London, and never had the opportunity to attend Astley's. Margaret tells me she can remember leaning so far out of the box that she almost tumbled into the ring," she recounted enthusiastically, her weariness miraculously a thing of the past.

He glanced pensively at her small waist. "I will take

great pleasure in coming to your rescue if that should occur, madam.''

"I heard you accompanied Ransley and his daughter to Astley's yesterday," said Hamilton, breaking the uneasy silence that had hung over them since they had left Kenton House.

Claire chose not to respond as Hamilton guided his curricle through the maze of traffic outside Hyde Park. She had been fairly successful at evading him over the past weeks, but had been surprised by his unexpected visit this afternoon with an invitation to drive out. Unable to offer a ready excuse, she agreed to accompany him rather than issuing a set-down that would sever their relationship forever. Now she regretted the temporary weakness that had put her in such an uncomfortable position.

"I'm amazed that my tame outings are of such interest," she said, slipping her hands further into her muff. The day was clear and bright with sunlight, but there was a dampness to the air that cut through her pelisse.

"I stopped by Kenton House yesterday afternoon," he explained, as they passed through the gates into the park and joined the procession of carriages. "Her Grace was at home and told me of your excursion. I must say I was surprised."

"I never thought to seek your permission, Hamilton, nor advise you of my plans." Her voice was stiff with anger and she made no effort to hide it.

"And I don't expect it, my dear, but shouldn't you be more particular in your choice of company?" he asked, as if conversing with an unreasonable child.

Hamilton's presumption that he had a right to judge her actions sent a flash of anger through Claire, and she found the afternoon was not as cold as she had previously thought. "I cannot conceive how a five-year-old child could ruin my reputation," she finally said, biting back the harsh words she could not utter in such a public place.

"It's not the child but the father, and you well know it," Hamilton responded, his lips forming a harsh, tight line.

"There's nothing about Lord Ransley that would cause me to avoid him," she argued. "He's accepted everywhere."

"He isn't for you, Claire," declared Hamilton, his composure cracking under her continued defense of the marquess. "He's been acting dashedly queer recently, locking himself away in the country."

"What do you expect of the man, Hamilton?" she returned heatedly. "He was attacked and nearly lost his life. Then his wife died in a tragic accident before he was fully recovered. I don't think it at all odd that he observed a decent period of mourning for her."

"You think he was mourning his wife?" he asked disdainfully, seeking to belittle his rival in her eyes. "How little you know, Claire. Ransley had discarded Lydia Courtney long before her death. He made her life so miserable that she turned to other men for comfort after he rejected her. Does that sound like a man who would mourn his wife? Does it sound like a man who could make you happy?" he ground out between gritted teeth.

"There is no question as to whether or not Lord Ransley can make me happy," she objected, "since there is nothing between us. Now, please take me home," requested Claire. "I find I have a terrible headache."

Too late, Hamilton realized he had misjudged both her loyalty to him and her feelings for Ransley. "Claire, surely you aren't going to allow a stranger to come between us?" he pleaded.

"And just who is the stranger, Hamilton? Today I feel as if I don't know you at all." Claire directed her gaze away from him, pointedly indicating the conversation was at an end.

The ride back to Berkeley Square was as silent as its beginning, and Claire left him with the briefest nod.

Claire pasted a smile on her face before greeting Lord and Lady Pentworthy. Her fatigue had only intensified, and she would have preferred to remain home before a warm fire rather than traipse out onto icy cobblestones in satin slippers. Only two things made the evening bearable: after their disagreement, Hamilton had not offered his escort, and tonight's gathering was one that promised to yield valuable information.

Pausing before her host, she made the appropriate responses to his welcome. Pentworthy was a tall, cadaverous man, with years of dissolute living etched permanently on his face. Lady Pentworthy appeared inordinately slight standing by his side. Her eyes, beneath lackluster gray hair, were weary from the effort of making do on their small means, further reduced by her husband's ruinous gambling.

The Pentworthys lived on the fringes of respectable society, and it was well known their financial stability rested on the way the cards fell. Thus Lord Pentworthy often attempted to lure more prosperous individuals to his home for a friendly evening of cards.

Passing into the drawing room, Claire's spirits sank as she glimpsed Hamilton across the room. He had been watching the door and as soon as she entered he made his way toward her, Harcourt and Carrington following close behind.

"Claire," he said, taking her hand as if their quarrel had never been, "I was growing concerned. I should have insisted on escorting you this evening. It isn't safe for a lady to travel alone on the streets at night."

"I wasn't alone," she snapped, astounded that he had elected to completely ignore their dispute. "Surely a driver and two footmen are enough to keep me from harm on such a short excursion."

Hamilton frowned, unaccustomed to receiving the sharp side of her tongue for the second time in the same number of days. He stood awaiting the apology which almost spilled from her lips. But Claire swore she would not give him the chance to further dominate her life. Instead, she turned to his two companions with a smile.

"Mr. Harcourt. Mr. Carrington. How pleasant to see you again," she lied sweetly, accepting their greetings.

"Lady Kingsley, I must apologize," said Harcourt, his brilliant blue eyes holding hers. "I didn't realize until recently that your husband was John Kingsley. He was an admirable man, and I offer you my condolences on his loss."

"Thank you," she murmured, lowering her gaze. "How did you know John?" she asked.

"We met on the continent some years ago. He was just beginning his career with the government, and was enthused about his occupation."

Claire hid her surprise at his admission that he had known her husband. As far as she was concerned, Harcourt was a prime suspect in Napoleon's rumored escape. He travelled freely, blended easily into all levels of society, and was an intelligent man. His admission that he had known John was even more telling. She concentrated on his thoughts, but intercepted nothing.

"I'm pleased to say he never lost that enthusiasm. It was a part of his attraction; people were drawn to John to see what gave him such a love of life." Claire swallowed the lump in her throat. Realizing that she might be speaking to his murderer brought back the pain of his loss.

"And you, Mr. Carrington," she said, directing her attention to the younger man, "have you travelled the continent also?"

"Indeed, Lady Kingsley. My father thought no son's education was complete without a Grand Tour. I was fortunate to be in Paris during the Peace of Amiens. I even met Napoleon briefly at the Tuileries before hostilities were resumed. Of course, I know you'll agree that the war was a dreadful inconvenience," he complained. Flipping open an exquisite snuff box, he offered it to both Harcourt and Ashford before helping himself to the aromatic blend.

"Absolutely dreadful," she agreed scornfully. "Imagine the nuisance of all those men dying where one wants to travel. It quite puts one out altogether. If you will excuse me, gentlemen, I think I will attempt to work off my disgust with a hand of cards."

Hamilton appeared shocked at her outburst. At best, she could hope he would condemn her barely civil manners and cease his involvement in her affairs. She returned Harcourt's smile with a nod as she swept away, noting what appeared to be a flicker of admiration in Carrington's eyes.

Seven

Claire's expectation that Hamilton might take a dis
gust at her behavior did not materialize. He appeared
on her doorstep the next morning as soon as convention
decreed it was polite. Claire was forced to receive him
alone since the duchess was still abed after a late night.
She greeted him with no hint of apology for the eve
ning before, and offered refreshment only to divert her
anger at his obtuseness.

After the initial courtesies were exchanged Hamilton
cleared his throat. "Claire, there's something I've
wished to ask for some time now, but I haven't wanted
to distress you."

Claire's curiosity was aroused by his unusual hesita
tion. "What is it, Hamilton?"

"I apologize for bringing up painful memories, but
I have long desired a remembrance of John." He
glanced away in embarrassment. "I know it's forward
of me, and perhaps the time isn't right, but it means
a great deal to me."

Claire immediately felt contrite for her ungrateful
thoughts about Hamilton and her remarks of the night
before. His pain at her husband's death must have been
great. He and John were closer than brothers, if their
tales were to be believed.

"Of course, Hamilton," she immediately agreed, soft
tening toward the man whose embarrassment over his

love for John prevented him from meeting her eye. Guilt washed over her as she remembered the harsh words she had spoken to him the day before. Evidently, he was sincerely attempting to look after her in his own misguided way, and she felt compelled by this new insight to be patient with him until he accepted that she was capable of standing on her own. In the meantime, she could easily grant his request as a first step toward a new understanding. "Is there anything special you would like?" she asked.

"I don't know. I haven't given it a great deal of thought. Just a keepsake to . . ." His voice broke and trailed off. After a moment's struggle, he continued in a normal tone. "Would you be able to part with his walking stick?"

Claire remembered well the silver headed cane that John was never without. She had often teased him about caring more for it than he did his wife because it went everywhere with him.

Hamilton observed her hesitation. "If you would rather not, I understand."

"Of course not, Hamilton. I was just thinking how right it would be to give it to you. It was so much a part of John and it would keep a small bit of him in the world he loved so well," she said, her eyes misting at the thought.

"I'm sorry, Claire," said Hamilton, taking her hand. "I've brought it all back to you, haven't I? That's the last thing I wanted to do."

At that moment Biggersleigh announced Mr. Harcourt and Mr. Carrington. The two men entered on his heels.

"It's all right, Hamilton," she said, seeing the worried expression on his face. "I'm fine."

"I hope we're not interrupting," said Harcourt, bowing over her hand.

It was all Claire could do not to pull away as she
remembered her suspicion concerning the dark man
before her. "Not at all," she replied in a civil tone. "We
were just discussing a keepsake of my husband's that
Mr. Ashford desired," replied Claire.

"I don't think I've offered my condolences on your
loss, ma'am," said Carrington, taking Harcourt's place
before her. "I didn't know your husband, but I understand he was an admirable man."

"Yes, he was," Claire replied briefly, unwilling to discuss John in front of the man who may have killed him.
Turning again to Hamilton she quickly finished their
conversation.

"I'm sorry the walking stick is not immediately at
hand, but after the accident Her Grace closed our home
and stored all our personal items in the attics here at
Kenton House," she explained. "As soon as possible
I'll have Biggersleigh show me where they're stored and
retrieve the stick for you."

"Are you sure you're up to it, Claire?" Hamilton
asked solicitously.

"Of course," she assured him confidently. "Think
nothing more of it."

"Thank you. It will mean a great deal to me."

She deftly changed the subject, bringing the others
into the conversation, wondering anew at the forces that
brought three such disparate men together in her drawing room.

As she conversed amicably with the gentlemen, concentrating on drawing out Harcourt, Lord Ransley arrived and was shown into the room. She felt a trace of
uneasiness that Hamilton was present in light of his
unreasonable reaction to her harmless relationship with
the marquess.

Claire carefully observed both men for any sign of
animosity. Ransley's face remained politely inscrutable

as he nodded and uttered unexceptional remarks of greeting to the other men present. Hamilton's response was equally commonplace, making Claire wonder if she had dreamed it all.

Hoping to keep the conversation impersonal, Claire addressed her remarks to the newcomer. "We were just discussing the possibility of a sparse Season, my lord, since so many of our countrymen are taking themselves off to Paris."

"Quite so," agreed the marquess. "After Napoleon's abdication, it wasn't soldiers who assaulted France, but English lords and ladies."

"Could you expect less when Bonaparte himself declared that there is nothing that surpasses Paris," remarked Carrington.

"Perhaps many will return by Spring," Claire suggested. "Since Napoleon is safely disposed of there will be plenty of time to enjoy the pleasures of Paris again."

I'll be damned! Napoleon will be back, and soon! There's too many of us involved for his escape to fail. In just a short time, my dear, your friends will either be dead or fleeing for their lives.

Claire's cup clattered in its saucer. She looked around to see who had uttered the blasphemy, but no one was standing fervently declaring freedom for Napoleon.

One of the men's thoughts had been strong enough to break through her normal wall of reserve. She glanced quickly toward Harcourt, but he and Carrington were ardently involved in recalling the delights of Beauvilliers, a Paris restaurant whose cuisine was said to be superior to all others, and she could detect nothing else from them. Focusing on Hamilton, she found he was vastly amused by food being described with all the passion due a woman.

Taking a calming breath, she met the marquess's quizzical eye. She knew he had travelled abroad quite fre-

quently before Juliana's illness, but she did not want to
believe he would betray his country.

Moreover, she had already learned that Harcourt was
somehow involved with Napoleon's escape. While usually inscrutable, his thoughts could have escaped control
just long enough for her to hear them. Or perhaps she
was underestimating Carrington. It was certainly possible he could be working with Harcourt. Did she dare
openly broach the subject? Smiling confidently she re-
plenished her tea and waited until there was a lull in
the conversation.

"I wonder that Napoleon remains so docilely in exile," Claire remarked, keeping her eyes lowered and
adding an unwanted teaspoon of sugar to her cup. "He
has his admirers, so I understand, and he must have
great charisma to have commanded such deep devotion
from so many." She allowed herself a peek at the men
around her table, and was assured she had their attention. "I passed through Leicester Square yesterday and
there was a crowd gathered outside the panorama to
see the model of his island prison. It did not appear
excessively forbidding. One would think Napoleon
could escape with little effort."

"I believe Talleyrand shares your concern," Harcourt
replied after a short silence. "He wanted Bonaparte ex-
iled in Corfu or St. Helena, where he could be more
closely guarded, but he's been unsuccessful so far."

"Is security so negligent then?" she asked, hoping to
find out how much they knew.

"It isn't easy to guard him on Elba, but beyond that
there seems to be laxity about the whole business," volunteered Carrington. "The prevailing mood is that he's
abdicated and all danger has been removed. I'm afraid
England may have to learn the hard way that all men
do not honor their word."

"There have been several rumors since his exile about

reinstating him in Paris," drawled Ransley in a bored tone. "I daresay we'll hear numerous more before the Congress is over."

Claire could detect nothing from the men, and was apprehensive about pursuing the subject further.

She must arrange to see Templeton immediately and pass on her recent discovery. She was convinced that Napoleon's escape was more than a rumor this time, and if one of the men sitting in her drawing room was involved, its success was a real possibility. She continued to sip the soothing blend of tea while impatiently awaiting her guests' departure.

Lord Ransley stepped into his curricle after bidding the other three men good day. Something had shaken Claire, of that he was certain. She had made a valiant attempt to hide her disquiet and had most probably succeeded with the others; however, he had studied her too closely to be fooled. Her comments on Napoleon had further disturbed him. Was she one of the Emperor's admirers? Did she wish to see him free?

He waited while Ashford's carriage edged out into the slow traffic of Berkeley Square, and watched Harcourt and Carrington step into a hackney bound for a session at Gentleman Jack's.

Removing the stickpin from his cravat, he stuck it in his pocket, then motioned the groom to take the reins again. Climbing the flight of stairs to Kenton House, he rapped sharply. "Is Lady Kingsley still in the drawing room?" he asked when Biggersleigh opened the door.

"Yes, my lord, but . . ."

"Never mind announcing me. I will only be a moment."

He entered before the butler could object and made his way down the hall. Claire was seated at a small writing desk near the window. Lord Ransley smiled at the frown creasing her forehead as she concentrated on the paper before her. She had just dipped her quill to continue writing when he spoke.

"My lady?"

She gave a start and swore under her breath as ink splattered the page.

He smothered a grin at her unladylike words. "I'm sorry. I didn't mean to startle you," he said, moving forward to help blot up the ink.

"It is of no matter, my lord, merely a note to my cousin. She enjoys the latest *on dits* from town."

Reaching the desk, he caught the ink with his handkerchief before it dripped onto the Aubusson carpet.

"Oh, Lord Ransley, you've ruined your handkerchief."

"Better that than your carpet or your charming gown," he said, running an admiring gaze over the green and gold morning gown she wore. He mopped at the remaining ink. "I fear you'll be forced to begin your letter anew," he said, looking at the ink splattered paper.

Only a few words remained legible, but they fairly leaped out at him: *Napoleon plans to escape. . . .* His hand remained steady as he wiped up the last of the ink and turned to meet the dismay in her eyes.

"There, I think you and your carpet are safely out of danger now," he predicted as if nothing was amiss.

"Thank you. But it certainly wasn't worth ruining your handkerchief. As I said, it was only a letter to my cousin who enjoys hearing the most outrageous rumors circulating. Biggersleigh will be shocked that I allowed you to sacrifice such a fine piece of cambric."

"Then it shall remain our secret," he replied, tossing the stained handkerchief on the fire.

"Was there something you wished, my lord? Not that

ou aren't welcome," she continued, blushing in her
onfusion. "But you have only just left and . . ." she
tumbled to a painful halt.

If the situation had been anything else he would have
ound her bafflement endearing, but after seeing the
etter confirming his suspicions, he could only admire
her acting ability. "I was in my carriage when I noticed
my cravat pin was missing. I thought I might have
dropped it during my visit."

"We shall search immediately," she said, ringing for
Biggersleigh. "What kind is it?"

"Hmm? Oh, gold with a small ruby. It was my father's
and has more sentimental value than real worth."

"Then we shall certainly find it if it is here."

"Thank you." He hastily consulted his watch. "I fear
I must leave you once more. I have an appointment
with my man of business."

"I understand, my lord. If we find the pin, I shall
send it around immediately."

"Thank you again, my lady." Giving a curt bow, he
strode out of the room as if glad to be gone.

Claire sank onto the rose-striped sofa, her heart beating wildly in her chest. It had been such a close thing.
If the ink hadn't spilt he might have seen everything
he had written.

After instructing Biggersleigh to search for his lordship's pin, she rose and went to the desk, intent upon
completing her note to Templeton. Reaching for the
ruined sheet of vellum, she was dismayed to see that it
had not been rendered completely indecipherable. She
crumpled the paper and quickly threw it into the fire.

Had he seen it? she wondered, pressing her cold
hands against flushed cheeks. He had given no sign.
Even if he had he most likely would have thought it
was exactly what she had said: a bit of gossip to enter-

tain her cousin. Comforted by her logic, she placed an other sheet of paper on the desk and began writing.

Lord Ransley's thoughts were far from logical as he tooled his curricle through the crowded streets. She had lied to him. She was no more writing to her cousin than he was prince regent. He now had proof that Lady Kingsley was doing more than flirting, and he was not at all pleased that he had been proven right.

Lord Ransley was irritated. Both his mother and sister had written, making it a point to tell him how delighted they were that he was going into society again. He admitted he had been in relative seclusion since Lydia's death, but that was to be expected. Although love had quickly disappeared from their marriage, he would not disgrace Lydia's memory by ignoring convention. But he was out of mourning now and there was no need to cut himself off from society.

And it was not altogether pleasure that lured him to the drawing rooms and clubs of London. There was still the question of what to do about Lady Kingsley and her influence on Juliana.

He had kept their relationship totally impersonal since seeing the damning evidence of her correspondence. When she came to visit Juliana, he retired to his library, reappearing only as she was leaving to gravely thank her for coming. In the evenings, he continued watching her flit from one gentleman to another, engaging them in conversation, touching their arms with a familiarity that hinted at something more. She seemed to gravitate to those who were barely clinging to respectability, listening to their discourse with an intentness that would flatter any man.

A wry smile twisted his lips. She made such a lovely spy he would probably spill every secret he knew for

er favors. The extent of his cynicism startled him, and
ifter much soul searching he decided he could not con-
lemn her on such flimsy evidence as four words in a
personal letter. Until he had more proof, he vowed, he
would accept her explanation. But like the toadeaters
who clung to the fringes of the *ton,* his suspicion re-
urned and was more difficult to dislodge each time.

Claire was very much aware of Lord Ransley's dark
eyes following her whenever they attended the same
function. His continued observation unnerved her, and
lrove her forced gaiety to extremes. She was disgusted
with her unsophisticated reaction. True, the marquess
was a handsome man, and he resurrected feelings that
had lain dormant for several years, but there was every
reason for her not to act like a green girl over him.

If she continued on her present path, her reputation
would not sustain her in the eyes of the *ton,* and she
could lose entree to their narrow world. Ignoring Lord
Ransley as much as possible, Claire continued searching
he drawing rooms of the *ton* for proof to convict John's
murderer.

A muscle twitched in Lord Ransley's cheek as he tied
his cravat. His frustration was not brought on by attempting to achieve the perfect oriental, at that he was
expert, but by his failure to discover Lady Kingsley's
true character.

He had no quarrel with her behavior when she was
with Juliana. As far as he could see they enjoyed one
another's company, and she exhibited no inappropriate
manner in front of the child. And although Juliana still
had not spoken, only the day before she had made a
sound somewhat resembling a giggle before clapping
her hand over her mouth.

It was that damned letter he now wished he had never

seen, and Lady Kingsley's continued association with
questionable gentlemen that drove him to the edge o
losing his formidable control.

He was not jealous, he assured himself as he patted
the immaculate white linen folds into place. He had
put aside that emotion as soon as he discovered he
could command a lady's attention as long as he desired

No, Lady Kingsley piqued his interest for another rea
son altogether; she was hiding something. While i
might not be spying—and he admitted to an overindul
gence in melodramatics in that instance—something
drove her to an excess of sociability. She was searching
and he wanted to know her prey.

Determined to uncover her secrets, Lord Ransley had
decided to pursue another avenue. As soon as he tied
this damnable cravat, he would call at Kenton House
He had known the duchess since his youth, and al
though they had only recently become reacquainted, he
descended the broad stairs of his town house secure in
the knowledge that the duchess would receive him.

He was not disappointed when he arrived at Berkeley
Square. He was shown into a small sitting room; obvi
ously a private chamber reserved for family use.

"Your Grace, thank you for receiving me," said the
marquess settling himself in a comfortable chair.

The room was heated by a well-laid fire, most wel
come even after such a short drive from Grosvenor
Square. The chairs and sofas were sturdy enough to
bear his weight, yet their soothing rose and green up
holstery would appeal to any woman.

The duchess welcomed him with a smile. "Ransley
I'm surprised you can spare the time to visit when there
are several reputed diamonds of the first water already
gracing the Season."

"You have them all beat, Your Grace," he answered
roguishly.

"Gammon!" she replied with an answering smile. "As soon as the duke's scrapegrace heir returns I'll take myself off to the dower house, returning only to supply my embroidery thread."

"You would never be so cruel as to deprive society of your company," contended Lord Ransley.

"After Lady Barringer's rout, it sounds extremely desirable," she complained sharply.

The marquess chuckled amiably at the memory of Hanora Maitland, Duchess of Kenton, dressed in purple silk with white plumes sprouting from an overwhelming turban. Observing the slight frown beginning to form between her eyes, he decided it might be prudent to change the subject.

"Do you mean that in all this time you've had no luck in locating the duke's heir?"

"Oh, he's been found all right, living on some island plantation. It seems he isn't at all impressed by a dukedom, and intends to continue living in his paradise instead of returning to our stifling society— his words, you understand," she explained. "Of course, he isn't married— too busy enjoying his freedom, I would imagine— so I remain duchess until he comes to his senses and accepts his responsibility."

"I'm sure it will happen soon," Quinton answered soothingly.

"Well, in the meantime, I do not intend to spend my time worrying over him when I have such pleasant company," she stated emphatically. "Claire will be sorry to have missed your call. She had a prior engagement, and left only moments ago."

The marquess well knew that Claire had agreed to go shopping with Margaret Lacefield. He had overheard them make the appointment the evening before and thought it an excellent time to see what the duchess would reveal about her granddaughter.

"You must convey my regrets," replied Ransley. "Lady Kingsley seems to be in great demand and the Season not even in full swing."

The duchess detected a hint of censure in his voice. "I'm pleased to see her get out more. She was confined for so long I was concerned that she might not easily return to a normal life."

"Confined?" repeated the marquess in bewilderment.

"You didn't know of her accident?" inquired the duchess.

"Actually I know very little about Lady Kingsley," he replied, sidestepping a direct answer. "Although we meet quite often, the surroundings never seem appropriate for exchanging confidences."

Speculation gleamed in Hanora's eyes. It was not a sudden whim that had brought Lord Ransley to her sitting room; he was interested in Claire. He would be a perfect match for her strong-willed granddaughter, the duchess reflected. She could not have chosen better herself.

But from what she knew of Ransley, he would not easily fall prey to a woman's charms again. If he was attracted, he would question his emotions and the woman who aroused them. It would do no harm to relate what was common knowledge of Claire's misfortune. The account might soften him, easing his struggle against feelings already strong enough to bring him here.

"It's certainly no secret, my lord. In fact it was a well publicized tale at the time. It happened in the summer of 1812, just before Salamanca."

"I was out of the country most of that year and part of the next," recalled Ransley. He had not returned to England for any length of time until the fall of 1813 when he learned of Juliana's predicament. "I'm sorry, I didn't mean to interrupt. Please continue."

"Claire and her husband were travelling to London when they were attacked by highwaymen," began the duchess. "Shots were fired and the horses bolted, running wild until the carriage overturned on a curve. Fortunately they were at the edge of a small village and help arrived in a few minutes. But it wasn't soon enough for poor John. When the villagers pulled them from the wreckage he was already dead and Claire was unconscious."

The maid entered and the duchess busied herself pouring out the hot chocolate she favored on cold mornings. After passing Lord Ransley a cup she continued with her story.

"Claire did not awaken for three days, and it was another week before she became cognizant enough to know what was going on. At that time we learned she was blind."

Hanora made no attempt to soften the blow. Lord Ransley's cup rattled in the saucer and he placed it on the table near his elbow. He closed his own eyes against the bluntness of her statement, unable to bear the thought of Claire's lovely sea-green eyes being sightless.

Once she had his attention again, the duchess continued. "We pursued every avenue, but finally Dr. James told us that only time could heal her if it was meant to be. For months we waited and hoped."

From his experience with Juliana, Ransley could vividly imagine the despair the two women had faced. Even knowing the outcome had been positive, he still felt anguish that Claire had to endure those months.

"It wasn't until the close of 1813 that the darkness began to lift for Claire. But she was afraid to raise my hopes and kept the knowledge to herself. She was able to see shapes before she finally told me. By spring of last year her vision was entirely restored. I shall never forget the moment when my granddaughter saw me for

the first time in more years than I wish to remember."
The duchess wiped a tear from her eye with a wisp of
fine lace-edged lawn.

The marquess wondered what had kept the two apart,
but the time was not right to pursue the matter.

His hands steady once again, he lifted the cup and
sipped the cooling chocolate. "Has she been well since
then," he asked.

"Oh yes," the duchess answered with a ready smile.
"And, as you know, she came through it with a wonderful ability to communicate with children." She smiled
again at her vast understatement of the fact.

She did not know the marquess's intentions, but was
determined he would not hurt her granddaughter. "I
will not have her suffer any more pain," she warned
him.

"I will do my best to see that nothing else befalls
her," he promised. She smiled smugly, and he wondered
what she had construed by his comment— he did not
know exactly what he meant himself.

An ache was beginning to make itself known just behind Claire's eyes and the evening had barely begun.
If she had not been convinced that the plan for Napoleon's escape from Elba was authentic, she would have
remained home. But, as it was, she felt compelled to
pursue the rumors despite the obvious skepticism of
Templeton's superiors.

Claire had wasted no time in meeting the government
man in front of Hatchard's, passing along the astonish-
ing news she had heard in her own drawing room.

Instead of rushing back to his office as she assumed
he would, Templeton leisurely lifted her hand to his
lips and saluted her. Anyone watching would think the

PRESENTING AN IRRESISTIBLE OFFERING ON YOUR KIND OF ROMANCE.

Receive 4 Zebra Regency Romance Novels (A $16.47 value) *Free*

Journey back to the romantic Regent Era with the world's finest romance authors. Zebra Regency Romance novels place you amongst the English *ton* of a distant past with witty dialogue, and stories of courtship so real, you feel that you're living them!

Experience it all through 4 FREE Zebra Regency Romance novels...yours just for the asking. When you join *the only book club dedicated to Regency Romance readers*, additional Regency Romances can be yours to preview FREE each month, with no obligation to buy anything, ever.

Regency Subscribers Get First-Class Savings.

After your initial package of 4 FREE books, you'll begin to receive monthly shipments of new Zebra Regency titles. These all new novels will be delivered direct to your home as soon as they are published...sometimes even before the bookstores get them! Each monthly shipment of 4 books will be yours to examine for 10 days. Then, if you decide to keep the books, you'll pay the preferred subscriber's price of just $3.30 per title. That's $13.20 for all 4 books...a savings of over $3 off the publisher's price! What's more, $13.20 is your <u>total</u> price...there's no extra charge for shipping and handling.

No Minimum Purchase, a Generous Return Privilege, and FREE Home Delivery!

We're so sure that you'll appreciate the money-saving convenience of home delivery that we <u>guarantee</u> your complete satisfaction. You may return any shipment...for any reason...within 10 days and pay nothing that month. And if you want us to stop sending books, just say the word. There is no minimum number of books you must buy.

A $16.47
value.
FREE!
No obligation
to buy
anything, ever.

ZEBRA HOME SUBSCRIPTION SERVICE, INC.
120 BRIGHTON ROAD
P.O. BOX 5214
CLIFTON, NEW JERSEY 07015-5214

two were conducting a light flirtation, and Claire fumed at his placidity.

"Aren't you going to do anything?" she had hissed, pasting a smile on her face.

He had smiled reassuringly. "Naturally, Lady Kingsley. I would be remiss if I did not, but I doubt anything will come of it. I am no further along than when we last spoke. In fact, I judge that our cause has been set back by the dispatches I received this morning. They report Napoleon's continued imprisonment on Elba and assurances that everything is as it should be."

"Of course everything is normal now," she had snapped. "Do you expect a message with the date and time of his departure? Everything will continue to appear normal until it's too late and that devil is free again."

"Please calm yourself, my lady," Templeton had begged, looking around to see if they were being observed.

"I *am* calm, Mr. Templeton," she said through gritted teeth. "I am also concerned that more of our men will be killed in a war that has gone on twenty years too long. If you will remember, one of those unfortunates was my husband. It's time to assure there will be no more deaths because of that monster."

"Lady Kingsley," he began in a tone meant to pacify, "I promise I will do all I can to convince our people that the threat is real this time, but I cannot promise success. If you would only confide your source, it would help a great deal."

For a moment Claire had considered passing along the names of the men who had been present in her drawing room, but it would not be fair to cast doubt on all their reputations. For Margaret's sake she could not even sacrifice Harcourt unless she was absolutely certain.

"You know I cannot do that," she had finally answered. "I have a confidentiality to maintain. As soon as I hear more I shall contact you." Then, allowing him to take her hand once again, she had accepted his help into the carriage, unaware of the marquess stepping down from his phaeton a few doors away.

That had been yesterday afternoon. Last night's musical had yielded nothing but insipid young ladies warbling uninspiring tunes. If that was the limit of their talent Claire surmised the Season would boast few marriages.

Since arriving at the Darlingtons' she had neither seen nor heard anything to confirm the planned escape. The evening was much as any other until Sylvia Beaufort, a dark-haired woman, no longer youthful, but with enough beauty to attract most men, had joined the group surrounding Claire.

"I have recently returned from the continent," confided Mrs. Beaufort, "where I lost my dear husband." She touched a scrap of lace to her eyes before noticing Claire's survey of her low-cut, scarlet gown.

"Of course, I am well out of mourning, but his memory is still with me," she hastened to add.

"I can well understand, Mrs. Beaufort. Perhaps the delights of the Season will keep you from suffering a decline," Claire replied, unable to keep the cynicism out of her voice.

"Is that Lord Ransley arriving," trilled Mrs. Beaufort, her gaze fastened to the entrance.

"It certainly seems to be," answered Claire, observing the imposing figure clothed in black evening attire. "Are you acquainted?" she inquired with an air of boredom.

"We met in France, a time I shall never forget," the

widow replied, feminine avarice gleaming in her dark eyes.

Claire was sorely tempted to see what thoughts were arousing Mrs. Beaufort to such a pitch, until she realized she had no desire to know. The woman was certainly not thinking of Napoleon as she gazed across the room at the marquess, and that was all that was of interest to Claire at the moment. Lord Ransley's and Mrs. Beaufort's personal alliance could remain private, she decided as she rejoined the main conversation.

Lord Ransley was still analyzing his protectiveness toward Claire Kingsley when he arrived at the Daringtons' rout that evening. He had seen her in front of Hatchard's yesterday, and had pulled in his team to greet her when Matthew Templeton had approached. His eyes narrowed as he remembered every nuance of the scene that had been played out before him.

To the casual observer they were just another attractive couple indulging in mild flirtation on a dull February day. However, the marquess had detected a hint of impatience that had been missing in Claire's previous meetings with Templeton. There had also been a sense of contained anger at one point in their conversation, and Claire had departed rather abruptly, leaving Templeton to stare after her for some time before walking away. A lovers' spat or two spies disagreeing? he wondered.

In light of Claire's letter, her meeting with Templeton took on a particularly sinister aspect. But even after all his doubts, Ransley still had the urge to rush to her side, pull her away from the crowd, and pledge to protect her from the world's cruelties.

He had seen a softer and, conversely, a stronger side of Claire through the eyes of the duchess. Hanora had painted a very poignant picture of a young woman who had the courage to overcome her own tragedies to help children whose problems were too heavy for them to bear alone.

After a great deal of soul searching he admitted he had judged her before she had spoken a word. Her relationship with Ashford and Templeton was probably just as Drew had explained, friendship extending from their association with her husband. And he could certainly not blame her for making the most of the Season when she had lived in darkness for so long. He was even more willing than before to concede that the letter which had nearly condemned her in his eyes was, in truth, written to a bored country cousin looking for excitement.

Lord Ransley drew in a deep breath of relief. He had not known how much the possibility of her guilt had weighed on him until it lifted from his shoulders. He felt like a young buck gathering his courage to approach an incomparable.

Drawing near to the circle that surrounded Claire, the marquess overheard Viscount Weatherby mention a masquerade ball being held at his home two days hence. As the conversation continued, he realized the Viscount had extended an invitation to Claire and she was actually considering attending.

Evidently, she did not know what she was getting into, he decided, barely able to restrain his disapproval of the scheme. But as soon as he got her alone, he would put paid to the idea for once and for all.

Absorbed by his annoyance with Weatherby's audacity, Lord Ransley was not aware that his attention was being solicited until a delicate hand closed over his arm in a purposeful grasp.

"Lord Ransley, what a pleasure to see you on my first evening back." Sylvia Beaufort stared boldly up at him

ith a decolletage barely containing her considerable
harms.

She caused him to recall a past he would rather for-
et, a sentiment the lady did not seem to share from
he way she leaned against his arm. Sylvia belonged to
time when the scars from his marriage and rejection
y Lydia were still fresh and painful. He had accepted
er offer of company, and she had answered his needs
or a short time.

Sylvia had known from the beginning of their brief
lliance that he was married, and he had made it clear
here was no future for them in any way. Evidently she
ad heard of Lydia's death, for she exhibited no sub-
ety in her approach.

"Mrs. Beaufort," he acknowledged, taking her hand
a an excuse to escape her hold. "I never thought you
ould give up the gaiety of Paris for London."

"I had a sudden yearning for the soil of England,
y lord."

More likely for a rich protector, he commented si-
ntly. "You will certainly brighten the drawing rooms,"
e commented, casting a speaking glance at her gown.

Taking his remark as a compliment, she leaned closer,
ffering him a better view of the attractions he might
ave forgotten. Looking up he saw Claire observing his
nd Sylvia's reunion. Abruptly excusing himself, he
dged through the throng to his tigress's side.

"Would you honor me with this next dance, my
dy?" he asked, flashing a smile that had successfully
helted many a lady's heart.

Claire was caught off guard. "I could not take you
way from Mrs. Beaufort, my lord. She is, after all,
ewly returned from the continent and still grieving
ver her dear, departed husband."

"Good God! Did she tell you that?" he exclaimed in
isbelief. "Beaufort's been gone these past eight years,

and Sylvia's been seeking solace continuously sinc
then. Indeed, I have heard she began in advance of th
sad event, just to be prepared."

Claire stared at him a moment before hiding he
laughter behind a delicately painted silk fan. "My lord
you should not be discussing such intimate knowledg
with me."

"Are your sensibilities so fine that I must tread care
fully?" he asked, his voice lowered until they were in
audible to any but her.

"No, but I assure you that if Mrs. Beaufort had over
heard you would have had to answer to her," replied
Claire, glancing quickly at the subject of their conver
sation.

"Then I am extremely fortunate her attention is nov
directed elsewhere," he concluded, a devilish smile on
his face. "Perhaps my luck will hold until you grant me
this waltz."

Something was different about the marquess tonight
reflected Claire. His manner had never been as warm
toward her, and the core of resistance she had nour
ished so deliberately over the past weeks melted in the
glow of his eyes. "How could I refuse when your hear
must be breaking to lose Mrs. Beaufort so soon," she
teased, proud of her ability to discuss his *chère amie* so
lightly.

"I shall endeavor to survive, my lady," he replied
leading her onto the floor. He experienced a rush o
satisfaction at seeing Ashford frown as they walked away

"I've been continually surprised to see you each eve
ning," she remarked archly, fitting into his arms as i
they were made for her.

"And why is that, my lady?"

The warmth of his hand burned through her gown
distracting her from their conversation. "I was given to

nderstand you didn't go out into society often," she
id, thankful to have found the right words.

"I've always been told it's a woman's prerogative to
ange her mind, Lady Kingsley. Surely a man can
aim that same privilege." His hold tightened, bringing
r closer until her skirt swirled about their legs seem-
g to bind them together.

Her laugh was artificial even to her own ears as the
at rose in her cheeks. She wondered if he had found
woman to replace Sylvia Beaufort or whether he would
sume their alliance despite his protestations. "Of
urse, my lord, but I am given to understand that it
unusual in your case."

"Then perhaps you should not listen to others, and
me to me instead," he suggested, tempting her to
quire further.

"And what would you tell me?" she chanced.

"That now there is a reason for me to attend enter-
inments," he answered gruffly, holding her gaze with
s.

Pulling her even closer, his arms tightened with a
ssessiveness that she did nothing to escape. The
nce became a near embrace, and they were slow to
lease one another when the waltz ended. Even then
did not disengage her hand, but led her to a corner
the room that offered a small degree of privacy.

She watched his lips move and wondered how they
uld feel against hers until she realized he was waiting
r an answer. "I'm sorry, my lord."

"I overheard Viscount Weatherby invite you to his
asked ball," repeated the marquess. "It isn't the place
r you, Claire."

Reality intruded on her dream world. She should
ve known there was a reason behind his asking her
dance. Angry that first Hamilton and now Ransley
lt free to order her life, Claire struck out. "And what

gives you the right to dictate my social engagements
my lord?"

The defiant challenge in her tone warned Quinto
that he had overstepped his bounds, and he attempted
to right his mistake. "None except friendship," he re
turned evenly.

"I did not know we could claim that relationship,"
she challenged contentiously.

"You're right. Perhaps it is something more." Fir
simmered in his dark gaze as he raised her hand to hi
lips.

Heat rose inside Claire as his simple salute ignited
spark that had long been dead. She wanted to feel hi
lips on hers, demanding and possessive. She wanted . .
Dear God, how could a respectable lady have such fee
ings? Closing her eyes, she fought for a semblance o
coherence. "Friends do not impose edicts, my lord."

"But they offer suggestions," he countered deftl
Turning her hand, he pressed the bare heat of his lip
against the pulse beating rapidly in her wrist.

His unruffled composure quickly brought her bac
to reality and whetted her irritation. He had questione
her from the moment they met, now he assumed a fe
honeyed words would turn her up sweet and she woul
willingly obey his every wish. "Which I am not boun
to follow," she retorted belligerently, jerking her han
from his grasp.

"No, you are not," he agreed, almost too amicabl
"But I know the gentleman in question very well, an
I assure you that the evening will not be to your likin
nor will his other guests."

"You know nothing about my preferences, my lor
so you cannot judge," she challenged, her mouth se
in a stubborn line.

He tilted her head upward, the edge of his han
warm beneath her chin. "I intend to learn, Claire,

promise you that." His thumb rubbed across her bottom lip. "I know we've gotten off to a bad start, but in this I wish you would listen to my advice. Weatherby is the most acceptable of his circle, and his manner changes considerably when away from the *haut ton.*"

Unwilling to allow herself to fall under his spell, Claire pulled away. "Thank you for your advice, Lord Ransley. Be assured I shall give it the consideration I feel it merits."

Ransley barely mastered the temptation to slam his fist into the silk-covered wall behind him in frustration as she walked away, her elegant figure stiff with indignation. He had made a mull of it from start to finish. If Claire had not yet decided to attend the ball, his heavy-handed dealing in the situation had just guaranteed it.

Eight

Doubtful that Claire would heed his warning, the marquess, in black evening dress and black mask and cloak, entered Weatherby's house late on the evening of the masquerade. Light was sparse in the ballroom, lending an air of intimacy and effectively concealing the worst of its shabbiness. After circulating, he was not at all surprised to recognize Hamilton Ashford at the edge of the dance floor wearing a half-mask that did little to conceal his identity.

Not long afterward, Ashford approached a lady wearing a red gypsy costume that Ransley recognized from Lady Barringer's event. Encircling her waist with his arm, Ashford drew her close and whispered in her ear. The woman quickly pulled away, tossed her head, and moved around the edge of the room. Ashford watched her disappear into the crowd, his mouth a grim line of displeasure.

Although black hair cascaded over the woman's bare shoulders, the costume and the graceful movement of her body was familiar to Ransley. She slipped into an alcove and as inconspicuously as possible the marquess followed her. She stood hidden in the deepest shadow, but he heard her indrawn breath as his form blocked her exit.

"Don't worry," he assured her, "I mean no harm."

Claire breathed easier as soon as she recognized Lord

Ransley's voice. She had feared that Hamilton had followed her. She should have refused his escort, but had
allowed the guilt she felt at her unaccustomed treatment
of him to get the best of her.

During their drive to Weatherby's, he had attempted
to bring their conversation around to Ransley again, but
she had quickly cut him off. As soon as they entered
the ballroom, he had begun drinking heavily, and his
unwelcomed familiarity and whispered suggestion had
shaken her more than she admitted.

"You don't look harmless," she replied, taking in the
marquess's black coat stretched across broad shoulders
and the mask which lent an air of mystery to his imposing figure.

"Appearances are deceiving, as you well know," he
replied enigmatically. "All I seek is my fortune, Gypsy,
and I'm told you can tell me that."

What did he mean? thought Claire. *Had word of her
unusual ability slipped out despite all of her precautions?*

"I'm very particular with my fortunetelling, sir. Those
who do not believe are not worthy of my time."

"I believe in your power, Gypsy. Do you need to read
my palm?" he asked, extending his hand to her.

His hand was much larger than hers, the skin hardened from years of handling reins. She ran her fingers
from his wrist down the length of his hand, heeding
the tremor as she caressed his palm.

"You're a very sensitive man," she observed, enjoying
the opportunity to touch him without social recrimina-
tion.

"Is that your fortune?" he asked, with a chuckle.

"Merely a statement of fact." Attempting to change
the direction of their conversation, she continued. "You
will experience a great joy in your life, sir. Something
you have longed for will soon be yours," she predicted,
thinking of Juliana's recovery.

For once, Juliana was not first in Ransley's mind. While the costume was the same and he was almost certain he recognized Claire's voice beneath the heavy accent, there was still a little doubt left. She made no move to stop him as he reached out and gently removed her mask.

Beneath the black hair, dark brows arched delicately over lashes that lay like a fan on her cheek. Expertly applied color highlighted the ridge of her cheekbones, altering the planes of her face as she stood in the shadows, her eyes downcast.

"Is there no beautiful, dark-haired gypsy in my future?" he asked, his voice husky.

"No!" she replied, glaring up at him.

Moving aside to allow more light to fall on her face, he finally saw her flashing sea-green eyes. "Ah. That's too bad, but then I've always been partial to a tawny-haired tigress."

"And how many have you known?" she asked pertly. Expecting anger because she had gone against his wishes, she was pleased with his reaction.

"None, but I'm open to new experiences," he answered with a heart-stopping smile.

Claire breathed deeply and slowly, hoping to slow down her galloping heart. "That is fortunate, my lord, for I see events in your future that may have you questioning what you have always held true."

Seeing her in the dim candlelight, Lord Ransley was vividly reminded of the hallucinations he had experienced after his stabbing. During his illness he had dreamed endlessly of a woman who came to him out of the mist, warning him of danger. He never saw her clearly, but remembered an old-fashioned beauty patch placed at the corner of the lovely curve of her lips. Her vision haunted him for months after his wound was healed, until he finally dismissed them as a product of his fever-ridden mind.

Tonight Lady Kingsley had placed a patch on her creamy skin in the exact location that the woman of his vision had worn hers. "Why did you wear this?" he questioned, reaching toward the beauty mark.

Claire turned her face away. She had completely forgotten the mark was uncovered. "It is, after all, a masquerade, my lord," she replied, shrugging.

"Intriguing," he murmured, her movement drawing his attention away from the mark to her bare shoulders.

I would like to kiss you all over, he thought as he touched her soft skin.

"That would not do, my lord," said Claire, unaware she answered his thoughts.

"But it would be so pleasant." Lightly gripping her upper arms, he bent toward her. His lips came to rest on her shoulder, paying tribute to each bit of warm flesh from there to the curve of her neck.

Claire was frozen with shock as his lips grazed over her skin. It had been almost three years since a man had touched her so intimately, and never had she felt desire rush through her as strongly as it did now. His warm breath feathered across her neck and she allowed her head to fall back, exposing the white expanse to his devouring gaze.

Ransley paused a moment to relish her capitulation, then his lips went unerringly to the pulse that beat rapidly beneath her silky skin, as if to claim her heart as well as her body.

He pulled her closer, one strong hand spanning her waist while the other pulled her hips into alignment with his. He held her firmly, but gently, watching for any sign of distress, any sign that she did not welcome his touch. What he saw were eyes darkened with unbridled passion to match the color of a storm-tossed sea;

what he felt was complete surrender as his lips settled over hers with an urgency that left them both reeling under the impact.

Without hesitation Claire slipped her arms around his neck and buried her fingers in the thick, dark hair that curled over the collar of his coat, pulling him down, insisting he deepen the kiss.

Quinton followed her willingly as her lips parted and he tasted the sweetness of her desire. He had never before felt this unusual mix of tenderness and intense craving which consumed him. This woman, above all others, had touched both his sensuality and his gentleness, confusing his emotions until he could not yield completely to either, fearing whichever he chose would reveal more than he wished.

Claire was being drawn into an unfamiliar world of sensation. John's touch had been playful, but Quinton's was of the tense strength that held a man's desires. She experienced a brief twinge of guilt at the pleasure she derived from his embrace, but it soon vanished as he pressed her closer. His strength enveloped her, numbing her mind until her body succumbed to its clamoring, melding intimately with his. Suddenly a raucous burst of laughter from the ballroom invaded their sanctuary and snatched Claire back from the edge of total submission.

She wrenched her lips from his, gasping out his name. "Lord Ransley, please! We must stop!"

His harsh breathing filled the small embrasure. He leaned his forehead against hers for a moment, then loosened his hold and braced his hands against the wall behind her, surrounding her with his masculinity.

Claire stood quietly as he brought himself back under control. She was as shaken as he when he finally pushed away from the wall and stood before her.

"I warned you not to attend this ball," he said with a wry smile. "Now do you believe I spoke the truth?"

At that moment Claire could only mourn the fact that they had not been private when their passion surged, but it would never do to admit her weakness.

"Indeed, I do. Rest assured I will heed your warning next time," she replied in an unsteady voice.

"Then come away with me, Claire. Let me escort you home," he appealed. Looking around the dim room, he could see couples who had gone beyond what had just happened between them. The scene reminded him of the Cyprian's Ball he had once attended. Looking back he saw her skeptical expression.

"I promise to be the pattern card of respectability," he volunteered reluctantly. "We'll sit on opposite sides of the coach."

Claire had regained her composure and was thankful she could respond in a normal tone. "Thank you for your concern, my lord, but I believe it will be best if I make my own way home."

"With Ashford?" he growled scornfully. "The last time I saw him he was being led away like a lamb by a simpering shepherdess. You won't see him again tonight."

"I know Hamilton very well and made provisions for his eventual desertion. I have my own carriage tonight, with men enough to protect me."

"And how will you insure escaping this hellhole unscathed?" he demanded.

"I'll manage as I usually do, Lord Ransley. You need not worry about me," she answered stiffly.

The marquess stared into her eyes, willing her to change her mind. *Come with me, Claire. Don't let me leave without you.*

"I cannot," she whispered, his silent plea too strong

for her to ignore. Only the thought of her vow kept her from accepting his protection.

All tenderness vanished from his face. "As you wish, my lady." With a slight inclination of his head, he turned and strode through the revelry until he reached the door. He halted a moment, hands clenched in tight-knuckled fists at his side, then stepping over the threshold he disappeared from sight.

For the first time Claire questioned her dedication. She wanted nothing more than to follow Lord Ransley from the room, fling herself into his arms, and beg him to take her to a private place. But now was a critical time. People were feeling the effects of the strong drink that had flowed freely all evening. She could find out more in the next hour than she had the entire evening. Replacing her mask, she stepped out of her hiding place to join the throng.

The room had become even dimmer and the people more abandoned while she had been with the marquess. She began to edge around a couple who were too involved with one another to notice her.

Dammit, you bitch! Do what I say!

Claire was not shocked, for she had heard all manner of things before she had learned to control her gift. Since she was trapped for the moment she turned her attention to the couple near her. The man was tall and lean, with light brown hair showing above his half-mask. The woman was a few inches shorter than Claire's average height, with dark hair and ample proportions barely concealed by the revealing cut of her gown.

"Eldon, my love, we need a bit more privacy if you mean to go any further." Her laughter was filled with feminine satisfaction.

The man slipped the tiny sleeve of her dress lower,

caressing the sensitive flesh he revealed. "Not until you agree, then I shall reward you."

Claire heard a rustle and a gasp from the woman as he bent over her.

"Can I count on you, Sylvia, to revive the old rumors?" he murmured.

"Oh, yes, Eldon. Just tell me what you want me to do," she groaned. "No, first let's go someplace more private."

So the widow Beaufort had found someone to assuage her grief. Claire hoped the unsuspecting Eldon had not imbibed too deeply, for she judged he would pay heavily for the favor Sylvia was so eager to grant. She pitied whomever would be the recipient of their plotting. Waiting until the couple moved away, she edged into the room again.

Lord Ransley's carriage rattled over the damp cobblestones following the ghostly parade of fog-draped lightposts through Mayfair. He must be soft in the head to allow himself to be played for such a fool. It was the beauty patch that had begun the whole mad episode. It reminded him of the woman whose vision had appeared during his fever, not allowing him to slip away when it would have been easy to do so.

He was the worst kind of nodcock to envision Claire Kingsley as his angel of mercy. She might not be the spy he had first thought her, but she was no more or less than others of her set: a lovely woman taking full advantage of her status as widow to defy propriety. No doubt Lydia would have been the same had she lived and he died. Rapping with his stick, he directed his coach to White's.

* * *

Although it was late, the liquor he had consumed did
not cause Lord Ransley's gait to falter as he entered his
home and made his way to the library.

He should have gone to his room where his valet
would be waiting for him. But though his body was
tiring, his mind was still too active to approach sleep.
He poured a brandy, more from habit than a craving
for another drink.

Standing in front of the fire, he swirled the liquor
in the glass, watching the flames reflect its amber glow.
Suddenly the door burst open behind him.

"What the . . ." began the marquess, turning toward
the noise. "Jason?" he questioned, setting aside his glass
before being encased in two strong arms. His younger
brother had never been backward about showing emotion, and he all but lifted Quinton from the floor in a
spirited display of brotherly camaraderie.

"Surprised to see me, brother?" Jason demanded, releasing the marquess.

"Astounded." Jason looked the same as always. His
dark brown hair was still a little unruly, and his hazel
eyes sparkled with a joy of life that Quinton envied. A
few more years would fill out the imposing frame which
marked the Courtney men. "I thought you were still at
Eversleigh," said Quinton, his spirit lifting with Jason's
company.

"I left a week ago," explained Jason. "I stopped by
Oakcrest, then followed you to town. You aren't going
to tell me I'm not welcome, are you?"

"Of course not. Juliana and I are rattling around
here all by ourselves. She'll be happy to see her uncle
again.

"Is she any better, Quin?" he questioned, his tone
turned solemn.

"It's early days yet, but she made a sound a few days

ago," Quinton announced with pride. "It seems a good indication."

"Dr. James must be an excellent physician," remarked Jason, cuffing him on the arm, his spirits high again.

"She isn't seeing James," Quinton admitted. "The doctor recommended someone else to work with Juliana."

"And he got a reaction from Juliana so soon?" he asked, surprised that Juliana, who had been exceedingly withdrawn over the past months, would respond so readily to a stranger. "Who is he?"

"*He* is a *she* by the name of Claire Kingsley. I tell you this in confidence. She's a lady of quality and prefers to keep her activity in this area private."

"You may trust me to keep silent," promised Jason. "It doesn't matter who she is as long as she can help. I say, she isn't the merry widow I've heard about, is she?"

"What do you mean?" the marquess asked stiffly.

"Why the news reached Oakcrest that you'd been seen in the company of a lovely widow quite often these past weeks," revealed Jason, enjoying his older sibling's rare discomfort,

"I'm sure our mother was overjoyed."

"You know she is. In fact, she's praying for better weather so she and Alura may leave for town earlier than expected."

"And our sister is no doubt in alt, too."

"Of course. She's already looking forward to another female in the family. Says we'll be outnumbered then." He laughed out loud before noticing the grim expression on his brother's face.

"Cut line, Jason. There's nothing going on between us. Lady Kingsley is attempting to help Juliana and I'm grateful for that. We see each other occasionally at various events and that's all there is to it," Quinton growled.

"Of course," agreed Jason, a roguish smile on his face. It must be serious, for he had never known Quin to take the time to deny involvement with a woman. He hoped sheer stubbornness would not force his brother to repudiate an attachment with the lady. "Is she pretty?" he asked impudently.

"Passing fair," acknowledged Ransley, privately thinking it a vast understatement. But it would be so far out of character for him to praise Claire's silky hair, the beauty of her green eyes, and the perfection of her figure, that Jason would commit him to Bedlam.

"Quin, you can't mourn Lydia forever," Jason said quietly, his voice filled with concern.

"My social life has not gone begging," Lord Ransley declared forcefully.

"Perhaps not," agreed Jason. "But you've allowed her memory to keep you away from the companionship every man needs."

"Because I don't keep a mistress doesn't mean I neglect my urges," retorted Quinton, not bothering to explain that lately those cravings had focused on one flirtatious, tawny-haired woman.

"That's not what I'm talking about. You didn't hesitate to satisfy your needs even while Lydia was alive."

"You become too personal," warned the marquess.

"Maybe so, but perhaps it's time someone did."

"Jason—"

"Lydia isn't worth ruining your life over," interrupted Jason.

"Explain yourself," demanded Quinton.

Jason hesitated at his brother's icy voice, but he was determined to finish. "Lydia wasn't faithful to you, Quin. She wanted someone to admire her, feed her vanity. When you were away, she turned to others."

The marquess's fists clenched and unclenched at his sides while a flush stained the ridge of his cheekbones. "Are you telling me my wife had an affair?"

"There was more than one, Quin. You know Lydia couldn't live unless being constantly showered with compliments. They were the breath of life for her. I'm not trying to hurt you, but I'd like to see you set free from whatever is tying you to her memory."

"You're lying," the marquess accused in a strained voice. Moving quickly he grabbed the lapels of Jason's coat. "I know you're lying," he shouted, drawing back his fist.

"Hitting me won't change anything," replied Jason, willing to accept the blow if it meant freeing his brother from the past.

Quinton released him, shoving him backward. "Get out," he ordered in a beaten voice. "Damn you, get out and leave me be."

Claire breathed a sigh of relief. She had arrived at Hatchard's early to assure herself that the marquess was not on the premises. She had neither seen nor heard from Lord Ransley since the night of Weatherby's masquerade. He had probably taken a complete disgust for her determination to remain at such a sordid event and was counting himself lucky to be free of her. She was surprised at the pain that shot through her at the thought.

When Templeton's message had arrived asking her to meet him at one o'clock, Claire had been happy for the distraction. It was rare that Matthew Templeton initiated a rendezvous with her. Usually he left it to Claire to let him know when she had some information for him.

"Lady Kingsley, what a delight to see you here."

Claire turned and smiled, wondering why he had never appealed to her as more than a friend. He was attractive enough, with warm brown eyes and hair a shade darker. His dress was subdued but impeccable, and expertly tailored. His cravat lay just so and the gold pin that adorned the pristine folds bespoke good taste. All in all, Templeton should appeal to any lady of a like age.

But Claire had kept him at arm's length, thinking that theirs was a professional relationship and anything more could jeopardize their task. In truth, even if they had met on a strictly social basis, he did not arouse the feelings that the marquess stirred up whenever he was near.

"Mr. Templeton, you're just in time to help me select a book. I know you are *au fait* in what is current. Can you spare a moment?"

"I would gladly make time for you, my lady," he replied gallantly, an amused twinkle in his eye. "There are a few volumes over here that might appeal to you." He took her arm and led her deeper into the shelves. "I am glad you could meet me at such short notice," he said when they were in private.

"It must be serious," she replied, accepting the book he held out to her and flipping through the pages.

"It is," he answered tersely. "We have received corroborating evidence from the continent that there is movement afoot to release Napoleon from his island prison. The French are pleading for the Emperor's removal to St. Helena, but the Congress is too busy entertaining and being entertained to listen."

Claire concentrated on keeping the book steady in her hand. "What do you plan to do?"

He gave a short bark of laughter. The amiable man who had entered the bookstore a short time ago had been replaced by a granite-faced, hard-eyed stranger.

The impossible. We must find the power behind the plot and put paid to it. I'm asking all our agents to put forth their best efforts. If you hear anything at all— the slightest whisper— report it to me immediately."

"I'll do my best," she promised.

"I know you will," he replied, his voice taking on its formerly pleasant tone. "You always do, and I am often unthankful. If I remember correctly," he said with a wry twist to his mouth, "it wasn't long ago that I dismissed your warning as groundless. I hope you will accept my apology."

"None is needed, Mr. Templeton. I am only happy that we have an opportunity to prevent Bonaparte's escape. I pray that we are in time."

"As do I, ma'am. Now, I will not keep you longer. Please take no undue risks. The men behind this plot are ruthless. They'll not hesitate to take extreme means to protect their plan."

"I'll be careful," she promised. "I have no desire to become a casualty. Thank you for the advice," she said in a slightly louder tone. "I'm sure I will enjoy the book immensely."

Templeton accepted her proffered hand and bowed slightly. "It has been my pleasure, Lady Kingsley," he replied, his grave eyes repeating his message of caution before he left the shop.

Claire made her way out of Hatchard's totally immersed in her thoughts. It wasn't until she arrived home that she realized she had already read the book she held.

Claire was so intent on garnering any bit of news pertinent to Napoleon that she took Lord Ransley's first note canceling her visit with Juliana at face value. His excuse of a conflicting appointment did not overly concern her at the time; it could happen to anyone. But the second note terminating the meetings altogether because "little progress had been made" commanded her attention and sent anger raging through her.

They had made considerable progress and the stubborn man knew it! He was only angry that she had not left the ball with him, and meant to use Juliana as a means of punishment. She had thought better of him, and wasted no time in setting out for Grosvenor Square to tell him."

Claire arrived on the marquess's doorstep filled with righteous indignation. Her social life had nothing at all to do with her relationship with Juliana, and she meant to inform his lordship of that very thing without delay.

"Where is Lord Ransley," she demanded as soon as his starchy butler opened the door.

"In the library, my lady, but—"

"There is no need to announce me. I can find my own way, and see that we are not interrupted," she ordered, without pausing in her march down the hall.

"Of course, madam," the dazed man murmured, certain he should immediately begin packing his bags.

Claire gave only one sharp rap before opening the door to Lord Ransley's library. She immediately drew out her handkerchief and applied it to her nose.

The room had evidently not been aired in days. It reeked of liquor, and a haze hung low in the room, spiraling up from a plate filled with the remains of smoldering cigars. Empty bottles littered the tabletops and lay abandoned on the floor, while others were balanced precisely one atop the other like a house of cards.

Walking carefully in order not to topple them, Claire moved further into the room. One wall was stained with dark rivulets running down to mix with the shattered remains of glasses laying on the floor. The sight cooled her temper considerably and nearly convinced her to take to her heels in fright. A man angry enough to do this was not one she wished to meet. But before she could beat a hasty retreat, the marquess rose from a chair next to the low-burning fire.

He was even more intimidating than the broken glasses. The impeccable, tightly contained Quinton Courtney, Marquess of Ransley, had been replaced by a disheveled, unshaven man looking more the devil than Claire cared to imagine.

"My lord?" she questioned in a tentative voice.

"My lady Kingsley," he drawled insultingly in a slurred voice. "So you have come to have your bit of me, too. Or are you just a dream again?"

Claire thought it better to say nothing.

"Damn you!" he cursed, slamming another glass against the abused wall. "Damn you for coming back again. It wasn't enough that you invaded my life and my dreams for months, was it? Making me think if I lived you would be there waiting for me. Well, look at me," he demanded, spreading his arms wide. "I survived and my arms are as empty as your promises. You're no better than Lydia. Nay, worse. She at least told me I repulsed her, while you . . ." His words tapered off and he dropped his arms, shaking his head in confusion.

"Did you save me just to torment me?" he asked, after a moment's consideration. "Hadn't I suffered enough, or did you think I deserved more?" His voice was full of bewilderment, and Claire wanted nothing more than to take him in her arms and comfort him. But before she could move to his side, he continued.

"If you hadn't warned me that I was in danger I wouldn't have been as alert. I would most likely have been found dead in front of Gunter's. But no, the Courtney luck held. It was New Year's Eve and too many people were about even in that damnable fog. I was alive and you have given me barely a moment's rest since then. Why did you do it, tiger lady? Why?"

The marquess dropped down into his chair. His eyes closed as he slumped back still mumbling to himself.

Claire gripped the back of the sofa in shock. Quinton Courtney was the man she had met last New Year's Eve! She had ventured out onto the fog-shrouded city street by herself in an act of independence and celebration. She was beginning to see shadows in her previously dark world, and was certain that the new year would bring back her sight.

As soon as she warned the man in the fog, Claire realized he must never know her name or it could jeopardize her mission. If he escaped the evil intent she felt surrounding him, he would surely pursue her until he found out how she came about her knowledge. Once the story made its rounds, the enemy— whether he was a believer or not— would avoid her. Claire had fled into the white swirling mist, praying the man would heed her counsel.

The restoration of her vision soon after their meeting in Berkeley Square wiped everything else from her mind, and since then she had given only a few fleeting thoughts to the occurrence.

Now she faced the same predicament she had all those months ago. If she admitted to being the woman in his dreams he would eventually ferret out her secret, and perhaps reveal it before her mission was complete. She could not let him know his drunken accusations were true. Hoping he would forget everything by the time he awakened, she tiptoed from the room.

It was late evening before Quinton came round again. After Jason's unwelcome revelation, he had spent the following three days striving to empty his wine cellar and reliving the shambles of his marriage.

It was true he had looked to other women for his needs, but it was at Lydia's request. She had made no secret of not wanting him in her bed. Although Quinton secretly thought she did not like the force of his ardor, she blamed it on the danger of having another child. When he mentioned there was a way to prevent the condition, she shuddered, saying she would not trust it.

No, he could not believe Jason; he had been misinformed. Lydia did not like the marriage bed well enough to welcome someone else into it. She had come between him and his family when she was alive, now she was haunting him, hurting him even after she was gone.

His family wanted only the best for him. His mother yearned to see him with a wife and more children. His sister and brother wanted him happy again, no matter what it took.

If he had stayed away from Claire Kingsley their hopes would not have been raised, and Jason wouldn't have tried to encourage his suit with such an unlikely story. Unable to find a full bottle, Lord Ransley made his way down the hall and climbed the stairs to his rooms where his valet still waited to help his master to bed.

He awoke the next morning to bright sunlight and a splitting head, but with a remarkably clear memory of what had happened in his interview with Claire. Calling for a bath and breakfast, he dressed with unusual care, then took himself off to Berkeley Square to apologize to a lady who had done no more than assert her rights as an independent woman, all in aid of his daughter.

He had not faltered once during his preparations to call on Claire. But now that he was in her drawing

room, he felt the urge to depart as quickly as he had
arrived. However, he had left it too late.

Claire stood in the doorway, hesitating a moment, her
eyes as cool as the depths of the sea. She did not offer
her hand, but greeted him with a regal incline of her
head.

"Lord Ransley." Her voice was cautious, but not condemning.

"Lady Kingsley, I'm grateful you received me this
morning."

Claire smiled. She had been afraid to spurn him because of Juliana, afraid to receive him because of his
memory. Juliana won.

"There is no reason I should refuse," she replied,
moving further into the room.

"Come, madam, let us have some plain speaking. Our
last meeting was not one you would wish to repeat."

Claire stopped directly in front of him, tilting her
head to meet his gaze. "I had no fear of that, my lord.
You would not have made it this far in such a condition."

He smiled bitterly. "You have the right of it, ma'am.
I'm here to apologize for that disgraceful scene yesterday."

"It was of my own making. I intruded on your privacy
and was deserving of your anger."

"No one warrants that level of rudeness. I had received some disturbing news and tried to hide in a bottle. I'm not proud of the fact nor am I trying to excuse
it, but I wanted to explain the circumstances so you
would understand it is not my usual state."

"I never thought it, sir. And since you have been so
generous, I must also apologize for bursting in unan-
nounced. Emotion also ruled me that day. I was angry
that you were denying me Juliana's company."

Lord Ransley had hoped he would not need to go

into a lengthy explanation, but he could see he owed her nothing less. It was not as if the story were secret, but he felt the veriest fool telling it.

"I would never keep you from Juliana. As soon as I came to myself I regretted my note to you. I feel I owe you an accounting concerning my ramblings yesterday," he said, leading her to a sofa and seating himself beside her.

As quickly as possible, the marquess described the attempt on his life, the ensuing fever, and the dreams that followed. He seemed embarrassed about believing she was the woman who had appeared to him.

Thankful he no longer believed his vision to be real, Claire accepted his apology and eagerly agreed they should not allow the incident to interrupt her meetings with Juliana.

Their business finished, Claire walked with him to the drawing room door. As he made ready to leave, Lord Ransley looked down at Claire, mesmerized by a face that had filled so many of his days and nights. Compelled by a force over which he had no control, he reached out for her and she came willingly into his arms. Their lips met, gently at first, then with a gathering intensity that neither of them resisted.

The first time he had kissed her, Claire had been caught off guard by the fierceness of her response. This time she was prepared, and honest enough to admit she welcomed the excitement that rushed through her. Her arms encircled his neck, firmly anchoring him to her as if she expected him to break and run at any moment.

Lord Ransley liked her holding fast and had no wish to move in any direction other than closer to her, which was impossible since their bodies were already molded together as one. He had never felt desired by a woman except for his title and money. But with Claire's arms around him, her body pressing urgently against him, and her mouth welcoming his invasion, he felt more complete than he had in his entire adult life.

What am I going to do with you? he asked himself as he placed kisses over her face.

"You mean you don't know?" she gasped as he reached her ear, lightly nipping the lobe.

He chuckled, his warm breath wafting through her hair. "I know very well what to do with a lady exhibiting such unrestrained ardor. It's the where that has me puzzled."

"Oh? Oh, my!" she said, finally realizing just where they were.

Lord Ransley wanted nothing more than to lock the door and relieve Claire's anxiety concerning his knowledge of lovemaking, but fate dictated otherwise. They were in her grandmother's house, surrounded by servants who might appear at any moment. Tamping down his passion, he settled for one last kiss before releasing her.

The loss of the solid strength of his body pressed against hers left Claire feeling cold and alone. Observing the bewilderment on her face, the marquess took her in his arms again, lightly stroking the curves and hollows of her back until her tenseness disappeared and she straightened, looking at him inquiringly.

Framing her face with large, capable hands, he held her gaze with an intensity that spoke far more than words. "I am extremely happy you aren't the woman in the fog, for the only way you could know to warn me was if you knew of the attack." He brushed his lips against hers again, lingering indecisively before giving her another quick hard kiss. "And I would hate to find I enjoyed kissing my enemy."

"I would never cause you harm," whispered Claire, held by the magnetism of his gaze.

He smiled at her confession, realizing better than she the depth of her avowal.

"It's the absence of the beauty patch that makes the difference," he teased. "Are you sure you've never worn one before the masquerade?"

Claire's breath caught as he raised his hand to brush the spot where it should have been, wondering if her makeup would remain if he did so. At that moment the duchess arrived home in a flurry of capes and muffs, curtailing their goodbyes to the commonplace.

There was a heightened awareness between them from that time on. Although Ashford still hung about Claire, Lord Ransley did not readily give way to her other admirers. And while she continued to circulate at the various routs and balls they attended, she spent more time with him. Since both had independent means, the *ton* had begun to speculate that a love match was in the offing.

Lord Ransley was not completely happy with the situation. Although Claire showed a decided preference for his company and his kisses, she still lavished her attention on too many other men for his own peace of mind. Someday soon he would need to confront Claire about her questionable actions, and their future. In the meantime, he would savor the time they had together.

Nine

"He just came in."

Claire was not surprised at Margaret's statement. She had made no effort to keep her eyes from searching the room for the marquess until she caught sight of him in a group near the entrance.

"Am I that obvious?"

"Only when you allow yourself to be, and I'm certain that's solely with me. I suppose you feel safe since I'm just as daft about Harcourt."

"And both our cases are equally as hopeless," Claire replied flatly.

"What could keep you and the marquess apart?" asked Margaret, her brows arching in surprise. "There can be no question about your suitability. You are equal in station, your families would no doubt be in alt with a connection, and it's clear that you would welcome his advances."

Claire spoke without thinking. "I have already welcomed his advances. Oh, not that way," she clarified, seeing the look of astonishment on her friend's face. "But I tell you truthfully, Margaret, it would take very little encouragement for me to do so."

"If you love him so much, what stands in your way?"

"Sometimes I see him watching me and there is more doubt in his eyes than I could ever hope to overcome. His marriage was far from being a happy one, and I'm convinced it's caused him to distrust women in general, for he hasn't mentioned anything permanent."

"Then you shall have to prove him wrong, my dear. And it looks as if you'll be able to begin very soon," she murmured behind her fan as Lord Ransley approached.

The marquess greeted both ladies, exchanging pleasantries until Harcourt joined them and drew Margaret into conversation.

"May I hope that you have a dance left, Lady Kingsley?" *And let it be a waltz,* he petitioned silently, *for I must hold you again soon.*

Claire studied her dance card to hide her confusion. When her emotions were involved, her restraint sometimes weakened. Several times she had found herself answering Lord Ransley's thoughts, and knew it would only be a matter of time before he questioned the occurrences. But for now she was just as anxious to be in his arms as he was to hold her.

"I have the next waltz free," she replied calmly.

"An answer to my prayers." He smiled in delight and offered her his arm. "Shall we promenade until the music begins?"

The solid warmth of his arm beneath her hand was a vivid reminder of their kiss. Glancing up she did not need to look any further than his eyes to know his thoughts were the same as hers.

Stepping out of the main flow of people, he slipped the ivory fan from her wrist. "Perhaps this will be of more help than a stroll," he said, plying the fan industriously before her.

"And perhaps we should both share it," she replied boldly, guiding his hand until the draft cooled the flush on his cheekbones.

He laughed, folding the ivory sticks and tapping her

on the chin. "Actually, I am here on a mission, you baggage," he said, still smiling down at her.

"Then it isn't my presence that drew you?" Claire had never flirted so openly before, not even with John.

"Never doubt that, my dear," he said seriously, his eyes hot with repressed desire.

Claire was suddenly out of her depth. She knew it would take only a slight indication from her and the choice would be removed from her hands. While she wanted to share his passion, she was not ready to join the ranks of widows who found their pleasure where they could.

"And what is your mission, my lord?" The tension uncoiled from his body as he accepted her decision.

"It seems my daughter has developed quite an appetite for excursions. We are going to take in the Royal Menagerie tomorrow afternoon and I wondered if you would wish to accompany us?"

"I would be delighted, my lord."

Satisfaction lit his eyes. "Good. We shall see you at two o'clock tomorrow afternoon."

The strains of the waltz sounded and she eagerly stepped into his welcoming arms.

The trip to the menagerie had been an unqualified success, thought the marquess, as the carriage rolled to a stop in front of Gunter's and he helped Juliana and Claire down. He still felt a bit uneasy returning to the place where he had almost died, but with his daughter on one side and his gypsy on the other the unpleasantness quickly vanished from his mind.

They were soon seated inside with hot chocolate and a tempting array of cakes before them when the duchess and Lord Moreland entered.

"Grandmama, I didn't know you would be here this

afternoon," said Claire as the couple paused by their table.

"It was a spur of the moment decision," replied the duchess, giving her hand to Lord Ransley and greeting him warmly. "You remember Lord Moreland?" she said, pulling the gray-haired gentleman into their circle.

"Of course," responded Ransley.

"Juliana, my dear, how are you?" asked the duchess. "I'm glad to hear that," she said in response to the child's brilliant smile. "If your father doesn't mind, I wonder if you'd like to join us. You see they have some very special cakes here that are made just for me, and I can't think of anyone I would rather share him with."

Juliana turned her pleading eyes on her father.

"Are you sure you want to be bothered, Your Grace?"

"It's no bother at all. I enjoy the child."

"Well, then," he still hesitated, looking again at Juliana who practically bounced in her chair. "All right, but don't make a pest of yourself, Juli."

Juliana slipped from the chair and took the duchess's hand, listening intently to every word the older woman said.

"I don't understand," said Lord Ransley. "It seems as if Juliana can actually converse with you and your grandmother."

"It's a gift," replied Claire, not wanting him to inquire too deeply. "Grandmama says it runs in the female line of our family."

"I'm glad you chose to share it with us," he answered, looking at her warmly.

Claire wished she felt as pleased as Lord Ransley, for although she and Juliana enjoyed one another's company, the child had hidden her fears behind a barrier that Claire had been unable to breach.

"I must admit that I'm discouraged by my lack of progress with Juliana," confessed Claire.

"She's happier now than she has been since my return."

"I don't question her happiness, my lord. But I'm at a standstill in reaching her," she answered with a distracted air.

It was obvious she was concentrating and Lord Ransley did not interrupt her. Instead he studied the small white teeth that were worrying her bottom lip, making it as rosy as when he kissed her. The memory of holding her created a possessiveness that reflected in his gaze, and Claire's breath faltered as she met his intense scrutiny.

Her thoughts escaped all bounds of a lady whenever she remembered the kisses they had shared. "My lord, where was Juliana when she stopped speaking?" she asked, determined to ignore his appeal and get back to the problem at hand.

"She and her mother were residing at Oakcrest," he replied shortly.

The mention of his wife had brought a slight hesitation to his voice which caused Claire to study him unobtrusively. There was hurt in his eyes— just a flicker— but enough to tell her how affected he was. He instantly extinguished it, as must usually be the case, and replaced it with steel again.

"Would you think it forward of me to suggest a visit to your estate?" she asked tentatively.

The marquess felt an excess of pleasure. He was suddenly eager to show Claire his home, and have her meet his family. If luck was with him Jason would be there and he could mend their relationship.

"I would be delighted to have both you and the duchess as my guests."

"Thank you, my lord. It's possible that being with Juliana where the trouble began will help me solve this puzzle."

"When would you like to come?" he asked, hoping
would be soon.

"It will take several days for me to complete my ob-
gations, but we should be able to leave by the end of
he week. That is, if Grandmama is agreeable."

"We will put it to her immediately," he replied as the
uchess returned Juliana to the table.

Seeing that her granddaughter was wholly in favor of
ccepting Lord Ransley's invitation, Hanora did not
esitate in agreeing. She realized that Claire wanted to
o for Juliana's good, but she also realized it was a per-
ect opportunity for Claire to become better acquainted
ith the marquess. The duchess agreed that the end of
he week would give them plenty of time to pack and
rrange details. The small party broke up with a sense
f anticipation in everyone's mind.

The next evening Claire sat at her dressing table star-
ng at her reflection. For the first time since she had
egun her search for the traitor, she was discouraged.
he evenings had merged into one endless round of
ocializing that was more torment than pleasure, with
o new leads to follow and no new secrets to uncover.
he rumors of Napoleon's escape had completely dis-
ppeared.

As she dressed for still another soiree, Claire admit-
ed her weariness, and longed to spend a quiet night
t home in front of the fire. Better yet, she would like
othing more than to put town behind her and retire
o Oakcrest immediately. Instead she donned yet an-
ther exquisite creation from London's most fashion-
ble modiste, and braved the cold London night once
gain.

Quinton saw Claire immediately when she entered.

He frowned as he watched her greet Lord and Lad
Ponsonby, then move further into the room.

Approaching, he captured her hand and carried it t
his lips. "It had grown so late I thought you were goin
to disappoint your admirers this evening."

"I could not do that," she replied, "it would ruin m
reputation."

Lord Ransley did not like Claire's frail look this eve
ning. Her smile was forced and her manner dispirited
Her face was paler than usual, with faint bruising be
neath her green eyes. He doubted she had missed a
evening out for weeks, and he was sure her calendar wa
filled with activities he knew nothing about. The woma
was running herself into the ground.

"I hope I find you well this evening," he said, stud
ing her carefully.

"Just somewhat fatigued," she replied.

"Then perhaps you should refuse a few invitations.

"And play gooseberry to my grandmother and Lor
Moreland?" she asked impatiently. "I think not, m
lord."

He was close to begging her to allow him to fill he
evenings with something more vitalizing than a mear
ingless round of social events. He could promise he
complete fulfillment when they were together for h
was experienced enough to know how to please
woman.

But he would not rush her. She would be beneat
his roof soon enough, he thought with a great deal c
satisfaction. He would make sure they spent time tc
gether and he would press his suit. Before they returne
to London she might be his.

"Then come with me," he urged, leading her ont
the dance floor. "We'll dance your cares away, and
you become too tired you may lean on me."

Claire wanted to accept his invitation and lay he

ead on his impossibly broad shoulder, to close her eyes
d forget the vow that now seemed futile. Instead, she
iled as his arm encircled her. "I feel revived already,
y lord."

As soon as the marquess left Claire, Templeton made
s way to her side. "I assume you have nothing to re-
rt or I would have heard," he said, disappointment
owing in his expression.

"Absolutely nothing," she replied in exasperation.
My usual sources of information are dried up. It's as
the subject of Napoleon is totally *du vieux temps.*"

"My other contacts tell the same story," said Temple-
n. "It only convinces me that the reports we had earlier
ere reliable. Evidently the leaks have been effectively
ushed, which worries me all the more."

They stood in silence for a moment, each thinking
the death and destruction that the successful com-
etion of Napoleon's escape could cause.

Claire had not considered that her upcoming trip
ould affect the investigation, and she was momentarily
mpted to find Lord Ransley and call it off. Only the
ought of Juliana and her knowledge that the people
ey sought had gone underground kept her from with-
rawing. But she did owe it to Templeton to reveal her
ans.

"It is unfortunate, but I'll be out of town for a short
hile," said Claire. "It's a personal matter that cannot
e delayed."

"I can't expect you to devote your entire life to our
rvice, my lady. Indeed, I'm grateful for the time
u've given so generously. The way matters are moving
ere's probably nothing for you to learn at the mo-
ent. Perhaps when you return, we'll have more luck."

"I pray that it will be so, and I'll do my best."

"You always do, Lady Kingsley. Now I see your ne
partner is coming to claim you. I hope you have
enjoyable trip. London will be much duller witho
you," he said, saluting her hand.

Several hours later, Claire was sitting in one of t
gilt-edged chairs placed around the ballroom. She h
just danced with Lord Davenport, whose whalebo
stays creaked loudly with every move he made. A le
sympathetic person might have laughed at his vani
but Claire's soft heart could do nothing more than se
him off in search of refreshments so she might sm
without wounding his pride.

Wiggling her bruised toes which Davenport had tr
on with his high heels, she sighed in defeat. She h
sacrificed her satin slippers for naught, for he kne
nothing further concerning Napoleon's escape.

Her eyes wandered over the room until she saw t
marquess's dark hair. Claire had danced twice with hi
that evening, and could still feel his strong arms arour
her. At that moment the crowd shifted and she observe
Sylvia Beaufort clinging to his arm.

"Sylvia's certainly wasting no time in picking u
where she left off."

Claire glanced up to find Hamilton standing by h
chair, his eyes trained on the couple across the roor
"I believe they met in France," she replied, outward
unruffled.

Her composure angered him. "They were more tha
mere acquaintances, my dear," Hamilton retorted, u
willing to pass up an opportunity to blacken his riva
name. "I'm sure you understand when I say they we
extremely close."

"And I'm convinced he's not the only man who ca

claim a close relationship with Mrs. Beaufort," snapped Claire, glaring at the blond man beside her.

A dull flush colored Hamilton's cheekbones. Claire had avoided him since the night of the masquerade, and now she was defending the marquess. He was accustomed to her flirting with other men, but they had never had a falling out over anyone before, and he did not like the significance it portended.

"Perhaps not. But at least Mrs. Beaufort has only indiscretion against her name. As far as I know she hasn't been accused of doing away with her husband."

"I thought I had made it plain that I don't wish to discuss the marquess any further," said Claire. "To do so degrades us and Lord Ransley."

"Don't be foolish, Claire, no man is a saint. It was a well-known fact that Ransley's wife had turned him away. A woman does not do that without just cause, and a man does not accept it unless guilty of some wrongdoing."

"Hamilton, I will not listen to any more. Not only do you malign Lord Ransley's name, but now you seek to denigrate his wife's memory."

"Make inquiries, Claire," advised Hamilton, undeterred by her indignation. "You'll find that what I say is common knowledge. The man is a murderer and everyone knows it, but there's no solid proof, so he walks free."

"What do you mean?" asked Claire, her body rigid with shock.

"Surely you've heard the rumors surrounding the late Lady Ransley's death. It is said she was last seen alive with Ransley late one night. He had some interesting scars on his face the next morning when she was found, but it seems he could remember nothing about his wife's visit or how he acquired the scratches."

"Rumors prove nothing."

"Of course not, or he would be behind bars instead of enjoying an evening with his mistress."

"If you will excuse me, Hamilton, I see Lord Davenport is returning." Claire rose and moved toward the short, rotund man, who was making his way carefully through the throng balancing a cup of punch in his hand. As much as Davenport bored her, his company was preferable to Hamilton's at the moment.

As she sipped her punch, Claire observed Lord Ransley bow over Mrs. Beaufort's hand, then disappear into the card room.

Sylvia Beaufort was not a happy woman. She had arrived just as Quinton completed a dance with Lady Kingsley. Lord Davenport had immediately claimed Claire's hand, leaving Lord Ransley frowning after the couple as they took the floor.

Seizing the opportunity, Sylvia had slipped her arm through his, smiling up into his startled face.

"My lord, you look as if you've been deserted," she had chided gently.

Lord Ransley had attempted to be subtle in refusing Sylvia's obvious advances, but the more his regard grew for Claire, the shorter his patience was with Sylvia. It was time to make it clear he was not interested in repeating their dalliance.

"Not at all. Unfortunately that was my second dance with Lady Kingsley, and being the lady that she is, she will not allow me another. However, I cannot like the way Davenport fawns over her."

He felt the woman beside him stiffen and withdraw her arm from his. Perhaps she had finally realized it would do no good to pursue him.

Sylvia flicked open her fan to cool her overheated face. She glanced about to see if anyone had been close enough to overhear Ransley's comment. It would do her reputation no good if rumor got about that the marquess had dealt her such a public set-down.

"I didn't know your acquaintance had progressed so far. May I wish you happy?" she asked through clenched teeth.

"No. It's much too soon for that," he replied hastily. "If you will excuse me, madam, I've promised Lord Stanford to make up a table." Bowing slightly he quickly disappeared into the card room.

Sylvia applied her fan even more diligently as her temper rose. How dare the man slough her off so casually! She had helped him through a difficult time in France after his wife had rejected him. Of course, she had greatly benefitted from their alliance, but that should not completely erase his debt to her. Now he thought to ignore her as if their past had never been. Well, the great Lord Ransley might be finished with her, but she was certainly not finished with him, not by a long shot!

The dance came to an end and she watched as Lord Davenport led his partner from the floor and scurried off toward the refreshment table. Hamilton Ashford had a brief, and what seemed to be a heated, exchange with the widow before Davenport returned carrying a cup of punch. Now was the time, thought Sylvia, as Davenport claimed his next partner and Lady Kingsley stood alone for the moment.

She moved quickly through the crowd. "Lady Kingsley, it's so good to see you again. I was just telling dear Quinton that your energy is amazing. I see you at every event I attend."

Claire had been attempting to erase the image of Quinton and Sylvia sharing a lover's embrace from her mind. She had met with little success, and now the brazen doxy had appeared at her elbow. "I didn't realize

my social life was of such interest to you, madam." Ice
dripped from her words and turned her eyes into green
chips.

"Oh la, my lady," replied Sylvia, appearing totally
oblivious to Claire's frigid response. "The *ton* thrives
on knowing all there is to know about everyone."

"So I have recently been reminded," remarked Claire,
recalling Hamilton's allegations concerning Lord Ransley. "It must be comforting to meet an old friend such
as Lord Ransley again."

Sylvia Beaufort had just suffered humiliation at the
hands of the marquess, and the reason for his rejection
was the woman who stood beside her. In a moment of
passion at a masquerade ball, she had promised Eldon
Garrick to revive the old rumors about Ransley. Eldon
would not reveal his reason for wanting to damage Ransley's reputation, but now the task of planting seeds of
doubt in Lady Kingsley's mind toward the marquess
would be all the sweeter.

"It is indeed. He's suffered so much since I last saw
him, the poor man. I'm glad to see that no one believed
he had anything to do with his wife's death despite his
threats."

Claire could not believe what she was hearing. First
Hamilton and now Sylvia assaulted Ransley's integrity.
"Threats?" she queried, already certain of what she
would hear.

Sylvia smiled. The silly chit had risen perfectly to the
bait. "Oh, my lady, it was nothing I assure you. In our
intimate moments Quinton often wished her dead, but
I'm sure he meant nothing by it," she confessed confi-
dentially. "Ofttimes men who are disappointed in their
marriages make rash statements."

"You would know better than most," replied Claire
grimly.

Sylvia ignored the thrust; destroying the marquess in

his current love's eyes was much more important than retaliating with a barbed comment. "Although I must say I was surprised that talk of murder was making the rounds," continued Sylvia, satisfied at seeing Claire's grip tighten around the cup. "It seems Lady Ransley and Quinton were together immediately before her fatal accident. I also heard from a reliable source that he had fingernail scratches on one cheek. Many people found it peculiar that he couldn't remember anything about it.

Claire could no longer stomach conversing with Ransley's mistress. "I'm sure you will excuse me, Mrs. Beaufort. I find my late nights have caught up with me."

"I know exactly what you mean, Lady Kingsley. I, too, cannot wait to feel my bed beneath me. Perhaps I will encourage Quinton to throw in his last hand," she replied suggestively, looking toward the card room.

"Goodnight, Mrs. Beaufort."

Sylvia smiled triumphantly as Claire turned abruptly and made her way toward the door. She would never let Eldon know that his instructions to renew the rumors about Ransley had given her so much personal satisfaction, or he would no longer be in her debt. She might never have the marquess in her bed again, but after tonight neither would Lady Kingsley.

It was a good hour later that Lord Ransley and Viscount Stanford stepped out of the card room.

"Off to Oakcrest tomorrow then?" asked Drew.

"That's right," replied Quinton, searching the room for the gleam of Claire's tawny curls. "I wish you'd reconsider and join us. You know how much Alura enjoys your company."

"Too old to keep up with the chit," complained Drew, with a grimace.

The marquess laughed and clapped his friend on the

shoulder. "She's grown up considerably this past year
I'm certain she would have compassion for your ancient
bones. Besides, Moreland's unable to make time in his
schedule, which leaves us outnumbered by females."

"Poor planning, I'll agree, but your own fault. Have
business myself, or I'd accept." Seeing Quinton's attention had wandered, Drew grinned slyly. "Looking for
someone?" he asked innocently.

"Claire. I mean, Lady Kingsley," Quinton answered
with a distracted air.

"Don't see her," offered Drew, scanning the room.

"She must have left," judged Quinton, satisfied that
she was getting some much needed rest, and also that
she was unavailable to the men who usually paid her
court.

He was more than glad for an early night himself
since he had planned to leave for Oakcrest at dawn. He
was disappointed in being unable to say goodbye to
Claire, but he would see her in just a few days. At Oakcrest he would have no competition for her time except
for Juliana, and he could always send her to bed, he
thought with a fond smile.

Ten

Claire spent the night overcome by indecision. What he had heard about the marquess had shaken her to he core. It was not at all unusual for a married man o have a mistress, but somehow she had thought better of Lord Ransley. She was also disappointed that he had liscussed his private life with a woman such as Sylvia Beaufort. The suggestion that he would murder his wife vas unacceptable to Claire, yet he was a strong man ind if his temper had gotten the best of him. . . . She lid not complete the thought, but rubbed her arms vhere the bruises he inflicted had been.

It was too late to cancel their trip to Oakcrest. Assured by the duchess that they did not need his escort, the narquess had already departed for his country estate o advise his family of their impending visit. There was nothing to do but carry through with their travel plans.

Yesterday Juliana had cried at their leave taking, her mile breaking through only when Claire promised to ee her in a few days. Juliana's recovery was the most mportant thing. Claire must put aside her preoccupation with the father and concentrate on the child.

The trip to Oakcrest was uneventful save for the luchess's complaint that Claire was entirely too quiet o be a diverting travelling companion. Claiming the

effects of too many late nights, Claire propped herself
up in a corner of the carriage and closed her eyes, feigning sleep to conceal her uneasiness. In her vulnerable
state she knew the duchess would make short work of
getting the truth from her.

Finding her claim to be real, Claire soon drifted off
but even in sleep she could not escape the troubling
rumors. She could concede that Lord Ransley would
turn to another woman if his wife denied him his mari-
tal rights; it was no more than any man might do. What
she could not believe was that a man who cared so for
his child could harm the mother.

She awakened with a jerk, a picture of the marquess
struggling with a woman at the top of an endless staircase all too vivid in her mind.

"Grandmama," she began abruptly for fear of losing
nerve, "did you hear any rumors about Lord Ransley
at the time of his wife's death?"

"What kind of rumors?" the duchess asked, removing
her gaze from the window and fixing it on Claire.

"That perhaps it was not . . . not accidental, and that
he might have had something to do with it?" Claire
held her breath, hoping her grandmother would forth-
rightly deny it.

"Who's digging up those old tales?" the duchess said
with a sigh.

"I've heard it from several people recently," Claire
replied, unwilling to reveal their identities to her grandmother. "Well, did you?"

"Yes, I'm afraid it was a nine day wonder at the time
but nothing came of it and another *on dit* took its place
Lady Delworth being caught *in flagrante* with her handsome, young footman, I think," she said, looking up in
amusement.

"It's no use attempting to change the subject, Grandmama," chided Claire.

"I'm not, but if I remember correctly Lady Delworth certainly did. Still hasn't returned from abroad," she mused, tapping her chin thoughtfully with one finger. "Probably has a new Italian footman by now."

"Grandmama," warned Claire.

"Oh, all right, all right," relented the duchess. "There was some foolishness that Ransley had scratches all over him the same morning that Lydia was found. But the man had barely escaped death himself and was still too weak to be up and around, let alone able to throw a perfectly healthy woman down the stairs. The authorities investigated and ruled it an accident."

"But what about the scratches?" Claire insisted.

"Who knows if there were scratches? You know the gossip mill as well as I do. A nick from shaving can be blown completely out of proportion by the time it makes the rounds. People are always looking for scandal where none exists."

"And are you so sure of him?" Claire asked.

"It's true I've lost touch with Ransley these past years, but I know his family and the Courtney men have always been honorable, treating their wives with respect. I can believe nothing less of Quinton."

While her grandmother's confidence in the marquess would not stand up in court, it was her only source of comfort, and Claire clung to it tenaciously.

The sun was just beginning to set when John Coachman guided the team through the gates of Oakcrest. The drive wound through a well-tended park of huge oak trees, their shade casting mysterious shadows this late in the day. The carriage rattled over a bridge spanning a rippling, rock-bedded stream. Peering out of the window to her right, Claire caught a glimpse of a lake through the trees. She was able to distinguish waterfowl

and a summerhouse before they disappeared from view,
leaving her anticipating a leisurely exploration of the
grounds.

The carriage slowed as it left the trees and moved
onto the sweep of drive before the house. Claire blinked
her eyes against the glowing rays of the setting sun and
observed Lord Ransley's home for the first time.

There was a graceful, classic line to the brick house
which rose three full stories. Small windows peeked out
from under the slate roof holding promise of a wonderful attic to explore on a rainy day. The house was
well maintained and sat in the midst of gardens and
shrubs and trees with a solidarity that conveyed the
strength of generations.

Claire soaked in the serenity of the setting while the
steps were being lowered and her grandmother prepared to descend.

Lord Ransley watched the carriage approach the
manor house feeling that for the first time in many
years his life was coming right. After returning to Oakcrest, his first matter of business had been with his
brother. He had hunted Jason down in the stables and
they had spent the afternoon riding over the estate.
Quinton had apologized for his display of temper in
London, Jason readily accepted, and they agreed to
avoid the topic of his marriage.

He had spent the next two days dealing with estate
matters that had occurred since his removal to London.
After handling the most urgent items, he endlessly
questioned his mother about the arrangements for the
comfort of their guests until she threatened to either
turn him out of the house or take herself off to town.

The marquess only laughed and kissed her on the
cheek, well aware that Lady Ransley was pleased to see

him show an interest in a woman again. He hoped she would not build her expectations too high, for although he was strongly attracted to Claire Kingsley he still had questions that could very well destroy her allure once they were answered. But as Lady Kingsley followed her grandmother out of the carriage his mind was far from the impediments in their relationship.

Descending the shallow flight of limestone steps, Lord Ransley greeted the duchess, welcoming her to Oakcrest. Turning to Claire he was immediately struck by the exhaustion conveyed by the droop of her usually squared shoulders and the faint shadows beneath eyes that had lost their sea-green radiance. The air of fragility that surrounded his gypsy merely made Quinton more determined to pamper her, and his heart beat a little faster when he thought of the intimacy that portended.

"It seems you've escaped the rigors of town just in time, my lady," he said, taking her hand between both of his while searching her face for a hint of pleasure at their meeting.

"Never say I'm that hag-ridden, my lord," she replied, summoning up a smile that was not altogether convincing.

"Never," he agreed returning her smile. "But the last time we discussed your health you combed my hair for not being honest, and you must agree that even the loveliest of ladies can benefit from a respite from endless routs and stifling city air. Being here at Oakcrest is just the tonic you need," he said, releasing her hand.

"Perhaps you're right," she returned, immediately missing the warmth of his touch.

Tearing his gaze from her face, he turned, offering an arm to the duchess. "My apologies for keeping you standing outside so long, Your Grace."

"Think nothing of it, Ransley," replied the duchess,

secretly delighted with the concern the marquess had displayed for Claire. "But a cup of tea would certainly be welcome."

"I believe it awaits us inside," he said, leading her up the steps. "Along with my mother, who is eager to renew your acquaintance."

"Ah, yes, Lady Ransley. I haven't seen her for years. It will indeed be a pleasure."

Claire followed in the wake of her grandmother, lending half an ear to her conversation, but concentrating most of her attention on the broad, blue-clad shoulders, and long muscular legs of the marquess.

Perhaps it was indecent, but Claire could not ignore the six feet of pure masculinity from Lord Ransley's dark hair to the soles of his polished Hessians. It was no wonder that Sylvia Beaufort had followed him from France. Intimacy with Lord Ransley would undoubtedly be impossible to forget.

Claire fought the heat that rose to her cheeks, determined not to feel guilty for admiring the marquess. If society decreed women should not entertain prurient thoughts toward men then it should not endorse a manner of dress that drew attention to their physical attributes.

While Claire struggled with the question of morals, Lord Ransley led them into a large marble-floored entrance hall panelled in beautifully grained oak. A graceful flight of stairs rose from the center of the foyer to a landing which separated and led to each wing. A door to the right opened into a spacious drawing room, furnished with Queen Anne furniture glowing from a rich patina of age and abundant polishing. French windows dominated one complete wall, giving onto a terrace which would be even more inviting when the summer's heat arrived. The room was a garden of pastels which blended harmoniously.

Three people were seated at the end of the room. Two footmen had just deposited several heavily ladened trays on an oblong tea table with slender cabriole legs and a raised rim. The man rose at their entrance and Claire knew he must be Quinton's brother, for although his hair and eyes were lighter, his build was similar and he carried himself with the same pride as his older brother. She noted the girl who was probably sixteen or seventeen, with deep honey-hued hair and hazel eyes, before moving her gaze to the older woman. Lady Ransley was lovely, and Claire found it hard to believe that she was old enough to be Quinton's mother. Her hair and eyes were as dark as her oldest son's and she radiated a vitality that Claire envied.

They had no sooner been introduced than Juliana burst into the room with a nursery maid in close pursuit.

"I'm sorry, milady," the girl said, bobbing a curtsey and reaching for Juliana who had climbed onto the settee beside Claire, clutching her arm and smiling broadly in welcome.

"There's no harm done," replied Claire returning Juliana's smile. "We are great friends, aren't we?"

Juliana bounced up and down, nodding her head enthusiastically.

Quinton was charmed by the picture they made. This was exactly how he had always envisioned his family, but Lydia had never been selfless enough to give Juli her undivided attention. She would certainly never allow her daughter to wrinkle her gown or muss her hair in a display of affection. He stood watching his dream come true and felt something shift inside of him, altering him forever.

Lady Ransley did not miss the obvious affection between the woman and child, nor could she ignore the expression of satisfaction and approval that lit Quinton's face. Perhaps her prayers were finally being answered and her son would find happiness at last.

After tea, Claire and her grandmother took time to settle into their rooms and change before dinner. Claire was still confused by her conflicting thoughts about the marquess. Her reaction at seeing him after such a short separation was proof positive that her feelings were much deeper than simple admiration. She could not reconcile the man she knew with someone callous enough to murder his own wife.

She went down to dinner still absorbed in her quandary, wishing she had never heard the vicious rumors about the marquess. Taking her seat at the right hand of Lord Ransley disconcerted her even further and she was barely able to choke down a bite of the delicious meal.

"Let me have cook prepare something more to your liking," suggested Ransley after watching Claire push food around on her plate for most of the meal.

"No, please don't bother. This is wonderful," she said, lifting a morsel of baked chicken to her mouth.

Lord Ransley was not reassured by Claire's half-hearted attempt to show an interest in eating. She still looked wan and was quite obviously ill-at-ease in his company. Since his explanation about the woman in his dreams and their shared kiss, he had felt a bond forge between them. Nothing had been spoken, but they shared an undeniable accord, and she had made no secret of the fact that she was looking forward to the upcoming visit to Oakcrest.

But from the moment she stepped out of the carriage he had felt her aloofness, and was puzzled by her attitude. Perhaps he had been overly optimistic when he thought she was looking forward to spending time with him and Juliana. The idea hurt far more than it should have.

The ladies departed for the drawing room, leaving the men to their port. A short time later, Quinton and

ason joined the women, only to find Claire had made
n early night of it, leaving the marquess to wonder
whether it was truly fatigue or an avoidance of his com-
any that drove Claire to her room so early.

Their relationship had been marked by several sharp
lisagreements, and early on he had made no pretense
t hiding his mistrust of her. Perhaps Claire had her
wn suspicions about his sudden reversal of attitude.
He would not rush his fences, he decided, but give her
oom to make her own decisions without undue pres-
ure from him. It would be difficult to remain detached
while she resided under his roof, but he was intent
pon making her a part of his life, and a few more
lays would be well worth the wait.

Tired and confused by her conflicting thoughts about
he marquess, Claire had retired almost immediately af-
er dinner, claiming the need to catch up on her rest
f she was to keep up with Juliana on the morrow. Cu-
iously enough, despite her inner discord, she went
straight to sleep. When she awakened, the day was well
advanced.

"What time is it?" she asked when the maid answered
her summons.

"Nearly eleven, milady," replied the fresh-faced coun-
ry girl who had been appointed Claire's abigail during
her visit.

"Why didn't you awaken me earlier? I should have
een up long ago," fretted Claire.

"His lordship said not to disturb you, milady. He said
you were to rest as long as possible. Then I was to bring
your breakfast up."

Observing the knowing look on the maid's face,
Claire did not make any comment. Being singled out
for such personal attention from the marquess would

certainly cause enough speculation below stairs withou
her adding fuel to the fire.

"I'll wear the yellow today," she said, as if Lord Rans
ley's interest in her sleeping habits was of no impor
tance.

The rest of the day progressed fairly smoothly. A
luncheon, the marquess treated her courteously, but n
differently from the other ladies present. In truth, i
seemed that the duchess received more of his attentior
than necessary, Claire thought uncharitably.

After luncheon, Claire's attention was claimed by
Juliana, who insisted she inspect the nursery, where the
child took great pride in displaying her treasures to
Claire. They spent the afternoon together and Clair
felt a new closeness with the marquess's daughter as sh
tucked her in for a nap.

The evening was similar to the night before, and
again Claire retired early, still feeling a great lassitude
despite sleeping the morning away. She mounted the
stairs thoroughly vexed that Lord Ransley had not ob
jected, but merely wished her a good night's rest.

Now, two days after arriving at Oakcrest, Claire stoo
staring out of the nursery window overlooking a barrer
rose garden wondering just how to go on.

She had awakened early, with a clear head and he
strength restored. Just as she was finishing an unusually
substantial breakfast, Juliana arrived ready for an out
door excursion. They had donned their warmest cloth
ing and explored the grounds that were just beginning
to green in the late February weather. Juliana had also
insisted they visit the stable to admire the small bay
pony she had received for her last birthday.

At no time during their wanderings had Claire sensed
any fear in Juliana. Even when they descended the

graceful staircase where her mother had fallen to her
death, the child had not demonstrated one bit of anxiety. Evidently whatever had occurred to render her
mute had not transpired in or near the house. Claire
was baffled. Juliana had stopped speaking while at Oakcrest, of that there was no question. It seemed she must
look further than the house and park for the problem.

Turning from the window, Claire ran an approving
gaze over the nursery. It was a pleasant room, painted
a light yellow that would remain sunny no matter how
dull the day. A fire burned brightly in the fireplace,
taking the chill from the room, and a thick carpet covered the floor. Books and toys filled the shelves and
tables. Maria and Lady Jane, immersed in a perpetual
tea party, occupied their own small table in the corner
complete with a tiny tea set. It was a room to delight
any child.

Claire's gaze came to rest on a chair near the fire
where Juliana's nanny sat sewing.

"Miss Juli's still asleep, ma'am," the woman offered.
"All the excitement of visitors has just tuckered her
out."

Claire nodded and wandered aimlessly around the
large nursery, straightening a book, touching a toy. "You
set a very fine stitch, Mrs. Benson," said Claire, noting
the impeccable workmanship the woman was executing.

The compliment brought a smile to the plump face
of the nanny. "I've done enough of them in my time,
I have," replied Mrs. Benson, as the needle flashed in
and out of the fine lawn. Her fingers were curiously
thin and graceful compared with the bulk of her ma-
tronly body encased in a gray dress and white apron.

"Did Lord Ransley explain why I am here, Mrs. Benson?"

"Yes, milady. He said you were trying to help Miss

Juli, and we were to answer all your questions. Although I don't know that I'll be able to help."

"Tell me about the day Juliana stopped speaking," suggested Claire, taking a seat near the nanny.

"I'm afraid I can't do that, milady," replied Mrs. Benson, never ceasing her stitching.

"Why not? I assure you no harm will come to you no matter what you say."

"Oh, it isn't that, ma'am. Nothing would keep me from helping my little darling, but you see I wasn't here. My mother passed away— God rest her soul— and I was gone a week or more travelling to and fro."

"I'm sorry to hear that, Mrs. Benson," murmured Claire. "You have my sympathy."

"It was the Lord's will," replied the older woman, accepting Claire's words with a nod.

Claire allowed a few moments to elapse before continuing. "Then I expect Callie will be able to help me," she said, naming the nursery maid she had met earlier in the day.

"No, milady, it was Bessie who was here then," stated Mrs. Benson.

"And what duty does Bessie now have?" asked Claire, praying for patience.

"I'm sure I don't know, milady," Mrs. Benson replied modestly, "I've never been to the Golden Bull."

Claire's brow furrowed, then she remembered seeing the inn as they passed through the village shortly before reaching Oakcrest. "The Golden Bull?" she questioned calmly, clasping her hands tightly to keep from pulling her hair in frustration.

"Why that's where Bessie works now," answered the nanny as if Claire were indeed a slow top.

"Did Bessie say anything about Juliana before leaving?"

"No, ma'am. Only that the child wouldn't talk and she didn't know why."

"Why did Bessie leave, Mrs. Benson? Surely she could not have been unhappy. The staff seems to be well treated here."

"She had no choice, milady. Madam threw her out. Such a screechin' you've never heard, but then her ladyship was like that. Took a dislike over any little thing and before a person knew it they were gone without a reference."

"Thank you, Mrs. Benson," said Claire, pasting a smile on her face. "I'll return later when Juliana is awake."

Claire admired her surroundings as she made her way from the nursery to her suite of rooms. The inside of the house was as beautiful and as meticulously maintained as the outside, filled with graceful furniture from an earlier period. There would be no crocodile leg sofas in this house, she wagered, as she opened her door.

Claire was struck anew by the beauty of her rooms each time she entered. The sitting room was large and airy. Light poured in from tall windows overlooking the park that sloped toward the lake. The walls were broken into panels filled with flat green damask trimmed with gold, stretching up to a white ceiling whose molding was touched with gilt. Valuable jade pieces adorned the richly carved mantelpiece, their graceful lines attesting to their worth. The chairs and settee were covered in green Gros de Naple silk, while a carpet of pale green, pink, and yellow covered the floor.

The bedroom and dressing room were no less sumptuous. The linens were the finest; the bedhangings were embroidered by a hand even the duchess would envy. Lavishly decorated perfume bottles, brushes, and combs were arrayed in precise order on the dressing table.

Claire felt certain it was no accident that she had been allotted a suite that was decorated predominately in the colors that flattered her most.

A flush rose to her cheeks and her heart beat a little faster when she reflected that Lord Ransley had, no doubt, personally chosen these rooms with her in mind. Could he be thinking of a future with her, or was she reading too much into the incident? Perhaps it was no more than coincidence that she had been given this particular suite.

She would not tease herself with such thoughts any longer. Instead of woolgathering, she should be concentrating on Juliana. Ringing for the maid, Claire changed into a dull gold riding habit with black braid. She perched a small black hat atop her head and set off on the short trip to the village.

The Golden Bull was no better or worse than any other village inn, judged Claire as she dismounted in the stableyard. Business was slow inside and she felt no embarrassment in entering and asking for Bessie. While she waited her eyes wandered over the patrons.

Several villagers were at the bar, but only one table was occupied by a man whose clothes marked him as gentry. He seemed unaccountably familiar, but Claire could not place where she had met him. Without warning, his pale eyes met hers and one eyebrow quirked at her interest. Irked that she had been caught staring, Claire turned away just as a plump, blond-haired young woman entered from the kitchen.

The owner indicated a room across the narrow hall where Claire might speak to the girl in private, and Claire ordered tea hoping to assuage any discontent he might feel.

After introducing herself and explaining the purpose of her visit she got right to the point. "Bessie, I'd like to ask you about your employment at Oakcrest." The sunny smile immediately disappeared from the girl's face.

"Oh, ma'am, I don't know what you heard, but I did nothin' wrong," she insisted, her hands twisting nervously in her apron.

"Of course, Bessie," Claire replied soothingly. "I'm not here to cause trouble. I'm merely striving to help Juliana."

"Oh, the little one. She sorely needs a body to care about her." Bessie stopped suddenly and looked away.

"It's all right, Bessie. You can speak freely. I promise nothing will come of it. I understand you were with Juliana when she stopped speaking. Will you tell me what happened that day?"

"Why, nothin' particular, ma'am. I wish I could help 'er, but I don't know nothin'. One morning she just woke up and wouldn't say a word, no matter how I begged. Nobody else hurt her a'tall that night because I was there."

"You spent the night in her room?"

"Yes, ma'am. She was restless like when I put her to bed. So I sat with her telling her stories my own ma had told me. She dozed off like, but kept crying out. So I stayed and fell asleep beside the bed. She cried out several times, but that was all."

"Did anything unusual happen the day before, Bessie?" prodded Claire.

Bessie's brow furrowed in thought before she answered. "No Ma'am, nothin' that I can recall. Mrs. Benson was away, so I gave Miss Juli breakfast, and after that she played with her dolls. Then I took her out for a walk. Mrs. Benson said Miss Juli should go out every day to keep her healthy."

"And your walk was unexceptional?" Claire asked, sure she would hear nothing significant.

"Well . . . Well, ma'am," stammered Bessie as a red flush covered her face.

"Come, Bessie," Claire said softly, "I promise everything you say will stay between us."

"It was only . . . It was only that I lost sight of Miss Juli for a time," Bessie admitted in a rush. "It wasn't long," said the maid, her eyes pleading with Claire to understand. "But George came by— his father owns the inn— and, well, we started talking and the next thing I knew Miss Juli was gone."

A chill washed over Claire. "Where did you find her?" she asked, endeavoring to keep her voice even.

"Oh, she come running back before I could even call. She wouldn't tell me where she'd got to. So I told her never to slip away from me again and we went back to the house."

"Did she mention that she had seen anyone?" asked Claire, praying Bessie held the key to Juliana's problem.

"No, ma'am. I couldn't coax a word out of 'er; she wouldn't even eat. So I bundled her up and put her to bed, all the time wishing Mrs. Benson was there."

Claire's hopes tumbled at Bessie's answer. "What happened then?"

"The next morning Miss Juli wouldn't say a word no matter what I promised. Mrs. Benson came back that day and her ladyship called me into her sitting room. She asked me what Miss Juli had said about her the day before. I told her nothin'. She called me a liar and threatened me if I didn't tell 'er. Before I knew it she'd turned me off without a reference."

Bessie's story only confirmed Claire's suspicion: whatever had robbed Juliana of the power of speech had to do with her mother. But Lydia was far beyond the reach of questions and Claire had nowhere else to turn but to the child.

Bessie was looking at her with a questioning expression, and Claire realized she had been silent too long.

"Are you happy here, Bessie? If you aren't I could talk to Lord Ransley. I'm sure he would take you back."

Bessie's face took on an expression of contentment that Claire envied. "Why thank you, ma'am, but I'm well satisfied. Me and George, we're plannin' on gettin' wed soon. We'll own this inn someday, so we'll be well fixed."

"I'm happy for you, Bessie. Perhaps everything worked out for the best."

After paying for tea she hadn't tasted and adding a good sum for Bessie, Claire left the inn. As she claimed her mount, she noticed a magnificent black horse with one white stocking tethered in the stable; no doubt belonging to the gentleman in the inn.

Claire rode slowly back to Oakcrest, pondering everything she had learned thus far. Even though she and Juliana had grown close over the past weeks, the child still buried her fears too deep for Claire to reach. She determined to put forth a stronger effort to find the source of Juliana's problem.

The next afternoon Claire had the gig harnessed and brought round. During the night she had decided to drive with Juliana hoping to come across the place where she had experienced such fear. It was not the best solution to the problem, but she could think of nothing else that would suffice.

Promising Juliana she could choose the path they would take, Claire coaxed the child into the small buggy. She felt Juliana's tenseness disappear as they took the road leading south from the house.

Several hours later, Claire guided the horse into the stableyard vastly disappointed with the outing. Juliana had exhibited nothing but a carefree demeanor during the drive. Uncovering the cause of the child's dilemma was not going to be simple, determined Claire as they made their way back to the house.

The only thing she knew for sure was that Juliana's problem had begun here at Oakcrest somewhere outside the house. Claire would drive over the entire estate if need be to discover the location, then she could begin the real work of revealing the cause.

Lady Ransley and the duchess were taking tea by the time Claire had tidied herself and made her way downstairs again. The two women had become fast friends over the past several days, discovering common acquaintances and a mutual preoccupation with embroidery to bind their rapport.

"My dear, I'm afraid we started without you," said Lady Ransley as Claire entered. "We had no idea when you would return, and as you can guess we're very informal here in the country."

"That is as I prefer it, my lady," replied Claire, bending to kiss her grandmother's cheek.

"Then, please, call me Sarah and I shall call you Claire. Your grandmother and I have already elected to be on a first-name basis," she said, exchanging a smile with the older woman.

"Nothing could please me more," agreed Claire, accepting a cup of tea from the countess.

Alura was picking out a soft melody on the pianoforte in the corner of the room, and Claire seated herself nearby. She had become fond of Quinton's sister in the few short days they had been in residence. Alura was an unspoiled young lady who gave no indication that she knew how lovely she was.

"You play very well, Alura."

"Thank you. It's one of my few accomplishments in

which I have confidence," she replied, ending the tune
with a flourish and turning on the bench to face Claire.

"Were you nervous at your come-out?" she asked
abruptly, hazel eyes solemn as only the young can be.

Claire could well remember her own apprehension
upon entering the *ton,* and gave Alura's question serious consideration. "Yes, even more so than you will be.
You see, I grew up on a remote estate. I had no play-
mates, and little contact with anyone except the servants
and my governesses."

Alura's eyes had grown wider. "Were you being held
prisoner?" she asked, already envisioning Claire as a
tragic heroine straight out of the Minerva novels she
secretly borrowed from her mother.

"Nothing so exciting," replied Claire, suppressing a
smile. "My mother was reclusive, and my father decided
I should reside with her. Perhaps if I had been a boy,
and his heir, he would have felt differently. So you can
see that you're much better prepared to face London
than I was when I came out."

"But you're so pretty, surely you had suitors falling
at your feet."

Claire laughed out loud at the compliment. "Thank
you, my dear," she said warmly. "I did have my share
of beaus, but I accepted my first proposal and married
before the Season was over."

"I'm sure I'll never receive an offer," mourned Alura,
resting her chin on her fists.

"Of course you will. You're very lovely and will probably become all the rage when you come out."

"Do you think so?" she asked, hope sparkling in her
eyes.

"I know so," Claire pronounced confidently. "And
the duchess and I will be there to see that you go on
well."

"Oh, thank you so much. When I ask Quinton and

Jason about the *ton,* they pat me on the head and tell me I have a long time before I need worry about it."

"You must attempt to ignore their remarks, Alura. You're their little sister and it will be some time before they'll admit you're a young lady. You're extremely fortunate to have such caring brothers. In time, you'll come to appreciate their concern."

"I can scarcely credit that," replied Alura dubiously, "but I will endeavor to be more tolerant of their attitude."

A moment later Quinton and Jason strolled into the drawing room. The marquess's gaze went instantly to Claire and she was caught in its dark boldness. He had been all that was courteous since she had arrived at Oakcrest, but Claire suddenly felt as if a barrier had dissolved which had previously held him at bay. A small shiver ran through her before she dropped her gaze. If she read him right, Lord Ransley was declaring his intent to pursue a closer relationship.

Claire had received her share of both proper and improper proposals since she had begun going into society again. They were neither unique nor unexpected. Any attractive, well-heeled widow could expect the same. Heretofore she had experienced no difficulty in turning aside the offers with tolerant amusement. But the marquess raised altogether different feelings inside her, and she did not know whether she was capable of refusing him, no matter what it was he offered.

Then she remembered Sylvia Beaufort, who was waiting for Lord Ransley in London. Had he gazed at the voluptuous Sylvia in the same manner when they first met? Perhaps he was looking for a suitable substitute for his mistress while he was rusticating. Well, his lordship would find she was not such an easy mark.

"I'm glad to see the two of you on good terms again," said Lady Ransley, smiling at her sons.

"It was just a small misunderstanding easily put to rights," replied the marquess, glancing at his younger brother.

"That's right," Jason acknowledged with a twinkle in his eye. "Surely you remember all the times we almost came to blows when we were boys," he teased.

"How could I forget? It's small wonder I'm not completely gray by now. I can only hope that all my grandchildren will be girls."

"We wouldn't dare deprive you of another generation of Courtney boys. I promise to produce three at the very least," Jason boasted.

Tea continued in a lively fashion and Claire forced herself to relax and ignore the marquess's dark, smoldering gaze. If she kept reminding herself of Sylvia— as distasteful as that might be— perhaps she could scrape through without an entanglement with Lord Ransley after all.

After their first drive, Juliana freely entered the gig with Claire, and nearly every afternoon they drove out with absolutely no adverse reaction from the child.

It was a week before Claire realized that Juliana had directed them north, south, and west from the house, but never to the east. The next afternoon she persuaded Juliana to let her choose the course of their drive. Juliana stiffened as Claire turned the horse east and gave it office to start. Tugging at Claire's sleeve, she pointed in the opposite direction.

"Now, Juliana. You promised I could choose our course today, didn't you?" asked Claire.

The small dark head reluctantly nodded in agreement.

Claire weakened as she witnessed the anxiety in the child's eyes, but quickly hardened her resolve, unable to relent when it appeared she was close to attaining her objective. They continued along the road, Claire chatting to Juliana as if it were just another drive. She would surely have missed the small lane leading off to the left if Juliana had not suddenly moved closer, staring toward the tree-lined corridor.

"Why don't we explore this path?" Claire suggested. The child had gone still as a cornered mouse and she huddled close to Claire on the seat.

After a short distance the lane suddenly ended in a clearing where a small hunting box stood. Juliana had hidden her face against Claire, refusing to look up. Claire was convinced that inside this small storybook house lay the secret to Juliana's silence.

"Juliana, there's nothing here that can harm you." Claire spoke soothingly as she held the child close, stroking her hair. "I promise, I won't let anything hurt you."

They sat in the clearing until Claire felt a lessening of tension in the child. Then she turned the buggy and drove back to Oakcrest.

The next morning Claire rose early enough to take breakfast with the marquess. "Juliana and I came upon a hunting box while we were driving yesterday," she said, after filling her plate and accepting a cup of tea.

Quinton watched Claire butter a muffin and thought how satisfying it would be to share breakfast with her every morning. "Yes. It's a parcel of land that was added to the estate when the Earl of Warburton died. He used it as an escape from his wife, or so I've heard," he said grinning. "It was unentailed and the countess couldn't get rid of it fast enough."

"May we explore it?" she asked casually.

"Of course. Though you'll be sadly disappointed. I haven't been in it for years, and it's probably filthy from disuse. I'll ride out with you after luncheon."

"I couldn't take you away from your business, my lord. Juliana and I will stop this afternoon on our drive. It will be a diversion for us both."

Quinton felt guilty at having forgotten the main purpose of her visit. "Have you made any progress since being here?"

Claire's appetite disappeared at mention of her futile attempt to resolve Juliana's problem. Laying aside her fork, she stared at her plate with distaste. "I'm sorry to say I haven't. Perhaps I was overly optimistic," she confessed, not looking up. "I had hoped coming to Oakcrest would bring me closer to the solution, but it hasn't happened as yet."

Her face and tone were so dejected that he felt guilty about bringing up the subject. "Don't fret," he said, impulsively covering her hand with his. "I'm happy that she's no longer a quiet shadow sitting in the corner. She's enjoying life so much more since being in your company, and that's a great success in itself. You're taking the responsibility for something that isn't your fault. Promise me that whether or not Juliana speaks again you won't blame yourself."

"I don't know that I can promise that, my lord," said Claire, knowing that both the child and father had claimed a permanent place in her heart.

Claire felt a bit guilty as she rode alone down the narrow lane. She was not really deceiving the marquess. She did plan on coming to the hunting box with Juliana, but she wanted to see it before she brought the child there.

Dismounting and tethering her mare to a low hanging limb, she observed the building. It was a small two-story structure built of gray stone common to the neighborhood, with a stable situated at the rear of the building. There had been no recent upkeep to the area outside. The woods had begun encroaching on the clearing, and last year's long grass lay dead and matted on the ground.

The door yielded with a slight effort, and Claire pushed it open with a belated misgiving at coming alone. Dank, musty air enveloped her as she stepped into the small entry. A single table, a straight backed chair, and a coat rack furnished the hall. A door opened to the left into a sitting room, sparsely furnished with several chairs, a settee, and tables. The door to the right revealed a dining table, half a dozen chairs, and a sideboard. Claire followed the hallway to the back of the house where a compact kitchen, adequate for basic meals, was located. Returning to the front door she climbed the narrow staircase to the second floor where she found two bedchambers connected by a small dressing room.

Here was the only sign of occupancy that Claire had found, and it was not recent. One bed was made up with fine linens and pillows. Women's items lay scattered on the dusty dressing table, unusual to find in what should be a man's domain. Claire examined the silverbacked brush and comb, the finish black with tarnish. She stirred the hairpins with her finger, wondering who had last used this room.

A feeling of dread came over her which she did not pursue, but quickly turned and retreated down the stairs. She had just pulled the door closed behind her when she heard a horse approaching. Shading her eyes against the meager afternoon sun, she recognized the large black that had been stabled at the inn. The man astride the horse was the same one from the Golden Bull's public room. A shiver ran through Claire as she met his pale eyes.

"I believe we've met before," he said, as smoothly as
they were in a drawing room.

"And I believe you're mistaken, sir," she replied. She
did not need to read his mind to interpret his look.

"Then I shall right that oversight," he responded dismounting. "I'm Eldon Garrick. I live not far from
here." He waited expectantly.

His name sounded familiar to Claire, but she could
not place where she had heard it before. She felt extremely uncomfortable being virtually isolated with a
man whose presence alerted her to danger. "I am Claire
Kingsley, a guest of Lord Ransley at Oakcrest," she finally replied, thinking the marquess's name might be
of some protection to her.

Garrick studied her a little more closely. "Ransley was
always fortunate to find the most beautiful ladies," he
said, offering a smile which did not reach his eyes.

Before she could open her mouth for a set-down she
was overcome by the animosity emanating from Garrick.
A kaleidoscope of emotions flashed from his mind to
hers: rage, jealousy, and deadly intent.

"You must excuse me, Mr. Garrick," she said quickly.
"I am already late in returning."

He did not offer to help her mount, seeming to know
she would refuse. He only nodded, watching silently as
she rode down the lane.

Claire breathed a sigh of relief as the house disappeared behind a curve. There was more to Eldon Garrick than she wished to pursue at the moment.

Quinton stood in the hall at the bottom of the stair-
way with a sense of relief that he had not been the one
to have found Lydia after her fall. He did not know
whether he would have been able to enter Oakcrest,

stepping over the spot where she had lain, and clim[b]
those stairs again.

That night was hazy in his memory. He had take[n]
his medication before Lydia had entered his roo[m]
sending his valet away so they could talk in private. H[e]
remembered suggesting they postpone their discussio[n]
until morning when he was clear-headed, but she ha[d]
only laughed and said it could not wait.

The remainder of the evening was virtually blank
They had argued, because he remembered Lydia's voic[e]
getting louder, then fading into the dark fog that over
came him.

Early the next morning, his valet had discovered hi[m]
lying on the floor near the door of his room, his fac[e]
marked with scratches. He had helped his master t[o]
bed before advising him her ladyship had been foun[d]
dead at the bottom of the stairs. Quinton had not bee[n]
able to explain being out of bed, nor the scratches.

There was speculation, but nothing could be proven
However, he had carried the stigma with him since, an[d]
he was not completely convinced he was innocent. I[n]
his drugged state Lydia could have pushed him too far
He might have had enough strength to follow her
struggle with her until she fell, then return to his roo[m]
before collapsing.

It was not merely his belief that beautiful women wer[e]
untrustworthy that had kept him from Claire. It wa[s]
also the fear that perhaps he had been responsible fo[r]
his wife's death, and that it could happen again.

But despite his apprehension, he had come to car[e]
for Claire Kingsley, and he thought that she returne[d]
his feelings. There had been tragedy in both their lives
but perhaps it was time they put the past to rest an[d]
accept the happiness they could find with one another

He still had questions, but for the remainder of he[r]
visit he intended to ignore any doubts he harbored an[d]

enjoy her company. Hearing a sound behind him, he
turned and found the object of his reflections entering
the hall.

"I was looking for you," he said, noting her hair
hung loose today, confined only by a primrose ribbon
that matched the color of her dress.

He had never admitted to seeking her company before, and Claire wondered what trespass she had committed.

The marquess smiled gently. "You have no need to
look so alarmed; our peace still holds," he said, remembering their pact. "I have something to show you." Taking her arm, he guided her toward the door. "It's warm
today and you should need no more than your shawl."

Lifting the paisley wrap that hung loosely from her
arms, he pulled it higher. His hands lingered on her
shoulders longer than necessary, but she did not com-
plain. Nor could she believe any longer that this man
could do harm to any woman, let alone his wife and
mother to his child. She would ignore his alliance with
Sylvia until it became an issue. She met his gaze and
knew that if the footman had not been present she
would be lost in his kiss again.

Blast it! Why can't we be private?

Unable to help herself, Claire laughed, delighted that
they shared the same idea. "It's nothing, my lord," she
said at his quizzical expression. "I'm just happy to be
out of the soot of London. It's quite beautiful today, is
it not?" she asked as they stepped through the massive
front doors of the manor house.

"It is indeed. I want you to enjoy some leisure time
while you're here. You don't need to be with Juliana
every moment."

"I will," she promised. "But I enjoy Juliana, and she
is the reason I'm here."

"I had hoped there was more," he answered a little stiffly.

"Oh, I don't mean that I'm not enjoying your company and the pleasure of meeting your family. They are all that is amiable, and Oakcrest is perfection itself. I would spend most of my time here if it were mine." She blushed and hurried on, embarrassed that he might think she was hinting at a connection between them. "Your stables are splendid and I've enjoyed riding almost every day."

This time it was the marquess who laughed. "You're doing it up a bit brown, my lady. I don't need words to convince me you're enjoying yourself. Rosy cheeks and a relaxed attitude will speak for you. You must work on it," he ordered, a twinkle sparkling in his dark eyes.

"Now that is a contradiction, sir. First you tell me to relax, then you order me to work," she shot back.

"Just now I want you to enjoy my favorite place at this time of year," he said, bringing their walk to an end.

Caught up in Lord Ransley's attention, Claire had been unaware of where he was guiding her until he released her gaze and she looked around. "How beautiful," she said, an appreciative breath leaving her lips slightly parted.

They were in a small sheltered clearing of the park where violets created a sea of purple blooms, with daffodils and snowdrops making bright yellow and white islands here and there.

"Yes," he agreed, staring down at her rapt face. "Absolutely beautiful."

"Thank you so much for bringing me here," she said, bending and picking one of the delicate purple flowers, studying it in something near to wonder.

"I would have brought you earlier had I known you

would enjoy it so much. They've been in bloom this
past week."

"I have a particular love of flowers," she replied.
'Someday I would like to have a garden all my own.
Not that I don't enjoy living with Grandmama," she
hastened to add, "but lately I've felt the need to have
my own establishment."

A flicker of hope filled Quinton. Surely her desire
for independence was a sign that she was over the loss
of her husband. If he had his way he would provide an
establishment for her with as many gardens as she
wanted. He would warm her bed at night and breathe
in her scent that was sweeter than any flower could ever
hope to be. His mind was so full of plans he hardly
heard her next words.

"I'm sorry, my dear. I'm afraid I was enjoying the
beauty so much I didn't hear you."

"Did you know," repeated Claire, mesmerized by the
violet she twirled between her fingers, "that it's said
the emperor will return in the spring with the violets?"

Nothing could have brought Quinton to his senses
faster. Here he was contemplating offering for the lady
and she forcefully reminded him that she was still suspect in his mind. Was it mere coincidence? Something
she had heard in passing? Or was it a belief she cherished as carefully as the violet she held?

"Is there something wrong, my lord?" Claire asked,
wondering what had brought such a bleak expression
to his countenance.

"No. I just remembered I am to meet my steward in
a short time. Come, I will escort you back to the house
before I leave."

"If you don't mind, I think I'll stay here. It's such a
beautiful place, I should like to enjoy it a little longer."

"As you wish, my lady. I will see you this evening."
Quinton turned and strode swiftly away without a back-

ward glance. His heart withered as he wondered if she lingered to reflect on the impossible dream of freeing Napoleon.

It was true he had suspected her when they first met, but as they became closer he could not believe he would be drawn to a traitor. He was all but ready to put aside his doubts with an air of relief and now she had stirred them up again, making him question the reliability of his decision. When he reached the drive, he turned. Claire's dress was a pale splash of color against the purple setting. Had he been wrong?

Eleven

Claire had looked forward to a more comfortable relationship with Lord Ransley after he had shown her the violets, but she was to be disappointed. After that brief time of accord, he returned to his courteous manner. He expressed concern for her comfort, but there remained an air of reserve about him which she doubted would ever disappear. After his experience with his wife, Claire judged he held an innate distrust of females which might never be broken.

In the meantime, Claire had a job to finish. She had come here for the express reason of helping Juliana, not to languish after a man whose mood changed from minute to minute. She should not have to prove herself because of another woman's failing.

In order to free her mind of the troublesome marquess, Claire dedicated herself to Juliana. They returned to the hunting box each day until the child's fear decreased, and Claire knew they could take the next step.

Claire held Juliana's hand as she opened the door. A palpable fear engulfed the child and Claire stooped to comfort her.

"Listen to me, Juliana. I know something bad happened to you here, but that was a long time ago, and there's nothing here that can harm you now. Will you

trust me?'' At Juliana's nod, she hugged her close an
rose, then taking her hand they stepped inside.

Stopping in the small hall, Claire sat on the wooder
chair and pulled Juliana onto her lap. "Juliana, I war
you to remember the last time you were here. You ra
away from Bessie, didn't you? Then you saw this hous
and decided to explore. I know something frightene
you then, but I'm here now and will keep you safe."

She hugged the child tightly and closed her eyes, con
centrating on the small body in her arms.

*Slipping inside the pretty little house. Bessie will never fin
me here. Giggling, but softly, because Mama's gig is outsid
and she'll hear. Surprise Mama and ride home with her, leav
ing Bessie behind. Looking through the downstairs and findin
no one. Creeping to the bottom of the stairs, then up each on
silently until reaching the top. Mama's here. That's her per
fume and there's her dress on the floor. Sounds and cries an
a man's voice that isn't Papa's.*

*Then Mama and that man in bed, hugging one anothe
He's hurting her, she's scratching him, crying out. He giv
a yell then lies still. Maybe he's like Uncle Thomas. Uncl
Thomas had lain there with his eyes closed until they took hir
away. Papa said he had gone to heaven.*

*No. Not like Uncle Thomas, because pale blue eyes ar
opening, staring at her, saying bad words. Mama's saying ba
words, too. Screaming at her to go away.*

*Back downstairs, hiding in the corner until Mama fina
her. Shakes and slaps.* "Keep your mouth shut! Do you hear
Not one word! If your father hears it will kill him! Do yo
understand? Don't open your mouth! Not one sound!"

'Fraid. Run. Bessie! Bessie! Want to go home.

Claire carried the child outside into the sunlight
Climbing into the gig, she sat cuddling her until th
shaking ceased.

So that was it. Lydia had used the cottage as an as
signation spot. When her daughter interrupted he

ryst, Lydia had threatened her, and Juliana had fol-
owed her mother's instructions implicitly. She had not
poken at all, terrified that a single word would endan-
er the father she loved so well.

"Juliana," she said gently, "I know what has frightened you so much, sweetheart. And I promise you, noth-
ng will happen to your papa if you speak. Your mother
s no longer here, is she?"

Juliana's dark head gave a negative shake.

"Then she cannot hurt either one of you any longer.
 would never do anything to harm you or your father,
out it would make him very happy if you would talk to
nim. He's worried about you for a long time now. You
vould like to please him, wouldn't you?"

Again, came the sharp nod, only this time up and
down.

"Then I won't press you, but promise you'll think
about talking again." The dark head lifted, and eyes
till shiny with unshed tears met hers. Smiling, she nodded and climbed off Claire's lap to the seat beside her.

"Good. Now we shall go see if cook baked your fa-
orite cakes today." Taking up the reins, Claire guided
he horse down the narrow lane toward Oakcrest.

Claire allowed several days to pass before approaching
he subject again. Juliana's spirits had risen considerably, and on several occasions she had stifled giggles
and hummed snatches of nursery songs before falling
silent again.

After one such occurrence, Claire led her to the win-
low. Lord Ransley was striding toward the house, look-
ng as fit as any man could. "See, Juliana. You were
inging, almost speaking, and your father is fine. He
vould be even better if you would talk to him, sweetheart. It would be the best gift you could ever give him.
'll be with you all the time, and I won't let anything
happen to either of you. I promise."

A short time later the sound of boots echoed dow
the hallway. Juliana looked toward Claire as the foo
steps came closer. The door swung open and the ma
quess was standing there staring at them both acros
the nursery. He was so strong and full of life, the fres
smell of the outdoors still around him.

"Claire? Juliana? What is it?" He appeared baffle
that they were gazing at him so.

Claire turned to Juliana. "Please, Juliana, for you
father," she urged.

Juliana touched Claire's cheek before turning an
walking toward Lord Ransley. She stopped and stare
up at him. "Papa," she said, giving him the sweete
smile he had ever seen and holding up her arms t
him.

The marquess stood frozen for a moment, then whis
pering her name he lifted Juliana into his arms an
held her tightly, making no attempt to hide the tear
of joy wetting his face.

Claire left father and daughter in the nursery, slip
ping out while the exhilaration of the moment rendere
them insensible to all else. A weight had been lifte
from her mind and she felt the need for a fast gallo
in the fresh air.

There was one last piece of the puzzle missing, s
she turned her horse toward the hunting box again
Once she reached there she was not at all surprised t
see Eldon Garrick approaching from the opposite di
rection. Fate had previously worked to her advantag
and she no longer questioned it.

"Mr. Garrick," she said, pulling her mare to a stop

"Charming to see you again, Miss Kingsley."

Claire made no effort to correct his address. "Thi
seems to be a favorite spot for you, sir."

"Yes, I must confess a liking for the hunting box. I've spent many pleasant times here."

Claire focused on his thoughts, hard put to remain emotionless in light of his erotic remembrances.

"Then you must be a good friend of Lord Ransley, since this is a holding of his."

"We're acquainted," he replied. "But it was our fathers who were friends."

"You aren't close with the current marquess?"

"No, our paths seldom cross, but I knew his wife well."

Claire did not allow him to see that she knew the real meaning of his innuendo. "I did not have the honor, but I've heard of her tragic death."

"Such a loss. She was a lovely woman," he remarked evenly.

Claire needed to shake his composure or she would never learn anything. "I understand it was a double tragedy, for she lost her unborn child, also." The shocking words of the confrontation came to her as clear as if spoken out loud.

You're crazy if you think Ransley will accept your bastard as his own! If you're to be believed, he hasn't touched you in months.

Before I'm through he'll accept whatever I tell him. After all, my husband is an honorable man.

Every man has his limits, Lydia. Ransley might raise the child if it's a girl, but he will not allow another man's child to stand as his heir. He's too proud for that.

We'll see how much he's willing to accept to protect his precious name.

I'm warning you, Lydia, be careful. I will not allow you to drag me into this.

I'll use whatever means I need to save my position. Even if it means claiming that you forced yourself on me. However, I'm sure it won't come to that, my love. Quinton has always been totally smitten with me. He will believe whatever I tell him. Just wait and see.

Claire was as silent as Garrick. Her suspicions had been proven correct. Garrick had been Lydia's lover and the father of the child she carried.

"I must be returning," she said, meeting his pale eyes and realizing just how alone they were.

"So soon, Miss Kingsley?" Garrick asked, regaining his usual aplomb. "I had hoped we might get to know one another better."

Before she could object, he captured her hand. His lips were hot and dry as they pressed against her skin. She was mesmerized by his pale, cold eyes, until his thoughts of what he would like to do to her shocked her into movement.

"I'm afraid not, Mr. Garrick," she replied, pulling her hand away. "I'll be returning to town soon."

"Then perhaps I shall see you there, ma'am. I don't stay buried in the country all year long."

"Goodbye, Mr. Garrick," she replied curtly, urging her mare forward.

Lord Ransley sat his horse until the clearing was empty. He had stayed with Juliana until she was put down for her nap, then he had sought Claire's whereabouts. In the excitement of hearing his daughter's voice again, he had allowed her to slip away without a word of thanks.

Discovering she had ridden out, he quickly followed in the direction the groom indicated. As he reached the lane to the hunting box he saw it had been well used recently and guided his horse down the path. Hearing voices, he cautiously moved forward, sheltering in a grove of fir trees. It was then he saw Claire and Eldon Garrick in conversation.

While Garrick had occasionally called during his marriage, Quinton had not seen the man since Lydia's death. Even though their fathers had been acquaintances, the men had not grown up friends. As a youth, Garrick had made no secret that he resented Quinton's titled wealth, and the two avoided one another as much as possible.

Lord Ransley did not like the intimate look of Claire's meeting with Garrick. Was it a chance encounter or the result of a prior arrangement? Although Quinton did not want to believe that Claire would be involved in such questionable goings on, particularly with Garrick, his suspicions were immediately revived. Anger coiled tightly within him as Garrick kissed Claire's hand, but he remained absolutely silent while the couple exchanged a few more words. Then Claire rode away, passing close by his position.

Garrick lingered a few moments more before also departing, leaving the hunting box to reign silently over the small clearing. Quinton rode to the front of the building and dismounted. It was obvious by the flattened grass and newly worn path to the door that there had been more than one chance meeting here.

Remembering Claire's interest in the house, Quinton realized it was most likely the two had needed a place to secretly rendezvous. Controlling the anger that still possessed him, he tossed the bridle reins over his horse's head and swung himself into the saddle.

Claire was still counting herself thankful for escaping Garrick so easily when she heard Jason hail her. He galloped across the field on a rangy bay, clearing a hedge with inches to spare before coming to rest beside her.

"Very well done," she said, commending his horse-manship.

"Thank you, but I fear most of the praise goes to my horse."

"But you provided guidance and that is important."

"I also provide the oats and that is even more significant," he retorted, white teeth flashing in a beguiling smile.

They continued toward Oakcrest riding side by side. Claire valued Jason's friendship. They had hit it off immediately, quickly coming to a first-name basis, and enjoying their time together. He had a carefree, almost boyish attitude, but she had glimpsed a much deeper nature hidden beneath his congenial facade. She was sure he would be just as intimidating as Quinton in a few more years.

"I met one of your neighbors today," said Claire.

"Not Squire Grayson, I assume, or he would still be bending your ear. He will never let a pretty lady get away."

"No, not anyone who sounds nearly as nice as the squire. He introduced himself as Eldon Garrick."

She glanced sideways at Jason, and found him staring straight ahead, his face set in rigid lines.

"What is it, Jason?"

"Garrick is a neighbor, but not a friend. It would be best if you avoided him in the future," he warned.

"But why?" probed Claire, searching for confirmation of her conclusions.

"Garrick is no gentleman. He brought immeasurable harm to our family and is no longer welcome in our home. Believe me when I tell you he's a dangerous man, and stay away from him."

Claire considered his comments. They substantiated the feelings she received when she was with Garrick.

Before she could reassure Jason she had no thoughts
of pursuing a relationship with Garrick, he spoke.

"Claire, I've seen how Quin regards you when he
thinks no one is watching, and I believe there's something you should know about his marriage."

"Your brother sees me as no more than a means to
restore his daughter's speech," she protested. "In truth,
we do not get along well at all, but agreed to cry peace
for Juliana's benefit."

"That just proves my point," Jason persisted. "Quin
gets along with everyone. The fact that you and he
strike fire only confirms that he's attracted to you. He
had sworn never to be taken in by a beautiful woman
again, and I think you should know why."

He held up his hand as she started to object. "Please
hear me out. You can forget everything I tell you if you
find it doesn't matter, but at least let me have my say."

He quickly related the story of Quinton's courtship
and marriage, then continued by telling of Juliana's
birth and the obvious rift between the couple. He hesitated slightly before recounting Lydia's unfaithfulness
to her husband, and ended with naming Eldon Garrick
as her last lover.

By then they were within view of Oakcrest and the
horses needed no guidance to continue toward the stables and the promise of a generous measure of oats.

"Are you totally disgusted with us, Claire?" he asked
when he finished.

"No. Only extremely angry that a woman could treat
such an honorable man as Lydia did Quinton."

"So, you do care about him? I thought as much."
Jason's smug expression brought a smile to her face.

"I care for him as I would any person who has had
a great wrong done to him," she replied piously.

Jason laughed out loud. "Come, Claire. We are good
enough friends and, if my brother has control over his

senses, soon to be more. Admit you care more for him than just a sorry victim."

"I will admit nothing, sir," she stated, flashing him a pert smile before sobering. "But I do thank you for being so frank. I know it wasn't easy for you to discuss your brother's personal life."

"I've never done so before," he acknowledged. "But I think it's important for his future that you know, and Quinton would never tell you himself. In fact, he will not yet admit that Lydia was unfaithful to him."

At Claire's questioning look, Jason briefly summarized the scene that occurred when he revealed the truth about Lydia to Quinton. "So you see, I don't think he'll be healed until he accepts Lydia's betrayal and puts it behind him. I have high hopes that you'll be able to help him do that."

"I don't want to disappoint you, Jason, but I can't see how I can work such a miracle when he hardly speaks to me except for courtesy's sake."

"With love, Claire. You already love Juliana, that's obvious. I can't believe you don't love her father, also."

And she did, admitted Claire as she dismounted and handed her mount over to the stable boy. She had fought it since they had first met, had called it physical attraction after being without the touch of a man for so long. But Jason made her face the reality of her feelings toward Quinton; it was love. Now she wondered if she was capable of Jason's trust in her. Could she reach Quinton's heart?

Needing a few minutes privacy, Claire made her way from the stables to the garden where she could consider all that she had learned from Garrick and Jason. She had no sooner seated herself on a white stone bench than Lady Ransley appeared.

"My dear, how pleasant to find you here. I see you share my love of gardens, even when they are sparse of blooms," she said, studying the plants just beginning to emerge from their winter dormancy. "Do you have a favorite flower?"

"I have many," answered Claire. "They're all beautiful in their own way."

Lady Ransley was pleased with her answer. Lydia's interest had never gone beyond her own mirror. Quinton and Oakcrest would be in much better hands if her son had enough sense to offer for Claire Kingsley.

"The gardens suffered after Quinton married and I moved to the dower house. We have excellent gardeners, but they still need guidance on occasion, and I'm afraid that wasn't one of Lydia's strong points. As soon as I saw what was happening I stepped in as unobtrusively as possible to fill the gap. Fortunately, Lydia didn't mind in the least that I took the responsibility."

Claire felt like a spy listening to Lady Ransley's confidences, but she could not help wanting to know more. "I'm sure you were often here to visit anyway."

"You might have heard that Lydia . . . well, that Lydia did not feel comfortable with Quinton's family. So, no, I didn't visit as much as I would have liked." Lady Ransley hesitated a moment before turning her dark eyes on Claire. She could read the regard that Quinton held for this woman, and hoped that it was her future daughter-in-law who was sharing the bench with her.

Lady Ransley also knew that Quinton seldom talked about his personal life, things that might sway a woman's decision in accepting or rejecting an offer. She would not let her son lose the woman he loved if she could help it.

"Claire, perhaps I shouldn't meddle, but attribute what I'm about to say to a mother's desire to see her son happy."

Claire thought of her recent conversation with Jason and wondered if the whole family was conspiring to impart bits of wisdom to her in support of Quinton.

"Quinton's marriage was not a good match," confessed Lady Ransley. "Although he has never said so, I'm sure he realized it early on, but by then it was far to late to turn back. I never saw Lydia impassioned about anyone or anything but herself and her desires.

"Quinton was abroad when Juliana stopped speaking and Lydia did not even advise him that something was wrong. I took it upon myself to write him. Of course, he came home immediately, but his presence made no difference in Juli's condition.

"Lydia was glad to see Quinton only because she wanted to go to town. She said she couldn't bear to be buried in the country any longer and insisted they spend the holidays in London. It was the first Christmas that our entire family had not been together at Oak-crest, and I felt a sense of impending doom the entire time.

"My feelings were valid, because early in January Lydia brought Quinton home. He had been attacked in London and left for dead. I questioned why she took the chance of moving him when his valet said the doctor warned her against it. She merely shrugged me off without answering.

"I know I shouldn't say it, for she isn't here to defend herself, but it seemed as if she wanted him to die, and she was almost successful. The long, cold journey brought on a congestion of the lungs which further threatened Quinton's life; for days we didn't know whether he would live or die. Lydia never once entered the sick room, saying it depressed her too much.

"It wasn't long after that Lydia was found at the bottom of the stairs early one morning. Her neck had been broken in the fall, which brings me to the point of all this outpouring of family secrets," she joked grimly. "I don't know if you've heard the rumors that Quinton was involved, but I know my son well and I want you to know that he would never have hurt her or any other woman.

"We have a neighbor who was . . . close to Lydia. He was here the morning she was found, and I suspect that he was the one who carried the rumors back to London. He's always been envious of Quinton and would give anything to see his reputation destroyed."

Lady Ransley studied Claire's countenance. "I know I've given you far too much to absorb at one sitting, but I didn't want to leave it too late. I would like to think you will consider everything should the occasion arise."

"I . . . I will, my lady," agreed Claire, unable to respond more fully.

"One other thing, then I will leave you alone," she said, taking Claire's hand. "I speak for myself, and Jason and Alura. We all wish for Quinton's happiness, and I feel that you're the key to his future. I don't mean to press if you feel nothing for my son, but if you do return his regard, I pray you won't let vicious rumors affect your decision. Quinton is an honorable man, loyal to his family and friends. He deserves someone who will return that loyalty." Lady Ransley released her hand and rose. "Now I'll leave you to your thoughts."

Claire took special care dressing for dinner that evening after the maid told her that champagne was chilling and the master had ordered a veritable banquet be served. The staff were to celebrate, too, the girl went on, since Miss Juli was well again.

She had spent the remainder of the afternoon before

dinner considering everything she had learned about
Quinton. She could well understand his doubts concerning women after his disastrous marriage to Lydia,
and forgave him for his hasty judgment of her.

She realized she had an unfair advantage over him.
For although she knew the reason behind his attitude
toward women, he had no clue as to why she acted the
flirt. He was completely justified in thinking her as
frivolous and as untrustworthy as his late wife.

After Lady Ransley had spoken to her, Claire again
admitted to what everyone else seemed to know. She
loved Quinton Courtney and would accept his offer
without hesitation if asked. But first she must tell him
the truth about her quest and, most difficult of all, her
gift. She wondered if his attraction could withstand the
test.

The marquess stood at the bottom of the stairs as
Claire floated down in a cloud of green net over a slip
of white silk. An exquisite necklace of diamonds and
pearls encircled her throat, while matching earrings
sparkled from the lobes of her ears. A rope of pearls
threaded through the tawny curls that glistened in the
candlelight. She stopped on the last step and looked at
him inquiringly.

Quinton had ridden for hours after leaving the hunting box, returning only in time to dress for dinner.
After his anger cooled, he admitted that Claire's meeting with Garrick could have been nothing more than a
chance encounter, and that he should not judge her
without facts. She had not deceived him for, as yet,
there was no understanding between them.

He studied the woman before him, determined to
right that oversight this very night. She was the essence
of all he could want, and he loved her beyond reason.
That was the cause of his outrage, and he owed it to
both of them to give her the benefit of the doubt.

"I wanted a moment alone before we join the others," he explained, raising her hand to his lips. "You're very beautiful this evening."

"Thank you." She could think of nothing else to say as he held her gaze.

"Claire . . ." They were of equal height as she stood on the bottom step and it took only a slight movement on his part to touch his lips to hers. This was unlike their other kisses. It was not driven by rage or passion, but was a kiss filled with commitment of what was to come.

"Claire," he began again in a husky voice. He uttered her name as if it were his right and she did not correct him. "There is so much I have to say to you—"

"Quin? Where the devil have you gotten to?"

Jason's voice caused Quinton to utter a muffled curse. Of all times to come looking for him, his brother could not have chosen a worse moment.

Dinner was festive that evening, as they all rejoiced at Juliana's recovery. Claire thought the marquess's eyes held an unusual warmth as they lingered on her throughout the meal.

"I know we have special reason to rejoice this evening," Quinton announced to the table at the end of the meal. "However, I fear I must be the bearer of several items of grim tidings. There have been riots in London to protest the Corn Bill." He waited until the buzz of conversation quieted before continuing. "I understand mobs gathered in the West End. They broke into some homes, smashed windows, and looted what they could." Silence fell over the table as he continued. "At the lord chancellor's home in Bedford Square they hung a noose from the lamppost outside to drape around his neck if the opportunity arose."

"We must return at once," cried the duchess.

"Your Grace, I'm certain that Biggersleigh is in total command of the situation in Berkeley Square and that Kenton House is safe. But I'll send a messenger tomorrow in order to relieve your mind," he offered.

"Thank you, Quinton. But I feel it would be better to start for town in the morning," the duchess replied, her voice stretched thin with anxiety.

"Why not think on it tonight? Perhaps in the light of day you'll see things differently," he suggested with a reassuring smile.

"Although I can't think of what could be worse, you indicated there was more," remarked Jason.

"I'm afraid there is." Quinton observed the solemn faces around the table and regretted that he had to add yet additional distress to the evening. "Napoleon has escaped from Elba," he announced baldly.

A concerted gasp rose from the dinner party. "He's gathering an army and marching toward Paris," Quinton finished quickly.

At Quinton's announcement, pictures began flashing rapidly through Claire's mind. A ball quickly turned into a battle scene where men fought in evening dress. Rain creating a quagmire of the battlefield which was strewn with the wounded and dying. The air filled with cries for help and frightened screams of cavalry horses. Wagonloads of wounded moving slowly toward a small town along roads nearly hub-deep in mud.

Dear God, I was right, thought Claire, and now I'm not there to help. I must return to London, Templeton will surely need me now.

Everyone appeared shocked, observed Quinton, but Claire especially so.

"I'm sorry to have unduly alarmed you, Claire," he murmured, while the others were involved in discussing the somber news.

"It would be unnatural if I were not disturbed," she replied, her hands clasped tightly in her lap. "I cannot remember a time when we haven't been at war with Napoleon. I don't want another generation to grow up in his shadow."

"They won't," he assured her confidently. "Napoleon will find it hard going to gather the men he needs for success. He'll be returned to his prison soon, and a more secure one, I'll wager."

"I pray you are right, my lord."

The joyous mood of the evening had been effectively dampened. The ladies took their tea quickly and quietly; the men drank their port in a solemn mood, and the company retired much earlier than usual.

Claire restlessly paced her room after reassuring her grandmother that Lord Ransley was most likely right in his conclusion that Kenton House was safe. Too much had happened that day for her to calmly lie down and go to sleep. Taking the back stairs she slipped into the garden.

The moon was just full enough to cast a dim light over the paths and she made her way to the bench she had occupied that afternoon. It was such a short time ago that her thoughts were filled with happiness at a possible future with the marquess; now everything had changed.

The news of Napoleon's escape had effectively squashed whatever romantic notions she cherished for the evening. She must return to London immediately and offer her assistance to Matthew Templeton.

Lord Ransley was staring out of the library window when he saw Claire in the garden below. He had been unable to get a moment alone with her all evening and after his announcements she did not look in the mood to welcome an avowal of love.

If there had been any doubt that he needed her in

his life, it had been completely erased today. She had given him a precious gift by releasing Juliana from her silence, and had stirred him to unreasonable jealousy when he had seen her with Garrick. She had responded to the news of Bonaparte's escape with anger instead of tears, proving her to be a woman of considerable mettle.

Without his tawny-haired tigress he would still be a lonely, bitter man, with a daughter locked in silence. But Claire had given him back the faith that Lydia had stolen, which allowed him to shrug off the doubts he harbored about her questionable associations in London.

It was time to put his troubled past behind him and be happy again. The occasion might not be as opportune as he liked, but he could wait no longer to ask her to marry him. Pushing open the French doors, he stepped outside.

Reaching the garden, he found himself suddenly unsure how to approach Claire. She had come to mean so much to him that he didn't want to lose her.

Claire turned at the sound of his boots on the gravel path. "In all the excitement, I neglected to properly thank you for what you've done for Juliana," he said, joining her on the bench.

"Seeing the two of you together was thanks enough," Claire responded, reminded that something good had come out of the day.

"Do you know what caused her to stop speaking?" he asked, all the while considering the best way to approach the subject of marriage.

Claire hesitated. After Jason's and Lady Ransley's revelations about Lydia, she knew Quinton would never be truly free of his wife's ghost until he accepted her duplicity and absolved himself of guilt. Chancing that her confirmation of the facts might help him break

ree, Claire gathered her courage and turned to face
him.

"She had been threatened, Quinton."

"What! What threat could be strong enough to si-
ence a four-year-old child?"

"Her father's death."

The marquess's mouth opened, then closed, without
a sound.

"She had seen something she shouldn't have," continued Claire. "She was warned that if she spoke a word,
t would kill you. A child that young takes everything
iterally, so not only did she keep the secret, she also
kept completely silent."

"I can't believe this! Who would be so cruel? Surely
hey could see what they had done to the child." Claire
watched as his incredulity turned to anger. "Tell me
who it is, Claire, and I'll make the wretch sorry he was
ever born."

"I'm afraid it's too late, my lord. It was your wife."

"Lydia? Dear God! Why?"

"Juliana saw your wife with a man . . . Eldon Garrick. They were . . . in an intimate situation," she said,
phrasing it as delicately as possible.

The first wave of shock was over and Quinton began
to think again. "You've been talking to Jason, haven't
you?"

"Yes, but . . ."

"He's convinced you of Lydia's guilt and you've attributed Juliana's problems to it," he insisted bitterly.

"That isn't so!" she protested.

"Then did Juliana tell you?" he persisted forcefully.

"Not in so many words, no," she admitted.

"Then how?" he demanded.

Claire bit down on her lip. Her grandmother said
someday a man would be strong enough to accept her

as she was. There was only one way to find out whether
Quinton was that man.

"I have an, ah, ability I have not told you about.
Indeed, no one but Her Grace is aware of it." She
waited for a response, but he remained silent staring
at her accusingly.

"At times, I'm able to perceive a person's thoughts
and feelings. I reconstructed Juliana's activities the day
she stopped speaking. She had been outside with the
nursery maid and slipped away for a short time. When
she returned, she wouldn't speak.

"And that convinced you that Lydia made love to a
man in front of Juliana, then was coldhearted enough
to frighten her own child into silence?" he asked coldly.

"The hunting box that is on the estate," continued
Claire, ignoring his question, "is where the assignation
occurred. It took me days to gain Juliana's trust and
have her enter it with me. When she did, I asked her
to remember the last time she was there.

"The day she ran away from the maid she saw her
mother's gig in front of the house. She was a happy
little girl when she entered the hunting box, wanting
only to surprise her mother. I saw what happened that
day. I saw Lydia with the man; I heard her threats to
Juliana. I felt her fear, Quinton, and it must have been
terrifying to be four years old and alone, for it was bad
enough for me."

"Very affecting, Lady Kingsley, but you have not yet
convinced me of this magical ability of yours," he
scoffed. "And if you think to gammon me with such
nonsensical talk then you're a fool."

"I'm telling you the truth," maintained Claire, de-
testing the pleading in her voice.

"Then if it's true, you obviously don't need me to
tell you my feelings, you should be able to see them
yourself."

"I don't intrude on my friends' thoughts," she spat out indignantly.

"If that's the case then there is no need to forego your talent around me any longer," he sneered, shattering her heart.

"I don't know your motivation," he continued, his tone filled with disgust, "but I believe nothing you've told me about my wife."

"Then why do you continually condemn me for the same things your wife did? She flirted— and more— if I am to believe everything I have heard." She paused for a quick, angry, breath before continuing. "You compare every woman to her, and if there is any indication of light-heartedness of even the most innocent sort, she is immediately labelled a loose woman."

"Since I first laid eyes on you, your actions have been far from innocent with any number of men," he snarled, unleashing the jealousy that had haunted him for weeks.

"And you think I'm cut from the same cloth as your wife, don't you?" she demanded, her eyes blazing.

"My late wife's conduct is none of your business," he replied in a low growl. The anger in his eyes alone would have stopped Claire had she been in control of her own formidable temper.

"It is when it's to blame for Juliana's misery. And yours. And now mine!" she recklessly charged.

"And, of course, you are well able to see the cause of all our problems," he ridiculed. "Well, I, for one, do not believe this nonsense about being able to see what others are thinking.

"But if you're convinced of your powers you would best use it to look into the minds of the company you keep. You'll find your so-called friends are neither loyal to you or your country, but perhaps you already know that," he taunted. "As far as secret assignations at the

hunting box, I assume you drew on your own experi
ences with Garrick. You see, I saw the two of you there
this afternoon looking all the world like extremely
friendly acquaintances.

"The only redeeming deed you can claim, my lady
is releasing an innocent child from her silence. And
that was probably brought about by sheer good luck."
He thrust her aside and stalked off into the night.

Claire listened to the sound of his steps fade into the
darkness before she dropped to a bench nearby. He was
right. She had succeeded with Juliana, but had failed
miserably with Lord Ransley. He had accused her of
lying about his wife's unfaithfulness, and would prob
ably carry the guilt of her death with him to his grave
He had all but denounced her as a spy against the
crown, and thought she was carrying on a secret alliance
with his neighbor. If he knew she was the woman in
the fog, he would undeniably believe she had conspired
to kill him.

The chill of the night drove her indoors. The house
was silent, servants as well as family and guests had all
retired. A light had been left burning in the front hall
and Claire paused in its glow. There was something she
had to know, something she had had flickerings of ear
lier, but it had been too dark, too horrible to pursue.

She moved to the foot of the stairs, hoping that what
control she had over her ability would be adequate to
obtain the knowledge she desired. Her hand trailed
along the oak banister as she climbed the graceful flight
of stairs. Reaching the top she made an effort to clear
her mind of everything but the present.

She concentrated on Lydia and the night that she had
stood in this very same place at the top of the stairs
A swirl of emotions surrounded her. She experienced
Lydia's anger and stumbled from the force of its impact,
grasping the railing to keep herself erect. There was

the shadow of a man, but too indistinct for her to identify. The anger was soon replaced by fear as she felt a hand at her back and fell into a void, suffering intense pain and, finally, welcome oblivion.

Breathing heavily, Claire opened her eyes. Beads of sweat ran down her body, soaking into the material of her dress. A white-knuckled grip on the railing was the only thing that kept her on her feet. She now knew for a certainty that Lydia's fall had not been accidental. The rumors she had heard in London of Quinton murdering his wife filled her head as she made her way back to her room, wondering whether Jason and Lady Ransley were blinded by loyalty.

Claire sat by her window until gray light broke, too unnerved by her recent revelation to sleep. She watched the marquess make his way back to the house in the early dawn, and heard his door close before she began packing.

Twelve

Claire and the duchess stood in the front hall of Oak-crest saying goodbye to Lady Ransley, Jason, and Alura while their trunks were being loaded onto the coach.

"I cannot think where Quinton has gotten to," said the marchioness, obviously embarrassed at her older son's absence.

"Promise you won't ring a peal over his head on our account," remarked Claire lightly. "I saw his lordship last evening and told him of our decision. He said all that was appropriate then. I'm sure it was an emergency that called him away so early."

"It had better be, for I'm still his mother no matter what his age and I will not tolerate ill manners," she declared decisively.

"I'm certain he means no disrespect, Sarah," added the duchess. "You know how men are. They get so in-volved in projects they completely lose track of time. We'll no doubt see all of you again in a few week's time."

The reminder that they would soon be in London for the Season cleared the frown from Lady Ransley's brow. "We'll be there sooner than that if it's at all possible. I'm looking forward to the Season this year; the winter has been so dreadfully severe that we were quite cut off from society for weeks on end."

"And Mama says perhaps I shall be allowed to attend

few small events," added Alura, enthusiasm shining
om her face.

"We'll see, darling," said Lady Ransley, putting her
m around her daughter and giving her a hug.

"Lord help London, I say," intoned Jason in a pious
ice, dodging quickly behind Claire to avoid Alura's
reatening hand.

"Now children," warned Lady Ransley in a stern tone
o doubt used many times over the years.

Their laughter was cut short as a tiny bundle dashed
own the steps in a flurry of ruffled skirts and dark
rls to clutch at the skirt of Claire's chocolate-brown
avelling dress. A nursery maid, eyes wide with alarm,
rived close behind.

"I'm all that is sorry, your ladyship. She slipped away
efore I could catch her," apologized the maid. She was
ut a child herself and no doubt worried about her
osition.

"No harm has been done," Claire assured her. "I
ould have stopped to say goodbye if I had known she
as awake." Claire soothed back Juliana's dark, baby-
ne hair, until she could see her tear-streaked face. "My
oodness! What are all the tears about?"

"You're leaving," sobbed Juliana as if her heart
ould break.

"But I'll see you soon, sweetheart," soothed Claire.
Grandmama and I are going back to town to make
verything ready for you and Maria to take tea with us
gain."

Juliana's sobs grew quieter and she peered up at
laire through tear-drenched lashes. "Really?"

"Really," declared Claire firmly. "In a few days you
nd Lady Ransley, Jason and Alura will be in town."

"Papa, too?"

"Papa, too," Claire agreed with a catch in her voice.
Then you shall all come to tea. You and Maria can

tell Grandmama's dollies all that has happened sin
you last saw them. Now isn't that something to lo
forward to?" she asked, using a lace-edged handke
chief to wipe away the child's tears.

Juliana nodded, a trace of a smile appearing on h
face.

"Good. Now promise me that you won't cry anymo
or I'll be very sad."

"I promise," said Juliana patting Claire's cheek.
don't want you to cry, either."

Claire closed her eyes and hugged the little gi
tightly. "I won't cry," she whispered, and knew it w
true, for her tears and dreams had dried to dust aft
Quinton had left her the night before.

"Come, child," urged the duchess, a suspicious husk
ness in her voice. "If we don't leave soon we'll be forc
to spend a night on the road. It will be late enough
it is when we reach town."

Exchanging goodbyes and promises, Claire and th
duchess entered the carriage which finally started dow
the long drive of Oakcrest. The four people remaine
on the steps of the manor house waving until it disa
peared from sight.

Another set of eyes watched the leave-taking from
protected spot which gave a clear view of the scen
They were heavy-lidded from a sleepless night, an
filled with a strange mixture of self-loathing for bei
taken in again and regret for what might have been.

If the duchess felt Claire's sudden insistence that the
return to town posthaste was unusual, she did not voi
it. They were on the last leg of their journey befo
Claire confessed to what had taken place the night b
fore. By that time the light was fading and the duche

uld not see the dampness on her cheeks, but she
uld hear the tears in her voice.

'I'm sure time and distance will make both of you
e things differently,'' said the duchess as they clattered
er cobblestones damp from the mist that was swirling
rough the streets.

'Lord Ransley has made his feelings perfectly clear,
andmama. He wants nothing more to do with me,
d I will not force my presence on him. I only hope
will allow Juliana to visit us occasionally.''

'I'm sure he will, my dear. He loves her very much
d will grant her anything within reason. After all,
's not a monster, Claire, only a man who has been
orly used by a woman.''

'But I've done nothing to him, Grandmama. If he's
o stubborn to believe that, then I want nothing more
do with him. And you should have heard him when
old him of my gift,'' she continued, tears threatening
ce again. ''He is certainly not the man to accept me
I am.''

'Give him time, Claire. Yesterday was an emotional
y for everyone, with Juliana speaking again, then
ws of the riots and Napoleon's escape.''

''That should be no excuse for him to hurl accusa-
ns of treason at me and call me nothing short of a
man of easy virtue.''

'I cannot fault you for being upset, but he was caught
surprise at your announcements. No doubt he al-
dy regrets his harsh words and will beg your forgive-
ss when he returns to London. Now here we are at
me,'' she said, as they pulled up before Kenton
ouse. ''I yearn to be in my bed with a warm brick at
feet.''

Saying goodnight to her grandmother, Claire retired
the familiar comfort of her room. Never had the
een and gold room seemed so inviting. A fire was

soon blazing in the marble fireplace, taking the ch
from the air, and a tray containing a steaming pot
tea and thin slices of buttered bread rested on a tal
nearby.

Claire hastily removed her travelling clothes a
donned a comfortable nightdress and wrapper. S
pulled a chair closer to the fire, poured a cup of te
and relaxed while her abigail turned down the bed a
warmed the sheets.

Claire was still sitting before the low burning fi
reliving the humiliating scene from the night befo
when she heard a scuffling sound outside her doc
Thinking her grandmother might have taken ill fro
the long journey, she took a candle, pulled open t
door and stepped into the hall to investigate.

She felt a surge of relief that all was quiet at t
duchess's suite. Hearing another sound, she turned a
saw a shadowy figure near the door leading to the atti
At her exclamation, the man cursed and ran towa
her, knocking her against the wall as he bolted past h
down the stairs.

Calling for Biggersleigh, Claire scrambled for t
candle that had fallen to the floor in the melee. T
front door crashed open and the intruder had made
safe escape before help reached her.

"I can't imagine why a thief would bypass everythi
of value and make his way to the attic," complained t
duchess for at least the tenth time the next morning

"Neither can I, Grandmama. Perhaps he thought v
kept the family treasures there," Claire teased.

"Bah! The only thing he would find is dust and po
traits of the duke's ancestors that I cannot bear to lo
at."

"Then my only other thought is that it was one

their ghosts wanting to rehang his portrait in its rightful place."

"I don't suppose you saw anything worthwhile during the encounter, did you?" asked the duchess hopefully.

"I'm afraid not. I only felt a great deal of surprise and fear, and I'm not sure whether it was his or mine."

"It's good you can retain a sense of humor through this ordeal," commended her grandmother. "We are fortunate to have inherited the strength from the women on my mother's side of the family."

"Those are the same women responsible for our gift of perception, aren't they?"

The duchess nodded.

"I suppose it's too late to disown them?"

"Claire, there's a limit to what I will consider humorous this morning," she said jabbing her needle into the fabric she held and sending her granddaughter a reproving glance.

"What I don't understand is how Forrest Harcourt just happened to be in front of our house when Biggersleigh and the footmen reached the front door," mused Claire.

"He explained he was on his way home and saw the disturbance."

Claire gave an inelegant snort of disbelief. "Berkeley Square is not anywhere near his rooms, and there was no one entertaining nearby last night. I consider it highly suspicious."

"Yet you didn't find out anything from him, did you?"

Claire looked up in surprise.

"You can't fool me, Claire. I've been at this far longer than you, and I did a little probing myself," she admitted with a smile.

"Were you any more successful?"

"I'm afraid not. Mr. Harcourt is very practiced in keeping his thoughts carefully concealed."

"I still believe he isn't as innocent as he would like us to believe," contended Claire.

"Well, no matter. I've instructed Biggersleigh to employ several additional footmen. We will have someone on duty at all times to insure the incident is not repeated. A person cannot be too careful with sentiment running so strongly against the Corn Bills. It seems we are all being blamed for a disagreeable act."

Claire was not at all certain they could ascribe the incident of the night before to the Corn Bills. From all she had heard, the disgruntled dissenters acted *en masse*, not individually. But she would not further distress her grandmother with her opinion.

"What is it, Biggersleigh?" the duchess asked, as the butler entered the room.

"Mr. Templeton to see Lady Kingsley, Your Grace."

"Show him in. I'm still fatigued from the journey and will rest until luncheon," she announced. The duchess greeted Templeton on her way out, and advised Biggersleigh to bring refreshments for the gentleman.

"Lady Kingsley, how delightful to see you again." Templeton took a seat opposite Claire, crossing his legs and passing along all the recent *on dits* until refreshments had been brought and they were private again.

"I'm sure you're aware our worst fears have materialized and Napoleon is free again," he said without preamble.

"So I had heard, Mr. Templeton. This is one time that I regret the accuracy of my information."

"If only I could have convinced my superiors of the urgency of the matter we might have avoided this calamity. The only good I can see coming of it is that it should squash the anti-corn riots and perhaps draw our people together again." He paused for a sip of sherry before continuing. "Lady Kingsley, I ask you to reconsider and tell me where you came by your information."

"I cannot, sir. You know my feelings on that subject."

"Everything we've learned thus far indicates that the man involved in feeding information directly to Napoleon is the same man who killed John. He instructed the French on how to bring about our complacency so that we would doubt the very facts you brought to us. If you truly want to avenge your husband's death, you will share your information."

Claire quickly reviewed the men she suspected. Even though she was at odds with the marquess, she did not want to believe he was the traitor. Harcourt and Carrington were the better suspects in her mind. With a rush of shame she realized she would rather it be anyone, even Hamilton, than the marquess.

"I could destroy innocent men in the process, Mr. Templeton. And for what good? John is dead and Napoleon has already escaped. Allow me to be sure of my information before I give you a name."

"There's no time to lose, my lady. If Napoleon receives accurate information on troop movement and details of our plan of attack, he can avoid being captured again. You could be withholding information that could lead us to the traitor. He has not only murdered your husband, madam, but is directly responsible for thousands of other deaths. It's urgent we capture him and cut off the flow of information."

"I'm aware of the gravity of the situation, Mr. Templeton," she said, clasping her hands in her lap. "But I must be certain. Believe me when I say I don't know enough to help you identify the man," she pleaded.

Templeton observed the woman sitting across from him. Her beauty had never shown to greater advantage. Her lavender morning gown draped gracefully around her figure and enhanced the air of fragility that surrounded her. But he knew that beneath that delicate demeanor lay a strength unusual for a woman. Beaten, he gave a great sigh. "I believe you, my lady. You have always dealt squarely with me, and I cannot think you would do less now."

"Thank you."

He drained his glass and returned it to the tray before speaking. "Do you think you can help us further?"

"Perhaps, Mr. Templeton, but I have just returned to town, and it may take some time."

"That is something we are extremely short of," he said with a grimace.

"I will begin immediately," she vowed, "but it may be several days before I learn anything."

"I will hope for the best, madam. And this time I will not doubt your word," he promised with a wry smile.

"Mr. Templeton," she said, as he rose to leave. "We had an intruder here last evening."

"What happened," he demanded, reclaiming his seat.

Claire quickly related her encounter of the night before.

"Could it have been one of the men you suspect?" he asked when she had finished.

"It could have been anyone," she answered in exasperation. "My candle went out before I could see anything but a large person in dark clothes. He had a cap of some sort pulled low and I assume his face was blackened with soot, for it was smeared on my nightclothes where he ran into me."

"Damn!" he swore, immediately offering his apologies. "Forget I asked for your help. I will not endanger your life any further."

"If I remember correctly, we have had this discussion before, and you lost that time, too," she remarked with a impudent smile. "I want this man brought to justice

s badly as you do, and I mean to do all I can to expose
im for what he is. Besides, there is every reason to
elieve that the intruder was most probably an ordinary
hief, who had nothing to do with my intrigues."

"But you do not know for a certainty," he argued.
You must listen to reason."

"No," she stated firmly, "but I will be reasonable. I
romise not to go out alone. I'll stay in the company
f friends as much as possible, and will only put myself
t risk if it's absolutely necessary. After all, I'm not anx-
ous to leave this life anytime soon myself."

He could see he would get no better compromise
rom her. Warning her again to contact him immedi-
tely if any other unusual incidents occurred, he left,
till uneasy with the situation.

The Season was in full swing, with the news of Bona-
arte's escape only seeming to drive the revelry to
reater heights. Claire was confident that if the spy was
perating within the relative safety of the *haut ton*, she
ould discover his identity. So, acting on her conviction,
he threw herself into the social whirl with renewed
igor in what might be the last chance to avenge her
usband's murder. She was impatient to fulfill her vow.
he would always love John, but the marquess had
hown her she was ready to accept another man in her
ife. And while it might not be Quinton Courtney, some-
ay she would get over him, too, and have a home and
hildren of her own.

Lord Ransley spent several solitary days following
Claire's departure scrutinizing the events of his life af-
er his marriage to Lydia. Admitting he had deliberately
losed his mind to facts that did not conform to his

view of how life should be was difficult. But, at heart he was a fair man, and could not settle for less than a sincere search for the truth.

On the morning of the third day he found his mother in the small saloon drawing up lists for their London removal. Adjuring the footman that they were not to be disturbed, he closed the door behind him and waited until he had Lady Ransley's attention.

"Quinton, I'm glad to see you've finally come out of your sulks," she teased.

"I've been acting appallingly childish, haven't I?" he asked self-consciously.

Quinton was her first born and held a special place in Lady Ransley's heart. His marriage to Lydia Grey had been his only failure in an otherwise charmed life, and it had wounded him deeply. She had grieved for the son she had lost and for the man he had become.

When the *on dits* reached her about Quinton and Lady Kingsley she had rejoiced, thinking it indicated he had healed and was ready to begin again. His arrival with the news that Lady Kingsley and the Duchess of Kenton would be visiting Oakcrest was a strong indication that Quinton had fixed his interest on the attractive widow. Seeing the special bond between Claire and Juliana only confirmed that the union would be successful. And after their chat in the garden, she had considered the matter settled. Thus, Lady Ransley had been inordinately surprised by the hasty departure of their guests, and Quinton's subsequent isolation.

"I would not call it childish. I think we all need to pause and take stock on occasion."

"You are always generous, ma'am."

"I'm your mother, Quinton. I'm allowed that privilege no matter how old you become."

"And will you be truthful with me, even though it most likely will cause me pain?"

She laid aside her pen. She had waited over a year for this time to come, and now that it had she found she was inexplicably unprepared to cause him further hurt. "If that is what you want," she replied steadily.

"I have heard . . ." he stumbled to a halt. His hands fisted at his sides and his eyes closed against the ugliness he had been unable to accept beforehand. "I have heard," he began in a stronger voice, "that my wi . . . that Lydia was unfaithful to me. Do you know this to be true?" His dark eyes opened and he met her gaze squarely, ready to accept the facts no matter how distasteful.

"Yes, I do."

He heaved a great sigh. "Then tell me," he requested, lowering himself carefully into the nearest chair as if he were an old man consumed with gout.

Several hours later Quinton left the room and made for the stables. He needed a ride in the fresh air after hearing the details of Lydia's activities while he was away from home. His mother had elected to move into the dower house when Quinton married. At the time, Quinton had attempted to convince her it wasn't necessary, but she had insisted. Now he understood why.

As Jason had divulged to him in London, Lydia had taken lovers after she denied him his conjugal rights. His mother personally knew of three, but she felt certain there were others. When confronted with her blatant activities, Lydia had protested that many married ladies had *cicisbeos* and that she enjoyed their flattery too much to discourage them.

Lady Ransley disclosed to Quinton his wife's callous treatment of the staff at both the London town house and Oakcrest. There had been a rapid turnover of servants while Lydia was alive, and only their length of service saved many of the older servants. Lydia had not

gotten quite brave enough to turn off retainers wh
had watched her husband grow up.

But more was still to come. Juliana had been totall
ignored by her mother. She was confined to the nurser
most of the time, for Lydia did not want any of he
visitors reminded that she had a child.

Quinton felt an unusual feeling of relief in reactio
to the disclosures. He had known all was not right wit
his marriage from the beginning, but he had done hi
best to save what he could. Juliana was the only goo
thing to come of it, and she was worth whatever pric
he had paid.

Quinton breathed in a great breath of air as h
stepped out the door. It was over and done with, h
thought, and a great burden lifted from his shoulders
He could admit that his marriage had not been th
success he had pictured in his mind when Lydia walke
down the aisle toward him. Now both he and Julian
were free of her shadow and could make a new life fo
themselves.

"So, you've come out of hiding." Jason stood in fron
of him, a defiant set to his face.

"For good, brother, but I have a lot of matters to pu
straight. I've just had a long talk with Mother; now
think it's your turn."

"It will do no good. I won't change my mind abou
Lydia, and I haven't even begun to tell you what I thin
of your treatment of Claire," he growled, the Courtne
chin jutting out aggressively.

Quinton clapped Jason on his shoulder and laughe
out loud. "It may come as a great surprise, but I totall
agree with you on all points. Now, I need to hear ev
erything you know that I wouldn't listen to before." Hi
expression became serious again. "Mother's told m
what she could, but I believe you were privy to more
I'm not wallowing in grief, nor do I expect to call any

one out, but I don't wish to be surprised by any more revelations."

"And what of Claire?" Jason asked, beginning to thaw toward his brother.

"She'll be difficult to convince, but I don't intend to give up. Lady Kingsley will become my wife as soon as convention will allow."

Jason gave a whoop and threw his arm around his brother.

"Come now," said Quinton as soon as the excitement had died down somewhat. "Join me in a ride and we'll finish our conversation."

Quinton was silent as he and Jason lingered over port after dinner. The evidence against his late wife was overwhelming, and Quinton accepted it as truth. Jason had confirmed that Eldon Garrick was Lydia's last lover. Garrick was not unattractive to women, and Lydia would not have seen beyond his outward appearance, for she was just as shallow as he.

"I must see Garrick," he said into the silence that had fallen over them.

"The man isn't worth risking your life or exile for, Quin." Jason worried at the lack of emotion in his brother's face.

"I don't intend to risk either. Love had long since disappeared from my marriage if, indeed, it ever existed," confessed Quinton, rubbing a weary hand over his face. "But honor demands I at least confront my wife's lover."

"There's more, isn't there?"

"I saw him with Claire the last day she was here. They were at the hunting box."

"You don't believe . . . ?"

Quinton interrupted before he could finish the thought. "Garrick was always envious of our family. I believe that the liaison with Lydia was more an act of reprisal than an affair of the heart. I'm afraid what he might do to Claire if he believes my interest lies with her."

"Then I'll go with you."

"If you insist," the marquess agreed dispassionately. "Jason?"

"Yes."

"When I was recovering from the attack, was it possible I suspected the truth about Lydia then?"

"I don't know. When you were feverish you rambled on about a woman in the fog, but never anything about Lydia."

"Damn! If I could only remember," he cried, rubbing his hand across his eyes.

"It doesn't matter anymore, Quin. That's over and done with."

"Not for me it isn't," replied Quinton roughly. "I was on the floor of my room, with scratchmarks on my face the morning Lydia's body was found at the bottom of the stairs. She had been to see me that night and sent my valet away. That was the last time anyone saw her alive."

"And you think you might have done it?"

Quinton gave a bitter bark of laughter. "If she had confessed her betrayal, who knows what I might have done. I'm not the only one who wonders, if one is to believe the rumors."

"The rumor mill never stops and is seldom correct. You could not kill Lydia no matter how many lovers she took. It was an accident, pure and simple," concluded Jason.

"Then why can't I remember what happened that night, and where did the scratches come from?" he demanded, his fist striking the mahogany table with considerable force.

"You were critically ill, Quin. You had taken a heavy

dose of laudanum. It's a wonder you were coherent enough to talk when Lydia reached your room. You certainly could not overcome a perfectly healthy woman, carry her to the stairs, and throw her down, then return to your room before collapsing on the floor," Jason reasoned.

It did sound unrealistic given those circumstances, thought Quinton. "Our child died with her," he said quietly.

Jason reached out and laid a supporting hand on his brother's shoulder. "I'm sorry, Quin. I know how much you wanted another child, but you must believe that it wasn't your fault. You and Claire can raise a houseful of children here at Oakcrest. Judging from the way she fusses over Juliana, I'm sure she wants a large family as much as you do."

"You're right," agreed Quinton, some of the strain slipping away from his face. "As soon as I finish with Garrick, I intend to concentrate on making Claire my wife."

"When do we leave?" asked Jason.

"At first light tomorrow," replied Quinton, a smile of anticipation curving his lips.

During the trip to London, Quinton's thoughts were almost exclusively centered on Claire. He did intend to make her his wife, and while he wanted to believe in her complete innocence, there were still questions lingering in his mind.

Admittedly, Claire had not lied about Lydia, but she did consort with questionable people. And although he now believed her meeting with Garrick was innocent, her relationship with Templeton remained unexplained. He disregarded Ashford, for he had noticed a distinct coolness between the two before he left London.

There was also that tarradiddle about being able to read thoughts. He had to know the answers before he could plan a life with her or continue his own.

Thirteen

"I cannot think why you are so set upon seeing Grandmother's orchids, Hamilton," complained Claire, as the tall, blond man led her toward the conservatory at the back of Kenton House. "I didn't know you were an admirer of such things."

"Despite our long acquaintance, Claire, there are things you have yet to learn about me," he replied, an uncommon grimness about his mouth. "But that is a minor detail which I hope will be altered after this morning." His smile was forced as he guided her into the glass enclosed room.

The warm, humid air closed around Claire, and suddenly she found it difficult to draw a breath. Hamilton had been particularly insistent on getting her alone and the tautness of his expression made her apprehensive about their *tête-à-tête*.

He had called after her return to town and picked up their relationship as if their disagreements over Lord Ransley had never occurred. Since then she had accepted his escort on numerous occasions.

The incident with the intruder had made her wary of going out alone, even with extra footmen on the coach, and Templeton had warned her to limit her companions to those she could trust. Now she was sorry she had encouraged him to reestablish their friendship to

such an exclusive degree, but at the time, she had n
taste for forming new acquaintances.

They stopped in front of the orchids, and Hamilton
stared at them as if he had never seen such bloom
before. He was dressed impeccably in a gray morning
coat, breeches which disappeared into highly polished
Hessians, and a cravat that was simply, but exquisitely
arranged. His hair gleamed almost silver in the sun
coming through the glass. But for all his elegance, he
somehow appeared awkward as he turned to her.

"Claire, there was a reason I wanted to see you
alone," he said capturing her hands with his.

His palms were without the faint roughness that
marked Quinton's, she reflected, then almost smiled
that her thoughts were taking such a turn at that moment. It had been a sennight since she had seen Ransley, but she remembered every detail of him as clearly
as if he stood before her. If Hamilton could read her
mind, he would be extremely annoyed that she was
thinking of another man.

"Hamilton, I don't think . . ."

"Please, Claire, let me finish. I've admired you from
the day we met. John didn't tell you because it would
have made things awkward between us, but I was prepared to offer for you the day you accepted his proposal.

"After his death, it was a comfort to be around you.
I felt closer to him. But as time passed my earlier admiration returned. I've waited patiently while you
mourned, while we both mourned. Then Ransley appeared and I thought I had lost you again."

"There is nothing between us," she protested half
heartedly.

"I know. When you returned to London without him
or his ring on your finger, I was the happiest man alive.
It gave me hope that there was still a chance for us."

"Hamilton— "

"Claire, hear me out. I will never forget John and I
on't ask that you do; however, I cannot help but think
e would be happy knowing we were together. Will you
o me the great honor, Claire? Will you marry me?"

The thought had crossed her mind the past few days
hat Hamilton was being more solicitous than usual, but
he was not prepared for his offer of marriage. It was
more in his line to offer a carte blanche, though per-
aps not to his late friend's widow.

Claire could not believe that Hamilton was in love
ith her. He had attempted no more than a brief kiss
o her hand. Surely a man passionately in love would
ant more than that, she reflected, thinking of the
isses she had shared with Quinton. Grateful he could
ot read her thoughts, she met Hamilton's gaze. He
id not have the look of a man waiting for his beloved's
eply.

"Hamilton, I'm honored and I cherish our friend-
hip, but I cannot accept your offer."

A muscle twitched in his jaw, and his lips tightened
ntil they were but a thin white slash. "It's Ransley; he
ill stands between us, doesn't he?"

"Lord Ransley has nothing to do with this," she an-
wered truthfully. "If I had never met the marquess,
y answer would be the same."

"Take your time, Claire, you need not answer imme-
iately. I'm willing to wait."

"A day, a week, or a month will not make a differ-
nce," she said, willing him to accept her word. "I trea-
ure your friendship. It helped me endure those
readful days after the accident, but it cannot be any
ore."

"Please reconsider," he begged, an air of desperation
 his demeanor. "Your decision is too important to
ake hastily, Claire, it will change the course of both
ur lives."

"I wish I could say yes, Hamilton, but I can't. Al though I admire and respect you, and will always cal you friend, I do not love you in the way a woman shoul love her husband."

"You will learn to love me, Claire, I'm willing to settl for that."

"But I am not," she answered gently, thinking of th man who had stolen her heart. If only it was Quinto who was asking for her hand, she would be the happies woman alive.

Hamilton turned away, a shudder running throug his body.

"Hamilton, I'm sorry," said Claire. "Perhaps it woul be best not to see one another for a while."

"No," he said, facing her once again. "I'll not los your company because of my foolishness. We will con tinue as usual and perhaps you'll come to see what a outstanding husband I would make."

"I have no doubt of that, my friend, but I'm not th wife for you."

"That's what you think now, but opinions can change In the meantime," he concluded, a forced smile on hi face, "I'll collect you this evening. I believe we have dinner, several routs, and a ball to attend before th dawn breaks."

Claire acquiesced with a nod and watched him de part, his shoulders stiff beneath the gray kerseymere o his coat. She would not change her mind, but coul not bring herself to argue with him any longer.

Claire had been hearing more talk about the maste spy at work. Evidently, since the escape plan ha worked, he was getting bolder. It was just a matter o time before someone would let slip the information tha would lead her to the right man. As soon as she fel safe enough to travel about without an escort, she woul limit her contact with Hamilton. A man with his look and address would have no trouble finding a woman who would welcome his advances.

Claire was overwhelmingly pleased when the coach turned into Berkeley Square early the next morning. She had spent a seemingly endless evening in idle gossip and longed for peace and quiet. She wistfully thought of Oakcrest, but that was denied her now. She must be satisfied with something else, perhaps a visit to Bath after everything was settled.

Claire accepted Hamilton's hand and stepped out of the carriage in front of Kenton House. When he made no move she looked up at him questioningly.

"Have you reconsidered my offer?" he asked.

"My answer hasn't changed, nor is it likely to," Claire replied shortly. She had thought he had understood she could never marry him.

She heard him exhale and he gripped her hands tightly for a few moments. "So be it, Claire. I had hoped things would turn out differently, but my luck seems to have run out." He guided her across the cobblestones to the bottom of the steps.

"Just a moment, my dear," said Hamilton. "I must instruct my coachman."

"Don't bother to escort me in, Hamilton. I'm too tired to stand on ceremony."

"I insist, Claire. Besides, you must offer me a glass of brandy to toast our friendship. I'll only be a moment."

Claire tapped her foot impatiently as he turned back to his coach. She could be in the house by now instead of standing on the cold cobblestones, their dampness seeping through the thin slippers she wore. Deciding to go ahead without him, she turned and started up the stairs. At that moment a shot rang out and Claire's eyes widened in shock.

Another carriage drew abruptly to a halt behind Hamilton's, and Lord Ransley leaped to the ground as Claire crumbled onto the marble steps. Reaching her a moment before Ashford, Quinton lifted her in his arms and carried her into the house, ordering Biggersleigh to send for the doctor.

Claire briefly regained consciousness. Blackness swirled around her and for a moment she thought she was blind again. But the pain in her arm and shoulder reminded her of the gunshot she had heard just before she had fallen. There was movement and muted voices around her, then someone called her name. Her vision was too blurred to clearly see the figure bending over her, but her senses were remarkably intact.

Damn! I'll have that bungler's neck. A simple shot and he botched it. I should have done it myself.

Claire blinked, attempting to clear the haze that clouded her vision, but to no avail. He was here. The traitor who had killed John was within her reach and she could not see him. He had tried to kill her and now she was defenseless. She drifted back into darkness, wondering if there was anyone present who would prevent him from succeeding in his goal.

When she again regained consciousness, both Quinton and Hamilton were at her side. A few feet away Forrest Harcourt and Tyler Carrington spoke in muted tones to the duchess. By now the initial confusion was over, and the men's emotions were too strongly contained for Claire's muddled thoughts to penetrate their defenses. She regarded the four men before closing her eyes against the light, wondering which one of them wanted her dead.

* * *

Lord Ransley called for a damp cloth, running it lightly over Claire's face. From his experience with wounds, he knew the injury to her arm was not life threatening; however, he would feel easier if she would speak to him.

Lifting the cloth, his eye caught a small spot of dirt remaining on her face from her fall. He brushed at it, but it stubbornly remained. Bending closer, he touched the small black spot at the corner of Claire's mouth. Smooth. Her skin was smooth and silky. The black mark was not a rough cinder clinging to her skin, but a part of it. A chill of recognition washed over him as he remembered another faced partly obscured by fog, previously differentiated by what he thought was an old-fashioned beauty patch.

Frozen by his discovery, Lord Ransley remained staring at Claire's face and the condemning black mark until the doctor arrived and drove everyone but the duchess from the room.

Quinton returned to Grosvenor Square long enough to change clothes and explain to Jason over breakfast what had happened. Asking his brother to keep himself available, he donned his coat and hat and stepped out into the morning light.

As his carriage rumbled along Pall Mall, Lord Ransley realized that he would rather not have known the truth. A few short days ago he had admitted he loved Claire Kingsley even though her acquaintances were questionable and she had the ridiculous idea she could see things that others couldn't. At that time he had consoled himself with the thought that there were worse things to find in a wife, and now it had come true.

Claire had kept her identity a secret from him; she was the woman in the fog. She had known of his attack.

True, she had warned him, but in such a manner he could not take her seriously. There was only one way she could have known of the assault in advance; she had been involved. He was in love with a conspirator against his life.

The carriage drew to a halt in front of York House. Lord Ransley stepped out and entered the side wing occupied by the War Office, making his way to Matthew Templeton's office.

Even though the hour was early, Templeton was ensconced behind a desk strewn with documents. His attention was immediately taken by the dark man who suddenly filled his doorway. He had been expecting Quinton since he realized the marquess had taken an interest in Lady Kingsley. Sooner or later a man as sharp as the marquess would want some answers. However, the conversation took a twist that Templeton did not expect.

"Is Lady Kingsley under suspicion by your office for spying?" asked the marquess, without offering a greeting.

"Why do you ask?" Templeton replied, more to gain time than for want of an answer.

"There have been a series of events that lead me to believe she is not just another fashionable lady of the *ton.*" Lord Ransley briefly summarized the circumstances surrounding the attack made on him in the fog, and his recent discovery that Lady Kingsley was the woman who warned him, indicating she knew of the assault before it happened. He recounted her contact with various individuals whose loyalty to England was questionable.

It would take a very dull man indeed not to see that the marquess's emotions were involved with Lady Kingsley. "I know nothing of the attack made on you last year," answered Templeton. "If it had been related to your work for us we would have heard of it by now."

Quinton had been pinning his hopes on Templeton being able to answer at least a few of his questions. But he knew no more now than when he had first entered the office.

"Then how could she have known of it beforehand? And why would she wish me harm? I'm sure we had never met before."

"I'm afraid I can't answer that, my lord; however, perhaps I can explain her association with the people you deem questionable." Templeton paused for a moment, questioning his judgment, before continuing. "You see, Lady Kingsley has indeed been spying—for us."

Lord Ransley was speechless with surprise.

"I don't know who her contacts are or how she obtains her information, but she is one of our most reliable agents."

Quinton's mind was spinning. Claire an agent for England! He should be ecstatic, but instead his anger rose.

"How could you let her put herself in such danger," he demanded.

"I had no choice. Her husband worked for us and—"

"Yes," Ransley interrupted impatiently, "I've heard all about Kingsley's accident."

"Except that it wasn't an accident, but deliberate and cold-blooded murder," revealed Templeton. "John was instrumental in insuring victory at Salamanca by intercepting messages to the French concerning Wellington's plans. He also discovered the same man had been responsible for passing along information to Napoleon for the past several years. He was carrying evidence of the traitor and his name with him." Templeton picked up a pen, twirling it between his fingers, as he proceeded with the story.

"Evidently he was found out, because a robbery was staged to retrieve the documents. The robbery went awry when the horses bolted, and the carriage overturned at the edge of a small village. It was too late for John, he had already taken a bullet and was dead. The locals who quickly gathered around the accident probably saved Claire's life by keeping the murderer at bay."

This time it was the marquess who uttered a curse. Templeton gave him a moment to absorb what he had told him thus far before resuming his account of John's murder.

"Lady Kingsley had no knowledge of the documents, nor their contents. We searched the carriage, but found nothing. We thought John might have sent them ahead for safety's sake, but nothing came by post after his death. The highwayman was questioned extensively when we caught him, but he had never known the identity of the man who hired him. The spy and the information had completely disappeared.

"I thought perhaps the documents had somehow been retrieved by the traitor, but he laid low for some time, probably waiting for us to make a move. When we didn't, he became active again."

"Why in God's name did you tell Claire her husband had been murdered?" demanded Quinton.

"I don't know how she came about the facts," confessed Templeton, "but it wasn't from me. I paid a call on her one day and before I knew it she was telling me she knew everything. I endeavored to assure her that the War Office was working to find the murderer, but she wouldn't listen. She swore to find the traitor, and there was nothing I could do about it short of clapping her in prison."

"That might not have been a bad idea," commented the marquess.

"At the time I didn't expect anything to come of it,"

said Templeton, in a hurry to finish his tale. "I thought she was another hysterical widow. Then she began passing along extremely valuable information. How and where she obtained it I don't know, and she's never broken the confidence of her informers."

Lord Ransley questioned his own sanity as he recalled Claire's ability to communicate with Juliana, and her warning to a stranger in the fog. He could vividly picture her circulating among the crowds at the assemblies, balls, and routs, then meeting Templeton at Hatchard's Bookstore. Lastly, there was the night in the garden at Oakcrest, when she reluctantly voiced her ability to perceive thoughts. Rubbing a weary hand over his face, he decided to think about it later.

"An attempt was made on her life a few hours ago," he announced abruptly.

"Again?" exclaimed Templeton, rising from his chair. "Good God! Is she all right?"

"Yes. It was a near thing. Fortunately, she turned aside just as the shot was fired and the bullet struck her arm. But what do you mean, *again?*"

Templeton told Ransley what he knew of the intruder at Kenton House. "She must be getting too close to the traitor," he surmised. "Only a man greatly threatened would take such a chance. Did she tell you who she suspected?"

"No. She was barely conscious for a short period of time, but didn't say anything. There's a man by the name of Eldon Garrick who might hold a clue, do you know anything about him?"

"A nasty piece of work," commented Templeton with a frown of distaste. "None of her reports have mentioned Garrick. He's skirted the fringes of respectability for years, but he isn't privy to enough information to interest anyone. It's possible he could be a middleman passing information along, but so far down the line our office probably wouldn't even be interested."

"Thank you for your frankness," said the marquess, offering his hand. "If I find out anything of interest, I'll let you know."

While the marquess had learned a lot about Claire, he knew nothing that would expose the identity of the person who attempted to kill her. Garrick was his only suspect. If Claire had let him know she was aware of his liaison with Lydia, he could have decided to silence her. According to Jason, Garrick was not the kind of man to welcome facing a cuckolded husband who was accounted an excellent shot.

Thanking Templeton again for his cooperation, Quinton left the office as abruptly as he had arrived. He would collect Jason and they would track down El-don Garrick. In addition to confronting Garrick about Lydia, Lord Ransley intended to see if he was involved in Claire's attempted murder.

Fourteen

A short time later Quinton and Jason called at Kenton House. After finding that Claire was resting comfortably, the two brothers set about locating Garrick. They found him registered at Stephen's Hotel in Bond Street.

"Ransley," acknowledged Garrick cautiously as he opened the door in answer to their knock. "You're the last person I expected to see."

"No doubt. Aren't you going to ask us in, Garrick?"

"My accommodations don't lend themselves to entertaining."

"That's just as well, for the only diversion I'm interested in is straight answers." The marquess pushed Garrick back into the room. Jason followed closely, locking the door and pocketing the key.

"What is this?" demanded Garrick, his pale eyes flicking nervously between the two men.

"Whatever you want it to be," replied Lord Ransley. "We can make it easy or hard, it's up to you. But either way I don't intend to leave until I have some answers, and they'd better be the truth or you won't live to see tomorrow."

Garrick turned a shade paler and backed further across the room. "What do you want?" he snarled.

"Answers, and I won't repeat it again. What was my wife to you?"

Garrick laughed in derision. "Nothing, my lord. Your fine lady meant absolutely nothing to me."

This time it was Lord Ransley who paled. "I know you were her lover," he stated, finding the truth hard to speak out loud.

"I was her last lover," Garrick admitted, regaining a measure of his confidence, "but I was not the first nor the only one. She had enjoyed other men before me, and would have had many more if she had not met such an untimely end," he goaded.

Garrick had hated the marquess for years. Ransley had wealth and a title, and any woman he wanted without so much as lifting his finger. Now Garrick held the power to hurt the man he had envied for so long, and he meant to enjoy his confession.

"It was all Lydia's doing, you know. She did the pursuing and insisted upon meeting frequently at the hunting box. She was bored in the country, she said, and weary of her well-born husband," he continued with a self-satisfied sneer. "So bored that she tried to do away with you altogether. We were going to live the good life at your expense, but your luck held."

"What do you mean?"

"New Year's Eve, my lord. You do remember that, don't you?" he jeered. "Lydia bragged that she could use her tearful blue eyes to send you right into the arms of a pair of cutthroats she had me hire. And it almost worked, didn't it? She tried again with that long, cold ride home, but it didn't do the trick, either. Too bad; we could have been in Paris now, your lady wife and I."

Jason grabbed Quinton's arm before he could launch himself at Garrick. Willing himself to remain calm, the marquess continued with his questioning.

"What is your connection with Lady Kingsley?"

Garrick's eyes narrowed as he wondered what was be-

ind the question, and how he could use it to his bene-
it. "We've met several times, that's all," he finally an-
wered, deciding not to test Ransley's restraint.

"For what reason?" demanded Quinton.

"You've no right to come in here threatening me,"
sserted Garrick, his temper finally getting the better
f him. "Why do you think a man meets with such a
rime article? Surely you don't mind sharing the widow
fter sharing your wife, do you?"

Too late, Garrick realized he had pushed his luck too
ar. Quinton's pent-up rage would not be restrained.
He landed blow after blow before Jason was able to pull
him off the man.

"You can't beat him to death, Quin," gasped Jason.
"And he hasn't enough honor for you to call him out."
Still breathing heavily, Quinton looked down at the man
sprawled on the carpet. "Go back to the house, Quin,
and send me two of our stoutest stable hands along
with a closed carriage. I'll take him to the coast. I know
just the captain who will drop him on the other side
of the world for the right fee, and he won't make it
easy on his getting there."

"It goes against the grain to let him off that easily,"
said Quinton, rubbing his bruised and bleeding knuck-
es.

"It's the best we can do, Quin. There's nothing we
can prove. He won't confess in front of anyone but us.
And we could never find the men hired to kill you,"
argued Jason. "Besides, you'd have to air Lydia's dirty
linen in public, and you can't do that to Juliana's
mother."

Acknowledging the wisdom of his words, Quinton
agreed and left Jason to guard Garrick until the carriage arrived.

* * *

Quinton was at a loss as to what to do next. While he now knew Garrick and Lydia had conspired to murder him, he still did not know who had attempted to kill Claire. Garrick had been caught off guard at his question concerning her, and showed only confusion then baited the marquess with a relationship that was extremely improbable. It was, however, possible that Garrick was one of Claire's informers. Realizing Garrick would not confess even if it were true, Quinton returned to the War Office.

Templeton was still at his desk frowning at what looked like the same stack of papers that had been before him that morning. He looked up at Quinton's entrance, pushing the documents aside with an air of relief.

"Have you learned anything more?" he asked anxiously.

"Nothing to tell us the traitor's name," replied Quinton, pacing the bare floor before his desk. "I can't question Claire because she's still asleep, and I don't have any other leads to follow. Would you allow me to read through the reports Claire gave you? Perhaps there's something I might recognize."

"Of course." Guiding the marquess to an empty office, Templeton called a clerk to bring the reports.

Quinton spent the rest of the afternoon and into the evening poring over the information Claire had gathered and passed along to Templeton. Over the past few months she had mentioned many of the men he had seen her with, but nothing that would indicate anyone suspected her enough to make an attempt on her life.

Something obvious nagged at Quinton as he finished the reports. He puzzled over the documents, pacing the confines of the small room until he eventually realized there was no mention of Ashford in Claire's reports.

Lord Ransley returned to Templeton's office. "Did Lady Kingsley ever mention Hamilton Ashford to you?"

"No. But then that's not unusual since they're good friends."

Suddenly the marquess understood the omission. Claire had stated she never invaded the thoughts of her friends. Lord Ransley leaped from his chair and rushed out the door leaving Templeton staring after him.

The hour was late and Lord Ransley wondered if he would be committed to Bedlam for bursting into Kenon House at this time of night.

While Lord Ransley was rushing toward Berkeley Square, Hamilton was sitting beside Claire's bed when she awakened.

"Hamilton?" she questioned, still hazy from the dose of laudanum she had taken earlier in the evening.

"Yes, my dear, I'm here. I stopped by to see how you were."

"Where's Della?"

"Your maid? I offered to sit with you while she refreshed herself with a cup of tea." He glanced toward the dressing room door where the girl was lying bound and gagged tightly enough to keep her quiet.

"You're a good friend," she said, her senses too vague to remember he was suspect.

A momentary flash of regret flickered across his countenance. "I promised to see you took your medicine when you awoke."

"But I took some not long ago," objected Claire.

"You've lost track of time. Now be a good girl and drink up," he urged, lifting a glass to her lips that had been lethally infused with morphine. Claire had taken only a small sip when the marquess burst into the room and knocked the glass to the floor.

* * *

When she next awakened it was daylight and Lor
Ransley was by her side, his hand tightly grasping her
"What happened?" she asked, wondering if what littl
she remembered had been a dream.

"I think you should have some tea before I tell yo
anything," said the marquess, smiling at her confusior

"Now tell me," she insisted a short time later as sh
accepted a second cup of tea.

Claire was propped up against a mound of pillow:
her hair loose and falling around her shoulders in dis
array. The lace-edged gown she wore had one arm cu
out and a white bandage marked where she had bee
shot. He wanted to hold her in his arms and promis
to protect her from harm. He wanted to breathe in he
sweet scent and know he would have her for the rest o
his life. But there were explanations to be made befor
he could find out whether she held him in disgust fo
his previous accusations.

"Ashford has been arrested," he said, watching he
closely. "He turned traitor in exchange for money t
reverse his family fortunes. He's also being charge
with your husband's murder and the attempt on you
life."

Claire's eyes were the only color in her pale face.

Quinton removed the cup from her cold fingers, lean
ing forward he cradled her hand between his befor
continuing. "It seems John discovered the facts of Ash
ford's betrayal, and was on his way to London wit
proof when his friend arranged for your carriage to b
held up on the way to town. Ashford says he only mean
to take the documents and keep John silent by threat:
but the robbery took a turn for the worse when one o
the bullets hit your husband and the horses bolted. Ash
ford swears he never meant to hurt either of you."

Quinton stopped a moment, but Claire did not take
advantage of the lull, so he continued with his explanation.

"As long as you were blind, Ashford wasn't worried
that the papers would surface, thinking no one else
would go through John's effects but his wife. However,
after you recovered your sight the situation changed.
Ashford attached himself to you, determined to retrieve
the damning evidence. He could not risk the documents
turning up some day to ruin him. He knew John used
his walking stick to conceal secret papers, and was certain they were in it."

Claire's exclamation caused him to pause in his nar-
ration. She described how Hamilton had asked for the
walking stick, but in the rush to pack for Oakcrest it
had slipped her mind. "Hamilton knew we weren't sup-
posed to be here the night I saw the thief in the hallway.
He must have been attempting to steal the cane."

Lord Ransley nodded, confirming her conjecture.
"Ashford admitted to the housebreaking." He raised
her hand to his lips. "He also said he asked you to
marry him, thinking you would never suspect your husband. He believed he could eventually find the papers
and destroy them if you were wed."

"And to think I felt sorry about rejecting his suit,"
Claire uttered in disgust. "I actually thought he wanted
to marry me."

"I think he cares for you as much as any man of his
stamp could," judged Quinton. "He was hoping right
up until you arrived home that you would change your
mind. The assassin was not to fire unless he left you
standing alone."

"So when I refused him again, he made an excuse
to talk to his coachman," Claire surmised.

"Yes, leaving you a perfect target beneath the gas

light. I'm only happy that your patience ran out faste
than the man could take aim.''

Quinton raised her hand and pressed his lips to th
palm. "I apologize for my behavior at Oakcrest, my love
If I hadn't behaved so badly you wouldn't have returne
early to London, and all this unpleasantness could hav
been avoided.''

"Perhaps it was for the best," replied Claire, "for
I hadn't returned early it's very likely that Hamilto
would have found the cane and destroyed the doc
ments.''

Lord Ransley kissed her lightly, thinking he woul
certainly have a brave wife if she would agree to marr
him. But she was in no condition to listen to a propos:
at the moment. He insisted she take another small dos
of laudanum, promising to stay with her while she slep

The marquess made good his word, only leaving he
side to change into the clothes his valet had brought t
Kenton House. When Claire awakened again, he wa
dozing in the chair by her bed. Evidently, the duches
had put aside propriety in allowing the marquess acces
to her bedroom. Claire smiled; her grandmother wa
willing to see her compromised if it ended in marriag

Her slight movement caused Quinton to immediatel
awaken. They exchanged a smile, content with one an
other's company. He reached out and touched th
beauty mark at the corner of her mouth.

"Your face has haunted me for over a year now. I
kept me alive when the doctors held no hope for me
I asked for you when I awakened, and could not cor
vince anyone you were real. They told me I had imag
ined you, and after that I didn't care whether I die
or not.''

"I am immensely relieved that you decided to live,
she said, turning her head to press a kiss against hi
hand.

"Why didn't you tell me you were working with Templeton? I spent every night watching you flirt shamelessly with the most obnoxious men in London. When I retired for the evening, it was only to spend a sleepless night tossing and turning, imagining you in their arms and wanting to kill each and every one of them who enjoyed what should be mine." His diatribe ended with a kiss that refuted his anger by its gentleness.

"I should beat you for putting me through such torment," he murmured against her lips. "In fact, once you're fit again, I may well do it," he teased, his look belying his words.

"Quinton, I'm sorry I couldn't tell you what drove me to act the flirt, or about my true relationship with Mr. Templeton," she said, eager to explain. "And I didn't realize you were the man I had warned on New Year's Eve until you told me about your vision. Even then I couldn't reveal my identity. You would have had too many questions to ask about how I knew you were in danger. I couldn't have told you the truth because you wouldn't have believed me."

He opened his mouth ready to deny her charge. "You're right," he admitted, "but perhaps you could have convinced me more readily." He leaned nearer. "I was weak and would probably have believed anything you said with the right encouragement," he murmured, his lips brushing against her ear.

"You don't believe me yet, do you? I mean about my ability?" she asked, afraid to hear his answer.

"I believe you are a very special, very perceptive woman, and I've not yet been able to explain away everything that has happened since I met you," he said, interrupting his speech to place a string of kisses from ear to lips.

"In other words, you don't believe me," said Claire, her voice flat.

"I didn't exactly say that," he hedged, seeing she was determined to pursue the subject.

"Then what exactly did you say," she fumed. "Must I put on my gypsy costume again and tell your fortune, then wait for it to come true before you will consider what I say to be accurate?"

"You'll never wear that costume again unless it's for my eyes only," he ordered. "It reveals far too much."

"That's not the point, Quinton."

"It is to me."

"You are determined not to take me seriously, aren't you? I suppose if we continue our friendship you will conveniently forget everything that's happened."

"There's no question that we will continue our relationship, and I expect us to be much more than friends, my love." There was no mistaking the message in his eyes.

"We must discuss this, Quinton, before we have any kind of relationship," she insisted.

"Later," he murmured. "Why do you hide it?" he asked, touching the mark again, a sensuous smile on his face.

"John didn't like it," she said, allowing herself to be distracted. "He jokingly called it a witch's mark and insisted I conceal the imperfection."

Lord Ransley's touch lingered, caressing the soft skin. "I don't want to speak against your late husband, but to me it's an intriguing beauty mark and is most assuredly on the right person."

Leaning over he placed a kiss over it, then moved on to the softness of her lips, a habit to which she had already grown addicted. Pulling away he lifted her chin, "Leave it uncovered from now on," he commanded gently, but firmly. "I have an uncommon urge to kiss it at unconventional times and would rather not have it hidden by powder."

After the marquess demonstrated his uncommon urges a few more times, he settled her back among the pillows. "I've told you of Ashford, now I must tell you about Eldon Garrick."

"I don't want to hear any more about the man," she insisted. "He's caused too much trouble between us already."

"You'll be interested in this, for it means I owe you another apology," he teased. Quickly, he related the tale of his confrontation with Garrick. "So you see, you were right again, my lady."

"Something I could have done without," she said, aware of the pain he must have felt admitting his wife's unfaithfulness.

"I didn't love Lydia, Claire. At first I was taken by her beauty, but living with her was altogether another thing from admiring her," he confessed.

She allowed a moment of silence to pass. "My meeting with Garrick was not by chance, Quinton. I wanted to see him again."

Quinton looked at her in surprise. "Why would you take such a risk, Claire? While he's no threat to a man, he would probably enjoy the chance to bully a woman."

"I had heard his name before, but couldn't remember where. Then I saw him with Sylvia Beaufort the night I was shot and recalled everything. He had been at Weatherby's masquerade ball with Sylvia, and I heard her promise she would help him revive some rumors. At the time the words meant nothing to me. Just before I came to Oakcrest, Sylvia told me it was rumored you had a hand in Lydia's death. She also went on about your affair in France."

Quinton grimaced. "I'm sorry you had to hear about it that way, Claire. It's true Sylvia and I had a short liaison. Lydia had just turned me away. I was hurt and

needed someone to bolster my pride; Sylvia was conve
nient."

"Please, Quinton, I do not need to hear this," ob
jected Claire.

"If we mean to have a future together you must hear
it, sweetheart. Sylvia engaged none of my emotions. She
knew that what we had was a temporary arrangement
and she accepted it. She was also well paid," he added
uncomfortably.

"When she returned to England, she learned that my
wife had died and attempted to renew our relationship.
I made short work of rejecting her offer. I'm sure she
was angry with me and happy to comply with Garrick's
suggestions that she stir up all the rumors again. I be
lieve he started them in the first place, because my
mother told me he was at Oakcrest the morning Lydia
was found.

"I wronged you and Jason by not believing you about
Garrick and Lydia. He admitted they were having an
affair. You see, he has always resented me and also ad
mitted he conspired with Lydia to put an end to my
life."

Claire clutched his hand tightly. "The attack in the
fog."

"Exactly. The fact that it failed incensed him further
and he became obsessed with destroying me. He
thought if he stirred up enough suspicion about my
role in Lydia's death, I would be forced to go abroad
or face trial. Fortunately, my friends were staunch
enough to render the rumors harmless to all but the
most vicious tattlemongers."

"Quinton, there's something more you need to know
about Garrick and Lydia, something I can't prove except
that I felt it strongly the last time I saw him at the
hunting box, then again on my last night at Oakcrest."

"More of your seeing," he teased.

"I know you doubt my gift, but you must listen. Quin-
on, I believe that Garrick— "

Claire's maid peeked into the room. "There's a gen-
leman here, ma'am, says he's his lordship's brother and
would like to see 'em."

"Have him come up, Della," said Claire, thinking a
ew more minutes before her revelation would not hurt.

"Are you sure you're up to receiving Jason?" asked
Quinton. "I can easily see him downstairs."

"Of course I'm able. I must thank him for saving
vou," she added, reaching up to caress his unshaven
cheek.

"Afterward I shall freshen up," he said, hearing the
rasp of stubble against her hand, "or my valet will likely
urn in his notice."

A few minutes later Jason entered, bringing the smell
of horses and leather with him. "Well, we've seen the
ast of Garrick," he remarked cheerfully. "I watched
him go aboard myself. The captain promised he would
not have the energy to try escaping before hitting the
Australian shore.

"Funny thing though. He wrote a letter to you. Said
t was important you receive it as soon as I returned to
own. Smiled like the devil all the while he was writing."
Jason searched his pockets until he found a rather
crumpled paper, and handed it over to Quinton.

Lord Ransley experienced a sense of dread as he
broke open the seal and began to read:

My dear Lord Ransley, Due to the hasty nature
of our little chat at my hotel, I neglected to relate
several items which you might find amusing. I
had thought at first to allow you to continue carrying the guilt on your very respectable conscience, but finally decided I could not forgo the
pleasure of imparting such joyful news to you.

The child your wife carried at her death was not yours, but the product of our coupling— such a common word for the satisfaction Lydia gave— don't you agree? She was very proud of the fact that she had tricked you into believing you were the father of her bastard, and described every detail of how she accomplished it.

Quinton needed no reminder. He vividly remem bered awakening one night, with Lydia in his bed and the act almost consummated before he was fully awake With tears streaming down her beautiful face, Lydia ex plained she had come to him for comfort from a night mare and he had fallen upon her like an animal.

Quinton had never treated his wife discourteously but he had long been without companionship, so he had accepted her word, guilt tearing at his conscience for putting his own base needs before thinking of the threat to her life. He had carried that guilt with him since, and now he found out he was not responsible He smoothed the wrinkled sheets he had crumpled be tween his fingers and continued reading.

I have already disclosed that Lydia was instru- mental in plotting the unsuccessful attempt against your life, and her subsequent outrage when it failed. What I neglected to relate is that she blamed me for hiring an inadequate assassin to carry out the plan, and threatened to expose me as the culprit. As you must recognize by now, there was no limit to Lydia's desire for revenge, and I was forced to take action to avoid her re- prisal.

With the house in turmoil because of your ill- ness, it was easy to plan an assignation with Lydia in the library late one evening. However, I met her in the hall at the top of the stairs, telling her I was too anxious to see her to wait below.

She had just come from your room, and was furious that you would not give her power to direct your affairs while you were ill. You see, she still had hopes that you would not survive, and meant to bleed every penny she could from your estate before your heir claimed it. If you survived, she meant to take what she could and live abroad. However, you thwarted her plan by refusing to sign the paper. She laughed like a mad woman and said although you wouldn't cooperate, she had left her mark on you. I found out later about the scratches she left on your face, and used them to begin the rumors about your part in her death.

After hearing Lydia's story, I knew that once you recovered it would not take you long to discover Lydia's perfidy, and she would not hesitate to cast the blame on me. Lydia was a fool for flattery, and I praised and petted her until she was distracted by my words. I assure you, my lord, your wife did not suffer when I pushed her down the stairs. Indeed she did not even scream.

Lord Ransley's lips tightened in fury and a string of curses followed him out of the room. Claire retrieved the letter from the floor. After reading it, she sank back against the pillows and prayed for his safety.

Fifteen

Matthew Templeton was the first visitor the duchess admitted to the sick room. Claire had been protesting that she was well enough to go downstairs and threatened to do so if the tedium of her days was not relieved in some way. She had not heard a word from Quinton and Hanora decided company might help take her mind off the worry.

Templeton entered the room quietly. Claire reclined on a green and gold striped chaise, staring pensively out the window into Berkeley Square, where the sun and greening plane trees in the small park announced that spring was surely upon them. He made a slight noise and she looked up expectantly, disappointment apparent in her face when she recognized him. He envied the man whose return she anticipated.

"You do not have to tiptoe, Mr. Templeton. Except for a little soreness, I'm perfectly fine. The bullet only grazed my shoulder. Please come in and have a seat."

"I'm happy to hear it, Lady Kingsley. You had us all worried for a time."

"My grandmother still treats me like an invalid," she complained peevishly. Her face brightened all of a sudden. "Have you heard anything from Lord Ransley?" she asked.

"Not a word," he admitted, unhappy with having to drive the hope from her countenance. "But I wouldn't worry. With Garrick gone and Ashford imprisoned, he's in no danger. I'm sorry about Ashford," he began awkwardly. "I know he was a special friend, and in his own twisted way he attempted to save you."

"You need not apologize. Friends do not kill friends," she replied coldly. Something shriveled inside of her at the admission, and she wondered whether she would ever truly trust again. She held that against Hamilton as much as his attempt to kill her.

They sat in silence for several minutes, these two who had been brought together by the tragedy of her husband's death. He had been John's confidant and she owed it to them, and to her country, to divulge what she knew even though it might hold her up to ridicule.

"Just outside of Brussels there's a place called Waterloo," she began, without removing her gaze from the sun-filled window. "There will be a final battle; a final, terrible, loss of life before Napoleon is defeated for all time." She heard a whisper of cloth as he shifted in his chair. "The sun will not shine as it does today. There will be rain and mud and misery on that last night. At first Napoleon will seem to be victorious, but Wellington must not give up. Thousands will never see the sun again, but the duke will defeat Bonaparte once and for all."

"When?"

Claire shifted her gaze to Templeton. He was staring at her intently. "You do not laugh or ask how I know?"

"I've learned the hard way never to doubt your knowledge, and perhaps— as you've always insisted— it's better I don't know your source."

She averted her gaze again, staring as if mesmerized by things he could not see. "The allies plan an invasion of France in July, but Napoleon will not wait till then. I don't know an exact date, but tell Wellington to be prepared the night of the Duchess of Richmond's ball.

He shall dance before he fights," she said with a small, sad smile.

Templeton knew he had experienced the unexplainable. Perhaps when he was an old man with grandchildren gathered at his knee, he would tell them the story of this unique woman. Until then he would keep as silent as she concerning his source.

"That's all I know at present," said Claire, regaining his attention, "but if I learn more I shall let you know immediately."

He rose and moved to the chaise lounge. "You have my utmost regard, my lady." Lifting her hand he saluted it, then left the room without another word.

Claire sighed. Whether she was right or wrong, whether it would help or not, she had done all she could for the moment. Strange that all she desired was to go back to bed and bury her head under the covers until the world was right again, when just this morning she was clamoring to be dressed and downstairs.

After a light luncheon, Claire returned to the chaise and not long after, another tap sounded on the door. To her surprise Forrest Harcourt entered close behind the duchess.

"Darling, I didn't know if you felt up to having another visitor, but Mr. Harcourt is leaving today and insisted it was important he see you."

"I feel fine, Grandmama, don't fret so. Mr. Harcourt was right in insisting, we do have some unfinished business between us."

"Well, if you're sure . . ." she said, hesitating again before leaving them together.

"Unfinished business, Lady Kingsley?" he inquired, one brow quirked inquiringly.

"I assume you came to explain yourself, Mr. Harcourt," Claire snapped, in no mood to deal in subtleties.

"I cannot believe you would put yourself out just to inquire after my health."

"You wound me, my lady. Of course, I'm concerned that you're well. You are Miss Lacefield's best friend."

"And you care about her, don't you?" she questioned mercilessly. "After all you've spent a great deal of time insuring that she cares about you. I'm certain you've explained to Margaret that much to your regret, you must leave immediately with no idea when or if you'll return."

"All that you say is true," he agreed stiffly, "except that I have not seen the lady."

"And do not intend to," she accused.

"Unfortunately, that is also true," he admitted, taking a seat near her.

"Then why are you here? Why waste your time in telling me you're more than just a questionable gentleman of leisure, or perhaps I should say less," she taunted.

"In one respect I'm the same as you, my lady. An agent for the crown."

Claire's senses whirled as everything settled into place. "Why didn't you tell me?" she asked, anger rising.

"For the same reason you kept quiet. I was unaware we were working for the same cause. I finally figured it out, but I didn't know irrefutably until this morning when Templeton gave me my next assignment. He mentioned he had seen you and that you were well on your way to recovering. I was certain the information had to come from you."

"Then everything I heard . . ."

"You interpreted wrong," he finished for her. "You will become more astute with time," he maintained in a consoling manner.

"That's what Grandmama says," mused Claire. Suddenly her gaze jerked up to meet his, her eyes wide with astonishment. "How do you know?"

Harcourt smiled. "I was raised by my grandmother who was a gypsy. She had the gift, and while I did not, I learned to recognize those who did. Particularly if they were new at the craft."

Claire blushed under his regard. "Was I that clumsy? I wonder if anyone else guessed."

"You've nothing to fear, most people don't even believe in the sight. And I assure you, your secret is safe with me."

"All those times you just happened to be nearby?" she questioned.

"I was watching you," he admitted. "I didn't know which side you were on, but I knew something was bound to happen and I meant to be there when it did. Unfortunately, I was too late on the night that mattered."

"And Carrington?"

"He's one of us also," confessed Harcourt. "Although do not let him know I told you. He may decide to keep quiet, but I think you deserve the full particulars. By the way, he's outside anxious to affirm your good health with his own eyes. I thought our confessions required privacy, so I asked him to wait. Shall I invite him in?"

"Why not?" said Claire, with a shrug of her good shoulder. "I'm convinced nothing he has to say could surprise me."

Harcourt opened the door and motioned Carrington inside. There was an alertness in his expression that had previously been disguised by boredom.

"My lady, I'm glad to find you better today," Carrington said bending over her hand.

"Thank you, Mr. Carrington. I understand Mr. Harcourt is leaving us. Never say we are losing your company, too?"

"I fear I must, Lady Kingsley."

"Oh, dear, the ladies will be devastated. They were so looking forward to hearing you read your poetry." Claire attempted to appear suitably downcast. "Perhaps when you return?"

"Oh. Um. Well, I don't . . . that is, my trunk has never been found."

"That's right, and it contained your— what did you call them?— your scribblings. Is that right?"

"Yes. They're probably at the bottom of the channel by now, put there by some clumsy oaf." Carrington ran a finger around the edge of his cravat and stretched his neck as if he were choking. Claire had never seen him so disconcerted.

"Well, perhaps you will have something new for us when you return."

"I've decided to give up my writing, ma'am."

"Oh, no, Mr. Carrington. You would surely not deprive us of your talent." Claire was quite beginning to enjoy his discomfort. He did not deserve to escape completely unscathed.

"Yes, well. If I change my mind I will certainly let you know, Lady Kingsley. I will bid you goodbye now, and wish you a speedy recovery." He quickly bowed himself out of the room.

Claire and Harcourt shared a smile in silent amusement. "I must leave also, my lady," he said, the laughter fading from his eyes.

"You will not change your mind and see Margaret before you go?" she pressed.

"I'm embarking on a mission that could turn out poorly for me." He smiled at his understatement. He never thought he would soften the truth to such an extent in order to spare a woman's feelings. Margaret's influence had been greater than he realized. "Seeing her would do neither of us any good, and I believe no explanation to be better than a lie."

Claire didn't like it, but she understood. "Is there anything I can tell her?" she asked, praying for some word of hope to pass along to Margaret.

Harcourt stood silent, his lips forming a firm slash in his strong chin. "Tell her I'm sorry." He took several steps toward the door before turning again. "Is that worse than nothing?" he asked, indecision clearly written on his countenance.

"I don't know," she admitted honestly.

"Try it," he ordered after a moment's hesitation. Bowing slightly he disappeared through the door.

Claire stared after him, wondering if the whole day had been one continuous laudanum-induced nightmare. She was exhausted and did not quibble when the duchess bustled in, insisting she return to bed.

Claire was a little more rested, but in no better spirits the next morning when Margaret called. The two traded insignificant chitchat until refreshments were served and the maid had withdrawn.

"Claire— "

"Margaret— " Claire waved her hand, urging her friend to continue.

"The duchess mentioned Forrest stopped by for a short time. I couldn't pursue the matter with her, but did you see him?" Margaret asked, her eyes mirroring her concern.

Claire cursed Harcourt for leaving her with the unwanted task of telling her best friend that the man she loved had left without a word of goodbye.

"He called yesterday," Claire replied shortly.

"I'm so grateful," Margaret said, breathing a sigh of relief. "I haven't seen him for several days and feared

e had met with harm. I don't mean to sound disloyal,
ut ofttimes I feel there's more to him than he shows."
he shook her head and smiled. "Silly, isn't it?

"But what did he say? Did he leave a message for
me? I'm sure he meant to call on me, but has been too
nvolved in his business. Now that I think of it he prob-
bly stopped by while I was out and I wasn't advised.
 must speak to the butler about such laxness.

"We had planned on the Lautertons' rout this eve-
ing. Although I feel badly because you can't be there,
 was sure you wouldn't mind. Oh, dear, I'm babbling,
ren't I? It must be because I'm in love. Oh, it's a won-
erful feeling, Claire." She finally finished, looking at
Claire with anticipation.

 Claire stared at her, not knowing what to say. Mar-
aret's smile slowly died.

"What is it, Claire? Tell me, I deserve to know."

"He's gone," Claire said bluntly.

"When?" Margaret's whisper was barely audible.

"Last night, or perhaps this morning. I'm not sure,"
eplied Claire with an impatient gesture of her hand.

 Margaret rose, went to the window, and looked out,
er movements as awkward as a marionette. "He just
eft with no word, no message to me?" she asked in a
ow, controlled voice.

"He said to tell you that he's sorry."

"He's sorry?" Margaret repeated, an edge of hysteria
reeping into her voice as she turned from the window.
'Isn't that comforting?"

"Margaret— "

"Don't, Claire," she warned. "Don't say you're sorry,
oo. I don't think I can bear so much solicitude in one
ay." Margaret turned to the tray holding brandy which
ad been brought to the room for gentlemen callers.
'ouring a generous measure, she swallowed it in one
uge gulp, coughing at its bite.

"Do you know what the worst of it is, Claire? We never shared more than a kiss. Even when I brazenly offered myself, he said he respected me too much to take advantage of me. And I thought— fool that I was— that he meant to make an honorable offer. You see, I was right, my friend. I have nothing attractive to a man except my money, and even that was not enough to tempt Harcourt."

"Margaret— "

"I'm fine, Claire, but I must run," she insisted, pulling on her gloves and keeping her eyes averted. "I have some shopping to do this afternoon. I believe it's time I bought some caps. Plain ones, suitable for a spinster."

The day had become cloudy, as if it were empathizing with the occupants of the house on Berkeley Square, and Claire's room had dimmed appreciably since Margaret had arrived. As she anxiously watched her friend, unable to offer any encouraging words to alleviate her distress, a glow began to surround Margaret. Claire blinked, thinking the strain of the past days was catching up with her, but the radiance had increased when she opened her eyes again.

It was then Claire noticed Margaret was dressed in a gleaming white dress, decorated with yards of exquisite lace and pearls. A veil was held in place with a spray of white flowers, and she carried a bouquet of white and pink roses trailing silk ribbons. But it was her face that held Claire's attention: her expression was one of absolute, unqualified joy. Claire felt that same happiness and fulfillment when she was in Quinton's arms, and she had no doubt she was seeing a vision of Margaret's destiny with Forrest Harcourt.

"Margaret?" she called out, hiding her smile of satisfaction.

Margaret turned, once again unexceptionably attired in her afternoon dress of bottle-green. "Yes?"

"About those caps . . . I wouldn't invest too heavily right now."

A week passed before the marquess returned. By then Claire was up and about, with only a sore shoulder left to show for her experiences, and a short temper for the man who burst into the room and swept her into an embrace.

"You're hurting my shoulder, Quinton," she muttered shrewishly.

"I'm being very careful, you baggage, and you know it," he murmured, placing a particularly passionate kiss beneath her ear. "Now tell me you missed me as much as I missed you, and that you're happy to see me," he demanded, loosening his hold.

"Don't expect me to believe it took you all this time to check on Garrick," grumbled Claire.

"Do I detect a hint of jealousy, my love," he teased. "Perhaps you won't be so annoyed when I show you my surprise."

Claire heard a giggle and saw a dark, tousled head a moment before Juliana launched herself at the couple.

"Juli, darling, I'm so glad to see you," cried Claire, her ill humor forgotten.

Ransley stood smiling at the picture they made. "That's what took me so long. I decided to return by way of Oakcrest and hurry the family to town. Since you cured Juliana, I thought she might return the favor."

"You could not have chosen a better surprise," she said, hugging the child once more. "We shall have a great time, won't we, love?"

Juliana cast an appealing glance at her father before

bursting into speech. "Can we have some ices now that it's warmer, and go to Astley's again, and—"

"Whoa, young lady," said the marquess, laughing. "Lady Kingsley has been injured and can't go romping around with you for a while yet."

Juliana met Claire's gaze. *I'm sorry. Do you hurt very bad?*

"Thank you, Juli, but I hardly hurt at all anymore," said Claire.

When you're better will you go places with us again?

"Of course, I will," she promised. Looking up, she saw the confused expression on Quinton's face. "Right now Grandmama is in the sitting room and Cook has been baking all morning. Run along and we'll join you in a few minutes."

"I'm so glad we can still talk this way," said Juliana giving them each a kiss and darting out of the room.

"What was that all about?" asked Quinton.

"My questions first," announced Claire. "I've waited too long. What happened?" she asked, unwilling to give in so easily.

"Garrick was long gone by the time I reached the coast," said Quinton. "I have accepted what he said was true, and I swear he will pay sooner or later."

"I should have told you my feelings about Garrick when I was at Oakcrest," confessed Claire, "but you were so angry when I accused him of being Lydia's lover, I was afraid to say any more."

"I can't blame anyone but myself. Even if you had told me, I probably wouldn't have believed it. I continually denied the failure of my marriage. I thought if I rejected the mess I had made of my life it would conveniently disappear."

"It wasn't all of your own making, Quinton. Lydia contributed more than her share."

He squeezed her hand in appreciation of her support.

"While that may be true, no one helped me make a muddle of our relationship. Only my unwillingness to believe in you did that. If I hadn't been convinced before, your conversation with Juliana just now would have persuaded me. After all my bumbling, I know of only one way to prove my faith in you and my sincerity."

He pulled her into his arms and kissed her. *I love you, Claire. More than I can express. More than I've ever loved before or will again. You are my life. Without you, my darling, I will be incomplete forever.*

Claire opened her eyes as his lips left hers. This time he spoke. "Did you hear me, Claire? Do you know how precious you are to me?"

"Yes," she whispered, "I heard."

"Then say you'll marry me," he urged, his dark eyes consuming her.

"Oh, Quinton. I love you so much, but think of what you're doing. Can you live with someone like me?"

"I cannot live without you, sweetheart. I'll accept your gift and be thankful for it— in most instances," he stipulated, placing a kiss on the controversial beauty mark. "But I won't have you tampering with my thoughts without asking," he continued in mock sternness.

"You know I don't do that," she answered indignantly. "I do have standards, my lord."

"And what do your standards say about dallying in the drawing room with your future husband, my lady?"

"Not at all acceptable, Lord Ransley."

"Then we had better plan a marriage with all haste or I'm afraid I'll be tempted to anticipate our wedding night."

Claire blushed, but did not draw away from him. Her fingers brushed across his cheekbones and down the strong length of his jaw. She traced his firm lips, allowing her fingers to linger until he nipped them lightly.

"You claim to be able to read my thoughts," he said in a husky voice.

"Only when you allow it," she reminded him.

"Please, help yourself. It would be most pleasant for you to anticipate my needs."

A moment passed and Claire's blush grew even deeper. Sliding her arms around his neck, she buried her fingers in his dark hair and pulled his head down to hers.

"The time and place are not appropriate to what you're thinking, Quinton, but will this do, my lord?" she whispered, just before her lips met his.

"Very well, indeed," he managed to murmur a few minutes later. Gathering her even closer, he added, "For the moment."

Taylor—made Romance From Zebra Books

WHISPERED KISSES (3830, $4.99/5.99)
Beautiful Texas heiress Laura Leigh Webster never imagined that her biggest worry on her African safari would be the handsome Jace Elliot, her tour guide. Laura's guardian, Lord Chadwick Hamilton, warns her of Jace's dangerous past; she simply cannot resist the lure of his strong arms and the passion of his *Whispered Kisses*.

KISS OF THE NIGHT WIND (3831, $4.99/$5.99)
Carrie Sue Strover thought she was leaving trouble behind her when she deserted her brother's outlaw gang to live her life as schoolmarm Carolyn Starns. On her journey, her stagecoach was attacked and she was rescued by handsome T.J. Rogue. T.J. plots to have Carrie lead him to her brother's cohorts who murdered his family. T.J., however, soon succumbs to the beautiful runaway's charms and loving caresses.

FORTUNE'S FLAMES (3825, $4.99/$5.99)
Impatient to begin her journey back home to New Orleans, beautiful Maren James was furious when Captain Hawk delayed the voyage by searching for stowaways. Impatience gave way to uncontrollable desire once the handsome captain searched *her* cabin. He was looking for illegal passengers; what he found was wild passion with a woman he knew was unlike all those he had known before!

PASSIONS WILD AND FREE (3828, $4.99/$5.99)
After seeing her family and home destroyed by the cruel and hateful Epson gang, Randee Hollis swore revenge. She knew she found the perfect man to help her — gunslinger Marsh Logan. Not only strong and brave, Marsh had the ebony hair and light blue eyes to make Randee forget her hate and seek the love and passion that only he could give her.

TODAY'S HOTTEST READS
ARE TOMORROW'S SUPERSTARS

VICTORY'S WOMAN (4484, $4.50)
by Gretchen Genet
Andrew—the carefree soldier who sought glory on the battlefield, and returned a shattered man . . . Niall—the legandary frontiersman and a former Shawnee captive, tormented by his past . . . Roger—the troubled youth, who would rise up to claim a shocking legacy . . . and Clarice—the passionate beauty bound by one man, and hopelessly in love with another. Set against the backdrop of the American revolution, three men fight for their heritage—and one woman is destined to change all their lives forever!

FORBIDDEN (4488, $4.99)
by Jo Beverley
While fleeing from her brothers, who are attempting to sell her into a loveless marriage, Serena Riverton accepts a carriage ride from a stranger—who is the handsomest man she has ever seen. Lord Middlethorpe, himself, is actually contemplating marriage to a dull daughter of the aristocracy, when he encounters the breathtaking Serena. She arouses him as no woman ever has. And after a night of thrilling intimacy—a forbidden liaison—Serena must choose between a lady's place and a woman's passion!

WINDS OF DESTINY (4489, $4.99)
by Victoria Thompson
Becky Tate is a half-breed outcast—branded by her Comanche heritage. Then she meets a rugged stranger who awakens her heart to the magic and mystery of passion. Hiding a desperate past, Texas Ranger Clint Masterson has ridden into cattle country to bring peace to a divided land. But a greater battle rages inside him when he dares to desire the beautiful Becky!

WILDEST HEART (4456, $4.99)
by Virginia Brown
Maggie Malone had come to cattle country to forge her future as a healer. Now she was faced by Devon Conrad, an outlaw wounded body and soul by his shadowy past . . . whose eyes blazed with fury even as his burning caress sent her spiraling with desire. They came together in a Texas town about to explode in sin and scandal. Danger was their destiny—and there was nothing they wouldn't dare for love!

Available wherever paperbacks are sold, or order direct from the Publisher. Send cover price plus 50¢ per copy for mailing and handling to Penguin USA, P.O. Box 999, c/o Dept. 17109, Bergenfield, NJ 07621. Residents of New York and Tennessee must include sales tax. DO NOT SEND CASH.